MAROON RISING

JOHN H. CUNNINGHAM

MAROON
RISING

JOHN H. CUNNINGHAM

Published by Greene Street, LLC

Book design by Morgana Gallaway

This edition was prepared for printing by
The Editorial Department
7650 E. Broadway Blvd.
Suite 308
Tucson, Arizona 85743

Print ISBN: 978-0-9854422-9-3
Electronic ISBN: 978-0-9854422-8-6

www.jhcunningham.com

This book is for Scott Roberts

"Every day a holiday, every meal a feast"

*One of his many Marine sayings I have borrowed on occasion,
and a great description of our friendship*

"Fire deh a muss muss tail, him think a cool breeze"

(Fire is at a mouse's tail, he thinks it's cool breeze)

— Jamaican proverb

CONTENTS

Redemption Song

1

"ALL RISE," THE BAILIFF SAID.

I took in a deep breath. The walls of the small meeting room on the ground floor of the Hibbert House closed in on me—or maybe it was the people. At the far end of the table was Jack Dodson, my former partner at our once successful company, e-Antiquity. Now my competitor, on the edge of his seat too as the Heritage Architectural Review Committee filed in: men and women in suits or dresses, a study in skin shades from beige to dark black.

I'd come to know a little about most of them as we tweaked our application during the review process these past months. Although my reputation preceded me, I was sure at least a few had come to know me as I am today and not as "King Buck"—a nickname that stuck after the *Wall Street Journal* printed it under a picture of me sitting atop a huge load of Mayan treasure at the height of e-Antiquity's success.

The history of the room pressed in on me as we rose. The seat of Jamaican government in the 1750s, the Hibbert House was named after its original owner—Thomas Hibbert, who'd come to Jamaica as a rich young English merchant.

I hoped his ghost would look favorably on me now. Harry Greenbaum and I had spent a sizable chunk of cash pursuing this opportunity. Harry was my financier, and the closest thing I'd had to a father since my parents' death. Even though he'd been e-Antiquity's largest investor, he'd chosen to back me over Jack. An old-fashioned British tycoon who invested in dozens of companies, Harry was a fount of knowledge, connections, and cash—not to mention kindness. He'd stuck with me through the lowest of low points.

Our respective applications had been sealed, only the HARC board knowing the differences. Mine was generous, offering 75 percent of whatever antiquities we found to the National Maritime Museum. It also included an assurance that the structures we exposed during the dig, some thirty feet under water on the eastern tip of Port Royal, would be restored and preserved in accordance with UNESCO's guidance for best practices in underwater archaeology. Depending upon the depth of the antiquities, most of the value for the 25 percent we sought to keep would be spent on the restoration of what we unearthed, so Harry and I viewed this as a skinny but noteworthy opportunity to launch our new antiquity salvage partnership.

I allowed myself another glance down the table, looking past Jack Dodson to his partner, Richard Rostenkowski, a.k.a. Gunner.

Was Gunner smiling?

Everyone sat down except the chairman of the Heritage Architectural Review Committee (HARC), Johnston Cheever.

"In the matter of the applications filed by Last Resort Charter and Salvage," he nodded toward me, "and SCG International," he nodded at Jack, "we have come to a determination."

My elbows pressed into the wood table.

"Both parties have filed applications to perform an archaeological dig within the waters of Port Royal—to exhume and preserve the structure known as the Jamison House, while also seeking to recover assets purported to have been owned and hidden there by former Jamaican Lieutenant Governor Henry Morgan, or privateers associated with him. We have found one of the applications superior to the other."

Johnny Blake, my Jamaican associate, elbowed me and pumped his eyebrows. Jack glanced my way, revealing nothing but contempt as our eyes locked. I just hoped his and Gunner's greed would make their application inferior. I'd bankrolled several months of application, pre-evaluation, and the final evaluation process on that assumption.

Chairman Cheever cleared his throat. A couple of the board members squirmed in their chairs. I suddenly realized nobody was looking at me.

"HARC has selected and grants an immediate salvage permit to commence operations to SCG International."

Silence.

The heartbeat I'd heard pounding in my ears stopped. My eyes flitted from face to face on the panel. Only the gray-haired professor, Keith Quao from the University of the West Indies returned my glance, albeit momentarily.

"Thank you for your submissions." The chairman finished with some final instructions to Jack and Gunner. He said something to me, too, but I have no idea what.

Henry Morgan's treasure had vanished in the earthquake of 1692, the clue to which I'd discovered here six years ago while on e-Antiquity business. Since then, I'd declared personal bankruptcy, lost my wife and all my money, and Jack had been convicted of fraud and served five years in prison.

How had he beat me out? Or should I be wondering who he'd paid off?

"That a bitch, mon." Johnny Blake frowned at me and slapped his palm on my back, then walked out the door.

The HARC committee had already left the room, leaving me with Jack, Gunner, and a number of photographers and reporters. One directed a question toward me.

"You didn't really think you'd win, did you, *King Buck*?"

Still frozen, I caught my breath as Gunner broke free of the reporters, walked to my end of the table, and leaned close. It was one of the only times I'd seen him without his reflective blue sunglasses, which were folded in the breast pocket of his open-collared tropical shirt.

"Hit the road, Reilly." He spoke in a hoarse whisper, his eyes boring into mine. "And don't make a mistake-a, stay out of Jamaica." His small square teeth appeared as he grinned at his witticism.

"Screw you, Gunner."

Sixty Days Later

KEY WEST HAD BEEN PACKED WITH SNOWBIRDS AND CRUISE SHIPPERS FOR the past month, the winter season in full swing. I'd adopted my in-season habit of avoiding the more crowded parts of Duval Street, spending more time in my top-floor suite at the La Concha Hotel. For the time being I'd put my treasure-hunting dreams on ice. Harry's agitation over Jack's besting our application in Jamaica had been slow to wane, and since I still didn't know why they selected Jack over me, my anger had continued to fester.

I checked my watch.

I pulled up the website for the *Jamaican Gleaner*, one of the best news sources on the island, but found no mention of the Port Royal excavation. The first few weeks after HARC's decision they'd run multiple articles on Jack, his company and history, their swift commencement of activities out on the waters of Port Royal. So swift, in fact, I suspected he had inside knowledge of his getting selected. How, I didn't know.

I went to my mini-fridge and pulled out a beer. As soon as I popped the top, my phone rang.

"Hey, Buck, how you doing, mon?"

"Any news?" I had Johnny Blake on retainer to keep me apprised of Jack's activities.

"No, mon, they out there in force, but no word of nothing yet."

I smiled. "Good. I hope it's costing them a fortune."

I could imagine the painstaking and tedious effort involved in exhuming the remains of the Jamison house, which had supposedly been a pub and brothel—and the pressure each fruitless day must be putting on Jack and Gunner.

With any luck it would bury them.

"JNHT keeping an eye on them?" The Jamaican National Heritage Trust was a diligent steward of Jamaican history and had only considered the salvage aspect of the application because of the value associated with the preservation.

"Yeah, mon. They got a boat out there every day, with divers in the water watching them boys."

"How many boats and people does Jack have on-site?"

"As of this morning there was seven boats out there, maybe twenty-five people. They working round the clock."

"Seven." That was two more boats than Johnny's last report.

Jack had to pay for JNHT's costs too. An operation of that size would run roughly twenty-five thousand dollars per day. After two months that's around a million-five in sunk costs—pun intended.

I bit my lip. "Is Betty there?"

"You mean the beautiful blond woman, Mr. Buck?"

Jack's wife was brunette. Did Gunner have a girlfriend?

"No, my old Grumman Widgeon."

"Oh yeah, his water plane." Johnny laughed. "Thought you was talking about that babe with them. Got all the boys on the crew distracted. Some famous supermodel or something."

Supermodel? "What's her name?"

"I don't know, mon. Hot bitch is what I call her."

I imagined the scene out on the water. All those boats, all those divers working through the grid, stabilizing and restoring each bit of exposed structure as they dug deeper. Slow, grueling, expensive. Good.

"Anything else?"

"Yeah, mon, that woman from the university still wants to talk to you."

"I don't know, Johnny—she works with the professor who was on the selection committee."

"Yeah, but she's for real. Deep Jamaican roots. Says she got some ideas to talk to you about."

"This has to do with the Morgan excavation?"

"She won't tell me nothing, but I suppose so," Johnny said.

I wanted to call, but it was no longer my hunt. While I enjoyed watching Jack and Gunner bleed money, their selection by the HARC was final—any meddling by third parties would be punishable by law, and I had no interest in the consequences of breaking the law in Jamaica. Johnny and I scheduled our next call for another week out and hung up.

I read the number I'd written on the scratch pad by my phone, but it was the name that made me pause. Nanny Adou. The name Nanny had historic significance in Jamaica, and anyone named after Queen Nanny would either have to be a powerful woman herself or a pariah for using the name of one of Jamaica's most important figures.

Curiosity got the better of me. What could a phone call hurt? I drained the beer and used my new cell phone to dial the number.

A young man answered. "History Department."

"I'm calling to speak with Nanny Adou."

"Professor Adou? One minute."

Silence filled the line and I debated whether to open another beer.

"Hello?"

"Is this the Mother of us all?" I said.

"I'm not *your* mother." She sounded young, and agitated.

"This is Buck Reilly calling. Am I speaking with Nanny Adou?"

"Mr. Reilly. You must be versed on Maroon history here in Jamaica. I'm impressed."

We bantered back and forth a few rounds, then she got down to business. Sort of.

"I'd like to meet with you, in person," she said.

"I have no plans to be in Jamaica, Professor Adou. You're welcome to come to Key West, or we can talk on the phone, now." I paused. "Is this to do with the dig your colleague helped assign to my competitor?" I didn't make an effort not to sound bitter.

"There's someone who would like to meet with you, Mr. Reilly."

"As I said, I—"

"To discuss the excavation project you referred to. Colonel Stanley Grandy, to be exact. He's not military—"

"The figurehead of the remaining Maroons," I said.

"Correct again—on the Windward side, anyway. But he's more than a figurehead and he's an old man now. He would like to meet with you. In Moore Town."

Moore Town was in the northeastern part of the island, just below the Blue Mountain range. The town had been founded and controlled by the Jamaican Maroons, known to the Europeans as runaway slaves, since the late seventeenth century. The research I'd done during the application process for the Morgan site had mentioned a couple of Maroon connections.

What Nanny said had the hair up on my forearms. But Jack and Gunner would know the moment I set foot back in Jamaica, and I had no doubt that whatever forces they'd rallied to manipulate the selection would turn against me. Nothing Nanny Adou or Colonel Grandy could say would be worth the risk of winding up in a Jamaican jail.

"I'm sorry, Professor Adou, but as I said, I have no plans to be in Jamaica. So, thanks, but no thanks."

"I wish you'd talk to—"

"I appreciate your thinking of me." I dropped the phone into the cradle.

A sudden sense of claustrophobia closed in on me. I jumped up, headed out into the sixth-floor corridor, and pushed the button for the elevator. After two seconds I took the stairs, my mind back in Jamaica as I hurried down the steps.

2

Thirty More Days Later

"YOU KNOW THIS PLACE IS GONNA BE PACKED," RAY SAID.

"Yeah, well, Thom Shepherd draws a crowd—"

"Two cruise ships came in today, Buck. That's like ten thousand people." Ray Floyd—friend, mechanic, and island philosopher—dodged and juked through the crowds on the Duval Street sidewalk. I walked a straight line, or as straight as I could, staring dead ahead.

I took a left on Eaton. Ray was right—as we approached the busiest end of town, the crowd had indeed thickened. Two cruise ships would clog Key West's arteries like a lifetime diet of cheeseburgers but without the satisfaction.

Ray brushed his palms down the front of his long-sleeved blue flowered shirt as if to wipe clean any public interaction. Getting him to go anywhere other than the airport, Blue Heaven, or his duplex on Laird Street was a rare event. Not that I was much better.

"And how do you know Thom, anyway," Ray said.

"You know him too."

I caught the arch of his brows as we took a right on Whitehead. At least the pedestrian crowd was now moving in the same direction as us. Sunset was approaching, and Mallory Square was a black hole sucking in all loose matter not affixed to a barstool or a real life.

"Wait, what do you mean—"

"He was at the Beach Bar in St. John when we were down there with Crystal."

"Oh yeah. Tall guy with a cowboy hat?"

"He's a country singer, Ray. They wear cowboy hats."

"But couldn't we meet him later for a beer at Blue Heaven or Rum Bar? The Tuna'll be packed."

I turned down Caroline Street and saw a crowd ahead around the Bull. Or maybe they were waiting in line to get to the Garden of Eden, the rooftop nudist bar.

"We'll see if we can catch him before his first set," I said. "God forbid you relax, enjoy some live music, maybe chat up a pretty tourist."

"Funny, Buck. I get plenty of live music at Blue Heaven, thank you very much."

"And?"

"And pretty tourist women too, all right?"

The truth was, neither of us had been on a hot streak in the romance department lately. Those months of work on the Jamaican salvage application had sent me traveling from Kingston to Key West and back so often I'd lost my last flame, Nicole on St. Barth's. I couldn't afford to live there, as much as I enjoyed her company, and her roots were too deep to leave. Besides, neither of us was ready for anything more permanent. And I'd been in a funk in the months since Jamaica. Harry Greenbaum had encouraged me to move on, even offered to go in on another project, but I'd burned half my nest egg on the expenses he wasn't covering. One more failure like that and I'd be dead broke again.

As for Ray, well, he might never have had a hot streak.

We took a left then a right into the back door of the Smokin' Tuna, which was indeed packed.

"Let's go over here." I nodded toward the side bar, where Robert, the bartender, waved to us. He brought me a Papa Pilar's dark rum on the rocks and Ray a Coors Light.

"Surprised to see you guys here," he said.

"No kidding," Ray said.

"Is Thom Shepherd here yet?" I said.

Robert said Thom was in the back room at the end of the bar tuning his guitar.

Ray held his palms up. "Well?"

"I'll go see what's up." As much as I enjoyed my friendship with Ray, he could be like a nervous old woman outside his comfort zone, whose radius was very small.

I pushed the door open on the back room, actually a private room in the front of the building. I'd been in there once for a book signing by Michael Haskins, a local author.

Thom was sitting on a table, hunched over his guitar, strumming it slowly while twisting the knobs on the neck. The brim on his cowboy hat covered his eyes.

"Howdy, pardner." My John Wayne accent.

A wide smile creased his face as he looked up.

"Buck Reilly, just the man I wanted to see. How you been?"

We didn't know each other well, so it didn't take long to catch up.

"What's on your mind?" I said.

He rubbed the stubble on his chin between his thumb and index finger.

"Didn't I hear through the Coconut Telegraph that you're working on some kind of project in Jamaica?"

"Yeah, well, I was a few months ago but lost out to another salvage company. Why?"

He stood up and laid the guitar gently on the table. I realized he was nearly as tall as my six feet two—taller with that hat on.

"You have any plans to go back down there anytime soon?"

Jack Dodson's smug smile flashed into my mind.

"Buck?"

"Sorry, I was thinking about my schedule. You have a show down there?"

"Not exactly. But I'm recording an album at Tuff Gong Studios, where Bob Marley used to record, then shooting a video on the beach." His smile lit up again. "Thought if you fly me down, I can use your plane in my video."

"Let me think a minute." Getting paid to hang out during a recording session and video shoot? Normally that would be a no-brainer. And the email and voicemail messages from Professor Nanny Adou had grown more urgent and filled with more assurances that meeting the Maroon elder would be mutually beneficial. And hell, I wasn't prohibited by anybody other than Gunner from going to Jamaica, I just had to stay away from Jack's site.

"You with me, Buck?"

"Yeah, sorry. Let me make a couple calls. What's your timing?"

"ASAP. Hell, I'd leave tomorrow if possible. I'm behind schedule on the new CD and I have an important meeting with a record exec. Plus this whole Tuff Gong thing has stirred some buzz. Got Noah Gordon and Jim "Moose" Brown to produce it. Moose wrote "Five O'Clock Somewhere" for Jimmy Buffett—"

"I've heard of Moose."

I took down Thom's cell number and said I'd let him know by morning. According to Johnny, Jack was still scraping a dry hole in Port Royal, and just yesterday their fleet of boats had actually increased. If my estimate of $25k per day was accurate, they'd spent another three-quarters of a million dollars this last month—over two million in total. They'd have to be nervous wrecks by now.

And what could Professor Adou or the Maroon leader have to tell me that was so damned important?

Ray was only too happy to leave after his one beer, which I paid for. He rambled on about gossip at the airport and his checklist of things the Beast needed while we walked, but my mind was far away—one hundred eighty miles south, to be precise. I already knew what I'd tell Thom and had begun my own checklist, but I did want to speak with Nanny Adou once more before committing. I glanced at my watch.

Still time to call tonight.

3

AFTER SCANNING THE INCREASINGLY SPARSE NEWS, ALL I FOUND WAS AN
article about the upswing in community concern for the project amid
accusations that SCG International was doing a shoddy job, stirring up
silt and overdisturbing the area around the salvage site. Some artifacts had
apparently been destroyed, resulting in fines imposed by the JNHT. SCG
had declined to comment.

A follow-up article had me laughing out loud. There was a picture of a
really big old brewer's vat hanging from a crane aboard one of the barges,
with Gunner standing to the side, hands on his hips and scowling up
at the dangling monstrosity. The caption: "One Man's Treasure, Another
Man's Cask." According to the story, SCG International thought they'd
zeroed in on a massive stash of treasure when their magnetometer found
the vat. While disappointed, they remained "committed to the preservation effort."

I laughed again. Preservation effort was just code amongst treasure
hunters for permission to tear up a historic site in search of valuable
antiquities.

Didn't sound like they'd found anything yet, but they were doubling
down in their efforts, which would include more restoration work at a cost
even higher than the treasure hunting itself.

If HARC had picked Last Resort, Harry would be furious and I'd be broke.

Again.

Sufficiently updated, I called Johnny Blake, who answered after a few rings. Based on the background noise he was outside.

"Surprised to hear from you, Mr. Buck—we just spoke a couple days ago, yeah?"

"Tell me more about this professor who wants to meet me?"

"Aside from being persistent, you mean?" He laughed. "She's Maroon by birth, got close connections with them." Johnny was a pseudo-Rastafarian, so not particularly close with the Maroons but not opposed to them either. "Says the old colonel wants to talk to you. Hasn't told me why. How come you ask?"

"I have a charter trip to Jamaica, thought I might as well meet her while I'm down there."

"When you coming?"

"Tomorrow, maybe the day after. Can you let her know I'll call her when I get there?"

Johnny whistled. "Buck Reilly's coming back to Jamaica. Yeah, mon, I tell her. Your old partner won't be too happy, though."

"No need for him to find out."

He laughed and we hung up.

I'D MET JOHNNY YEARS AGO—IN FACT, HE WAS THE ONE WHO SOURCED THE old document that eventually led to the Port Royal salvage project. He was furious when Jack was selected, since I'd promised him 1 percent of Last Resort's cut of any profit, plus his expenses, but given that the site had been a bust so far, he hadn't really lost anything.

I sent Thom Shepherd a text message saying we were on and that we should plan to leave tomorrow around noon. Jamaica was ninety miles southwest of Cuba, which was ninety miles south of Key West. A 180-mile flight was well within the Beast's range, so no need to plan a refueling stop, and given the now thawed relations with Cuba, flying over the island no longer bothered me. My old nemesis Manny Gutierrez continued to have a role in Cuban government, or so my sometime handler FBI Special Agent

Edwin T. Booth told me. And Gunner had once bragged that Manny was a silent partner in SCG International and the reason they'd wound up with my old Grumman Widgeon.

Betty.

Having left her a smoldering ruin on a beach at the western tip of Cuba a couple years ago, I'd been shocked when she'd reappeared last year in the possession of Jack and Gunner. My old partner's rise from prison inmate to owner of a well-financed salvage operation was bad enough—Jack's getting his paws on my beloved plane had been a knife to my heart.

But if he thought he'd seen the last of me just because I couldn't mess with his Port Royal expedition, he had another thing coming. Paybacks, as they say, are a bitch.

4

THOM SHEPHERD WAS A FEARLESS FLIER AND HAD NO ISSUES WITH THE
Beast's age, semirestored condition, or the turbulence we encountered
over western Cuba. As for me, every bump brought back the trauma of
crash-landing Betty in the marl flats of the island, to the point that my
palms were clammy.

Perhaps sensing my anxiety, Thom volunteered the nature of his special
meeting.

"So aside from the songs I'm recording at Tuff Gong Studios, I'm meeting
with Chris Blackwell at his GoldenEye Resort."

"Why do his name and GoldenEye sound familiar?"

"Chris was the founder of Island Records. He discovered Bob Marley,
U2, Cat Stevens, and other name artists. And he owns GoldenEye, which
includes the house where Ian Fleming lived and wrote all the James Bond
books."

"Now, that's cool." I vectored the Beast further west and was now aimed
directly at Kingston, about forty miles away. "Does he have something to
do with the CD you're recording down here?"

Thom glanced out the starboard side window, then turned back to me.

"Guess I can trust you, Buck. I'm actually trying to get him to invest in
a record label I'm thinking of starting."

We began our descent toward Norman Manley International Airport in
Kingston. Air traffic control had me vector west and circle back around as

one large commercial jetliner took off and another landed. We had plenty of fuel, and Thom enjoyed the scenery—lush mountains and the blue water below—so I followed orders and waited our turn to land. After we looped around, ATC sent us north again, then instructed us to land on runway 12, which at nearly 9,000 feet long was four times the length the Beast would need.

On our final approach I realized we'd be flying right over Port Royal, so I dropped altitude to steal a glance at Jack's operation. Too bad I wouldn't see the look on his face when he found out I was back on island.

Emerald blue water shimmered below us as we flew parallel to the isthmus of Port Royal, when—there! I spotted Betty anchored adjacent to the big barge with the crane on it from the picture in the *Jamaican Gleaner*.

I choked up at seeing my old plane, and the sentiment knotted my stomach when I saw Jack's people—

"We kind of low, Buck?" Thom said.

ATC began shouting in our ears that we were too low and to change our angle of attack. I spotted several people looking up and pointing at us from the various boats—was that Gunner?

A flame leapt up from a cabin cruiser—

Gunfire!

I kicked down on the starboard pedal—Thom shouted—the Beast lurched. I spotted several holes in the far end of the port wingtip.

"Son of a bitch!"

"What's going on?" Thom said.

"Motherfucker shot us!"

I leveled off, now well past Jack's armada but askew of the runway. ATC started shouting in our ears to abort the landing, but I continued to descend and gradually edged back into position. Thom wedged himself into the seat and wrapped his arms around the shoulder harness—to his credit he didn't whine or start freaking out.

The Beast's port wheel caught asphalt, the starboard one touched gravel. We bounced. I shoved the wheel forward and we set down hard on the tarmac. In my ear the ATC was threatening to file a report about unsafe piloting, but I wasn't really paying attention, too furious at Gunner—or one of his henchmen—for shooting at us. I took a quick glance out the side window. At least there wasn't any fuel spewing from the holes—must have just missed the tank, though.

They'd pay for this.

"Damn, son," Thom said. "Folks told me trouble clings to you like a pair of tight jeans. I figured it was mostly talk, but damn if it ain't so." He laughed. "You going to radio the authorities?"

While I was grateful he'd shown grace under pressure, it wasn't easy to stem the stream of obscenities that pressed against my lips—not for Thom but for those sons of bitches on the water.

"No, I'll take care of this myself."

Once out of the plane, I inspected the damage. But for my kicking down on the starboard pedal in time, any one of the three bullets that tore through the wing would have hit the fuel tank and vaporized us in a ball of fire.

We made it through Customs. Thom did his best to calm me down, but I was so angry I could barely speak. He said he'd rent a car to drive up to Oracabessa and meet Blackwell at GoldenEye.

"But I'll wait around until you get back, make sure everything's okay. Sure you don't want to call the police?"

"I'll be fine."

He patted my shoulders with both hands. "Don't do anything crazy, now. I still need a ride home." He smiled, but my lack of warmth sent him on his way.

I ran outside into the heat of the day, already soaked with rage-born sweat—why had I intentionally buzzed them?

Would I ever learn?

Still, trying to *shoot me out of the sky?*

I hopped into a taxi, on a mission.

5

THE FISHING BOAT I'D HIRED TO TAKE ME TO PORT ROYAL HESITATED WHEN
I pointed across the blue water toward Jack's anchored fleet. I grabbed
a sunscreen stocking the boat captain had on the top of his center console
and pulled it up over my face to just below my eyes. I rolled the sleeves of
my fishing shirt down and buttoned them at the wrists. The boat owner, a
young commercial fisherman, shook his head.

"Boats are prohibited from approaching the archaeological site, mon.
We been warned by the Coast Guard."

A fistful of Jamaican dollars changed his mind.

The sight of Betty covered in salt and brine, her wings swaying uneasily
in the chop, caused me to clench my teeth so hard a shrill sensation shot
through my back molar and I let up. Men on the boats pointed and waved
their arms at us as we approached. More than one held fully or semi-auto-
matic rifles.

"I don't know, mister," the boat captain said.

"Just pull up to that first boat and I'll get out."

He glanced from me to the boat, a big cabin cruiser that likely held
Jack's offshore office. He looked back to the men with guns now pointed
at us.

"I don't know—"

I stood up and he slowed the boat to a crawl.

"I'm here to see the representative from the Jamaican National Heritage Trust and Jack Dodson!" I shouted this twice before Jack emerged from below deck of the fancy fishing boat.

"Who the hell are you and what do you want?" Jack's shout carried across the water.

I pulled the sun mask off my face. His face twisted into a grimace that matched mine. He waved his arm, and the men with the guns lowered them slightly. The captain sped up until we were close enough for me to grab hold of a rubber dock bumper, and then the railing.

"Just wait a hundred yards over there," I said. "This won't take long."

I climbed from the side of the fishing boat onto the side of Jack's boat, then over the railing onto the deck of what I recognized as an old custom-built Merritt fishing boat. My feet landed flat on the deck and Jack's men started for me—

"Leave him be," Jack said.

He squared off to face me. My heart thudded in my chest.

"You fucking bastard—you shot at me, nearly killed me!" My jaw quivered with anger, but I tried to control my breathing. I had a purpose here. "Where's your observer? I'm going to file a formal complaint and demand this site be shut down!"

I shoved Jack hard. He took a step back but remained steady.

"Our observer's underwater on the dive site, he didn't see or hear anything." Jack's lips were taut. "And I didn't shoot you, Buck. One of Gunner's men did. As bad as the blood between you and me is, it's all I can do to keep him from killing you, but I manage." He paused. "And what's with the mask? These men thought you were trying to rob us—"

"Recent skin cancer, asshole—"

"Fuck you, Reilly!" Gunner's voice, from several boats away. "I warned you to stay away from our site!"

I spun around to see him holding his gun up. It was an M4A1 assault rifle in desert camo, no doubt a souvenir from his days as a mercenary in the Middle East.

"You can't keep me out of Jamaica," I said. "But don't worry, I have no use for antique brewery vats!"

His eyes cut to slits and he lowered the assault weapon toward us.

"Gunner!" Jack said. "Don't point that thing over here. Simmer down, go diving!"

The fifty-foot distance between Gunner and me was so charged, I'm not sure I didn't feel a shock when he stabbed his forefinger at me.

"Last warning, Reilly! Authority or not, nobody will stop me next time." He shoved the gun into the arms of one of his goons and disappeared into the cuddy-cabin of the small cruiser.

"What's all the ruckus?" A woman's voice turned the blood in my veins to ice.

I spun around to see—no.

NO!

"Buck?" she said.

Her clear blue eyes shot from me to Jack, then she stepped forward out of the air-conditioned salon. She wore a silk blouse and short shorts that showed off her long, lithe, tanned legs. Her ash-blond hair fell across her face. She brushed it off with a graceful sweep of her hand.

She was stunning.

I reached toward her before I caught myself and dropped my arm.

"Fancy seeing you here," she said.

"Heather."

My voice trembled, but not so much that they could hear. I felt my legs shudder and locked my knees so they wouldn't buckle.

The beautiful blond supermodel Johnny Blake had raved about: "Hot bitch is what I call her," he'd said. Jack Dodson's constant companion, he'd said.

My ex-wife.

6

"**W**HAT IN THE HELL ARE YOU DOING HERE?" MY EYES WERE RIVETED ON Heather.

She turned to face Jack and they held a long glance. No words were exchanged, but her reaching forward to grasp his tattooed bicep, ever so briefly, was not lost on me. A wave of hot nausea hit—it was all I could do to swallow the bile shooting up from my stomach.

"You have no right to be here, Reilly," Jack said. "But since you are, why don't we go inside and talk for a moment—"

"I have no desire to talk to either of you. Heather, I asked you a question. I want an answer."

Heather's 36Cs lifted toward the cobalt sky as she drew in a deep breath. My mind rewound to the years of our marriage, her travels as a model in global demand, my time spent in the armpits of third-world countries negotiating with crooked government officials for salvage rights while Jack held down the fort and schmoozed investors in our Northern Virginia corporate headquarters. Heady days, a jet-set lifestyle, anything goes—but how far? Images of us together, including Laurie, Jack's wife, played in my mind like an old home movie.

"So?" I said.

"Jack and I have been together for a while—"

"Since when? Since he got out of jail?" I turned to face Jack. "What about your wife?"

Heather pursed her lips. Jack stared at me without a trace of remorse or guilt—hell, without any emotion at all.

"Since *when,* Heather?"

"Before jail." A tear slid from a sky blue eye and down her bronzed cheek.

No nausea now. Just three words like bullets.

"How. Long. Before."

Jack crossed his arms. "Years before."

My vision blurred. For just a minute, I froze.

"Buck, I'm so sorry, you were always gone—"

"So were you!"

"I was lonely, Buck—I'm not a suburban housewife type, you knew that. I'd go to your office and wait to hear from you. Because you never called—"

"No cell reception in jungles—"

"Jack was always there, he listened to me, cared about my career, my dreams, my needs . . . Buck, you can't understand—"

"Oh, I understand, all right."

"Buck—"

"Spare me the tears, Heather. You vanished while I was fighting to stay out of jail, my parents got killed—and now I find out you were off with *him*?" My finger stabbed Jack in the shoulder. He brushed it away, still calm and in control. Fucking accountant. "You cleaned out our bank account—took *everything* that wasn't bolted down—and fucking disappeared!"

Jack shoved me away.

"Back off, Buck."

"Don't tell me to back off, *partner*! And you were pissed at me for not visiting you in jail? Are you fucking kidding me? You were banging my wife!"

I felt the eyes of Jack's crew on us. Mine were now aimed at Heather.

A twinge of guilt stabbed at me. I *had* been gone a lot. I remembered our discussing it at one point, but there was always the next treasure waiting to be found. . .

"And what about your billionaire husband—the one you married before the ink was dry on our divorce papers?" Spittle shot from my mouth and made Heather wince. "What the hell was that about?"

"I didn't . . . When I went to see Jack, I realized I didn't love Barry, and—"

"Now you're with Jack, he has Betty, and he's using the fruits of *my* time in those jungles to take what should have been ours!"

The sound of laughter brought a cold numbness over me. Gunner must be loving this.

My breathing settled. My heart rate became steady and my vision intense, as if I were seeing the teak deck of the fishing boat through the most sophisticated of camera lenses—reminding me that Jack still had money he'd hidden from the investigators after our bankruptcy, while I'd mostly lived like a pauper ever since filing Chapter 11.

Jack got the girl—*my* girl. He got the salvage contract—the one *my* research led to. That last thought made me smile. I waved and the fishing boat idling a hundred feet off the port side instantly accelerated, its Yamaha motor the only sound. Again I smiled.

They looked at each other then back at me, confused.

"Maybe there's justice after all," I said. "Your salvage efforts—sorry, your archaeological reconstruction project—has been nothing but a dry hole. What have you spent, Jack? Couple million? More?" I smiled again. "And this one here?" I tipped my head toward Heather. "You'd better damned well find some treasure—and a lot of it. Between the two of you, you'll need it."

7

THE GRAY CONCRETE SKYLINE OF KINGSTON GREW CLOSE AS THE CAPTAIN took me to shore. I caught a taxi back to the airport to check on the Beast. Thom had needed to head up to the north coast, Oracabessa, and I planned to fly to the airport near Ocho Rios, now called Ian Fleming International. I was surprised to find Thom sitting in the lounge at the General Aviation terminal when I arrived at Norman Manley Airport.

"Thought you rented a car," I said.

"Was about to, then I found out how long it would take to get all the way up there, so I decided to wait around for you. Truth be told I was also a little worried, as pissed as you were when you left. You kick some ass?"

A long exhale was all I could muster. Thom read the signal and didn't ask any more questions.

It only took twenty minutes to file my flight plan and get squared away to head north. The afternoon sun hit hard as we stepped out onto the tarmac. Thom carried his suitcase and guitar, and once to the Beast, I let him inside to air her out while I inspected the holes in the port wingtip. Unbelievable. There were only six inches separating the closest hole and the edge of the 110-gallon fuel tank, and miraculously, the bullets hadn't hit the flap or the vacuum lines that control the flaps. I pushed my finger into the holes, one by one, to feel around for anything sharp, wet, any kind of damage invisible to the naked eye.

The holes felt clean, though I'd have felt better about them if Ray were here.

I spotted Thom watching me from the cockpit window. Back at the open hatch, I leaned inside.

"Do me a favor and grab the roll of duct tape in the file box next to my seat," I said. I heard him rooting around.

"This gonna work?" he said when he held it out to me.

"I'm not planning any water landings, and there isn't any internal damage, so yeah. It'll help preserve the aerodynamics at least."

I rolled up little pieces of duct tape, stuffed them in the holes, then covered each hole with a strip and rubbed it smooth. Ten minutes later I'd done a preflight check, confirmed we still had plenty of fuel, and closed the hatch.

Should I take the Beast getting shot as a bad omen, drop Thom off, and head home? Probably. Was I going to do that?

Hell no.

"What time's your meeting with the record producer?"

"We're having dinner."

I completed the preflight inspection, paying careful attention to the flaps and the vacuum system, which seemed fine. I turned on the fuel valves, moved the mixture control to idle cutoff, pumped the throttles, hit the ignition switch, and engaged the starters. Once the warm-up was done, I checked the oil and fuel pressures and waited for word from Air Traffic Control. Once it was our turn we taxied out, cranked up the manifold pressure, and lit off down the runaway.

As we climbed over the azure bay between Kingston to the north, with Port Royal to the south, I didn't so much as glance at Jack's armada for the big Merritt where I'd found him and Heather. I kicked the starboard pedal instead and banked hard over Kingston, another place I had no desire to gaze down upon. The recollection of the HARC selection meeting at Hibbert House was still an irritant.

Dry hole or not, I hated to lose.

"Wow," Thom said.

Out his side window were the Blue Mountains, some of the tallest in the Caribbean. Our passage, which ATC instructed us to maintain at seven thousand feet, kept us eye to eye with the highest peak to our east. The interior of Jamaica is rugged, green, and full of surprises.

The flight took only fifteen minutes before I hurried through the landing checklist, circled the airport once as we descended, then announced our final leg and approach onto runway 9, the lone 4,700-foot asphalt strip that ran parallel to the sea.

Once we came to a stop and shut everything down, I removed my headset and saw a big grin on Thom's face.

"I really appreciate you bringing me down here, Buck. Sorry we ran into trouble there in Kingston, but man, I can't tell you how excited I am to meet with Chris Blackwell."

"How you getting there?"

"Taxi. I got you a room at GoldenEye, too, man."

I nodded my appreciation. I hadn't really given any thought to where I'd stay, and I had yet to contact Nanny Adou or Johnny Blake to let them know I was here. So might as well spend the night at Ian Fleming's old digs and see whatever inspired him to write thirteen James Bond novels and launch the most successful franchise of spy movies in history.

That, and get a belly full of Appleton's Rum.

8

GOLDENEYE WAS NESTLED INTO A PRIVATE LAGOON ON ONE SIDE, LOW CAY beach on another, and the ocean on yet another. Private villas tucked into mature vegetation blended earth tones with the brilliant blue water and crashing white surf. It was peaceful, private, isolated: just what I *didn't* need, given my highly agitated state of mind. After dropping my bag in the lagoon view single villa, I opted to try and swim off some anger rather than heading straight to the bar.

The warm water welcomed me, and I could see clearly even without goggles as I swam around the large oval-shaped lagoon and the perimeter of the green island in the center. After an hour of semi-mindless freestyle swimming at as strong a pace as I could maintain, I lost track of how many times I'd circled the island.

I climbed out by the water sports station and crossed over the big pedestrian bridge, illuminated with large multicolored lights reminiscent of holiday festivities. I sat in the gin-clear water by Low Cay Beach, where I watched the few guests snoozing, drinking, and reading in colorful chaise lounges scattered along the sand. Daylight faded to oranges and pinks, and I could picture the amazing sunset visible from Negril on the western end of Jamaica.

MY MARRIAGE HAD ENDED OVER FIVE YEARS AGO. KNOWING HEATHER TO be shallow, narcissistic, and spoiled, her disappearing when I filed for bankruptcy had not come as a surprise. Or when she married the elderly oil tycoon less than a year later. By recognizing the inevitability of her need for wealth and the good life, I could justify losing her, and even marrying her. If the entire relationship had been based on a mirage, I could tell myself I hadn't really lost anything.

But seeing her today, for that split second before my brain connected the dots, I'd felt my heart shudder. It sickened me to face it, but of course I'd married her because I loved her. My trophy wife and I had been the toast of the town, young, beautiful, successful. The world had been ours for the taking. And oh, the fun we'd had.

It was easy to now see that I'd not only been a fool, but a blind, ignorant, self-centered fool. My darling wife and my business partner had found each other while I was out killing myself in third-world shit holes, bribing academics, digging through jungles, negotiating with criminals—all the while seeing myself as a real-life Indiana Jones.

I'd been good at it, too. I'd found incalculably valuable lost antiquities, treasures worth hundreds of millions of dollars, even helped to connect missing gaps of world history for cultures that had vanished centuries ago.

While Jack and Heather had been left alone in Virginia.

Back at my room, on the bed there was an envelope with a handwritten note requesting my company for dinner tonight with Chris Blackwell and Thom Shepherd at Blackwell's private villa. A quick glance at my ancient Rolex Submariner made me skip a shave and dash into the shower. Cocktails would be served in twenty minutes in the Bizot Bar, at the far end of the beach.

BIZOT WAS AN OPEN-AIR STRUCTURE OVERLOOKING LOW CAY BEACH. As I walked through the white sand I saw torches burning, candles flickering, and heard laughter filter through the foliage that separated the beach from the villas. Underneath the covered patio was a bar supported by columns entirely wallpapered in photographs, pictures, stories, and album covers from Blackwell's friends and clients back in the days of

Island Records. On the corner seat of the bar was a tall man in a cowboy hat with his back to me.

Chris Blackwell had a casual elegance: gray hair almost as long as mine and a trim beard, open collar, linen slacks, a deep tan from a lifetime in the Jamaican sun. Thom introduced me.

"Buck Reilly, welcome to GoldenEye." Chris shook my hand with a firm grip that belied his seventy-plus years.

"It's a pleasure to meet the man who introduced reggae to the rest of the world," I said.

Blackwell gave a brief nod. "And equally, a man who has cut such a romantic and dashing swath as a treasure hunter." This said in a British accent undiluted after his many years in Jamaica.

"It seems those days are long past," I said.

"Not so long." He smiled. "I'm quite familiar with the Port Royal salvage project you pursued."

I suspected a lot of people recognized my name from coverage in the local press.

"A brief attempt to revisit past successes," I said.

"Harry Greenbaum is an old friend," he said. "An investor, in fact, in the early days of Island Records."

"Really? He's never mentioned that, but given Harry's prolific portfolio I'm not surprised."

The bartender handed me a Black and Stormy, Blackwell's own version of a dark and stormy using his brand of rum.

"Your competitor has been luckless in Port Royal."

I managed a brief smile. "At this point I'm glad Last Resort wasn't selected."

"You're luckier than you know," Chris said.

"What's that supposed to mean?"

"According to Jamaican island legend, it's all a sham. The so-called Port Royal treasure, that is."

"So called?" I said. "The evidence that Henry Morgan spirited away a vast treasure was in a document identifying the location, dated late seventeenth century, and connected to a former slave who sailed with Morgan to the raid of Panama. I found it myself nearly six years ago through various connections here on Jamaica."

"Oh, I don't doubt it. The letter you acquired all those years ago was certainly authentic." He paused. "But legend here among Jamaicans whose family roots run back to those times has it that the content of the letter was intentionally bogus."

I sat there in shocked silence long enough for Blackwell to take a swig of his cocktail, put it down, and smile at me.

"You still there, Buck?" Thom said.

"Ah, yeah. Well, I suppose anything's possible, but a nearly four-hundred-year-old sham? Seems unlikely."

Yet nothing sounded unlikely coming from this man, who had an omniscient presence about him. Who'd been around the world and back many times, had built music legends from nothing, and still had a glint of Peter Pan in his bright blue eyes.

"It's academic for you now, of course, but as I said, lucky for you. Assuming local legend is true."

I sat on a barstool and gulped half of my Black and Stormy, the ginger beer tickling my nostrils.

"And I thought the music business was tough," Thom said.

Blackwell raised his empty glass.

"We should adjourn to my villa for dinner."

"Before we go," I said, "do you know a Professor Nanny Adou?"

Blackwell's eyes lit up. "Of course. She's at the University of the West Indies, and her ancestors have been here as far back as Morgan himself. Why do you ask?"

"She's been asking to see me. Says she wants me to meet an elder from the Moore Town Maroons but hasn't said why."

He was quiet for a moment.

"She's the genuine article, given her history and stature within the community. Have you met her yet?"

I shook my head.

"Well, it would be worthwhile, I'm sure. As I was saying, her family lineage goes back to the matriarch of Maroon leadership—Nanny herself."

"A mystery, wrapped in a conundrum, surrounded by legend," Thom said. "You'll be right at home here, Buck."

9

BECAUSE PROFESSOR ADOU WAS DRIVING UP FROM MOORE TOWN, JOHNNY Blake suggested we all meet at the Trident Hotel in Port Antonio. I rented a Jeep through GoldenEye and set out after breakfast.

The drive east along the coastal road cut in and out of wooded areas, weaving through small bays and towns: Port Maria, Annott Bay, Palmetto Bay, Buff Bay, and Hope Bay. An hour and a half later I finally found the Trident, just past the heart of Port Antonio. It was an elegant resort, geared to recapture the success of the 1950s, when the region's proximity to the Rio Grande had made it a strategic location for banana exporters.

Johnny was seated on one of the red couches in the courtyard out back, sipping a Coke. He jumped up when he saw me, and true to his outgoing personality gave me a quick hug and a fist bump.

"Mr. Buck, welcome back to Jamaica, mon."

"Thanks, Johnny. Can't say I'm happy to be here, but at least SCG is striking out." I glanced around. We were the only ones on the patio. "Speaking of which . . . have you ever heard a rumor the letter you sold me might be some kind of ancient scam?"

Johnny's ever-present smile vanished.

"Never heard nothing like that, mon. You saying I—"

"Whoa! I'm not suggesting you knew anything. But Jack hasn't found dick, and I heard the rumor from a source who knows local history, and it got me wondering."

Back came the toothy smile.

"Bad for your old friend Jack Dodson if it's true, huh?"

"Wouldn't break my heart, Johnny."

"Things real tense in Port Royal. Their work getting sloppier, and the Heritage Trust getting pushy."

Now that I'd seen Jack's operation firsthand, my estimate of $25,000 per day may have been conservative.

Good.

"By the way, I found out about that blond," Johnny said. "Name's Heather Drake—"

"I know." I took a deep breath. "I mean, it turns out I knew her."

He laughed. "Why am I not surprised, King Buck?"

"Do me a favor—don't call me that."

A waiter in a black uniform delivered cups and a pot of coffee. Johnny requested another Coke, and once the waiter poured my coffee, he bowed and walked away. I turned back to Johnny.

"I'm still curious about Professor Adou. You haven't told me much."

Johnny grinned, then reached into his pocket and pulled out a roll of Jamaican cash. He removed the rubber band and peeled back some bills until he found a five-hundred-dollar note. He held it up to show the image of Nanny, the leader of the Windward Maroons back from the late seventeenth and early eighteenth centuries.

"Named after the Mother of us all. I know who Queen Nanny is, but why's the professor named after her? Is there any significance?"

"Plenty significance, mon. She's the product of modern education but got a lot of old connections. Good thing you finally meet her, 'cause I'm not sure whether she be an Obeah like her great-great granny, but you don't want to take no chances—"

Suddenly Johnny's eyes bulged and he nearly fell out of his chair trying to stand up.

I glanced over my shoulder to see a tall, lithe woman in tan slacks and a bright yellow short-sleeved blouse walking toward us. I realized I was staring with my mouth open. Neither Chris nor Johnny had bothered to mention that Nanny was beautiful: fine features, mocha skin, short high-lighted hair, gorgeous figure, and a confidence that pulled it all together. I pushed my chair back and stood up.

"Miss Nanny," Johnny said. "Thank you so much for coming to see us."

She nodded at Johnny and stopped in front of me, tall but not so tall she didn't look up into my eyes.

"I'm glad you finally returned to Jamaica, Buck Reilly." She extended her hand and took mine in a firm grip.

Johnny extended his hand too, but still focused on me, she took a moment to give him a shake.

"Thank you for arranging the introduction, Mr. Blake. But at the risk of being rude, I'd like to speak with Mr. Reilly alone." She continued to study my face, her eyes probing mine.

I saw Johnny's shoulders slump.

"Excuse me," I said, then walked with him toward the lobby and patted him on the back. "Thanks, Johnny. I'll fill you in on what I learn and we'll see where this goes, if anywhere. In the meantime I know you'll be keeping an eye on Port Royal for me."

"All right, mon." He walked away, and I returned to Nanny Adou.

"Coffee?" I said.

"No, thanks." She sat on the couch across from me.

Questions filled my mind, but I held back. She leaned forward.

"Are you free for the next two hours? "

"I am. May I ask why?"

"I'd like to take you to Moore Town. A man's there waiting to meet you—Colonel Grandy."

"You'd mentioned him before. What does he want with me?"

"You're no stranger to Jamaica, Mr. Reilly—"

"Buck, please."

"The way you went about your recent pursuit of the Port Royal excavation leads us to believe you might be an advocate for the Jamaican people."

"How so?"

"Your application with its lack of . . . up-front fees and its promises to the selection committee was either naïve or honorable." A faint smile. "Given your background, nobody believes you're naïve. It's possible you've changed since your days as King Buck. That's what Colonel Grandy wants to see for himself."

A tingle ran up from my fingertips.

"To what end?"

She smiled, revealing white, straight teeth. Her almond-shaped eyes, while narrowed, looked alert but not unfriendly.

"You won't be disappointed, I assure you. And to anticipate your next question, yes—it does have to do with the Port Royal effort."

I sat back in the chair and sipped now lukewarm coffee.

"A friend and I had dinner with Chris Blackwell last night," I said. "He had an interesting theory about a legend related to the old letter that led me to the Port Royal project. What do you know about that?"

She smiled. "I'd rather you discuss this with Colonel Grandy, but I'll be happy to share some history with you first."

We both leaned in. A breeze swirled her light scent into my nostrils, inviting me closer.

"Some of the story is true, some parts are not. As you noted in your historical assessment in the application—"

"Wait—the applications were confidential."

Now the smile was almost a smirk. "Many of the former slaves who sailed with Henry Morgan on his privateering campaigns were Maroons. One of these men was connected to the letter in question."

"Connected how?"

"He wrote it. You need to understand that even though the Maroon community has been diluted over the years, there remains a core of elders who still speak the African dialects, practice the ancient ways, and curate our historic details. This piece of history has been held close, and given the value involved, you can imagine why."

I could only nod.

"The letter you acquired some years ago was originally a diversion planned by the man, or men, who helped Morgan hide the valuables from the attack on Panama. After Morgan's death in 1688 there was a massive search for the treasure conducted by former family members, privateer associates, and the authorities that felt swindled by Morgan. Just four years after Morgan's death came the earthquake that sank a good portion of Port Royal, so those who had helped Morgan hide the loot produced the letter stating that it had been buried in the bowels of the Jamison House, a part brothel Morgan was known to frequent. This letter had been hidden with the rest of his papers."

I felt as if I were filling with helium, getting lighter and lighter headed. If the treasure wasn't buried in the sunken ruins of the Jamison House, where was it? What else did she or Colonel Grandy know?

"Of course the Jamison House had been selected because it was buried under tons of rubble a league beneath the sea." She stopped and wet her lips with the tip of her tongue. "And the letter was the document you acquired."

The wheels inside my head spun, but I could find no angle to refute what she'd said. It made a lot of sense.

"If the Jamison House was only part brothel, what was the rest?"

"I thought that would be obvious. It was a rum distillery."

A giddy tingle danced through me with the thought that Jack might have run off with a bad luck charm when he stole my archives, but only for a moment. The professor may have been wrong about me. I wasn't naïve, but I wasn't necessarily honorable.

"Tell me, Nanny, do you know where the treasure is?"

"Don't jump ahead, Buck, it's not that simple."

We held a long stare. I raised an eyebrow but she didn't flinch. Hard one to read, this Nanny Adou.

"So what do we do from here?" I said.

"I take you to Moore Town, and depending on how that goes, we'll see what the next steps will be."

She suggested we go in my vehicle so I'd have a way back later.

"Would it be possible to get another permit to dive on Port Royal?" I asked as we walked to the open-topped Jeep.

She gave a short laugh. "Why?"

"An associate of mine wants to perform an underwater, high-quality photographic archaeological survey of the western section of the sunken city."

Her eyes narrowed. I held my silence.

"I think that could be done quite easily." She mentioned the name of an associate at the Jamaican National Historical Trust and said I could use her name.

I gave her my best smile.

"Thanks, I will."

10

THE ROAD TO MOORE TOWN WAS DUE SOUTH OF PORT ANTONIO. GOOD thing Nanny was with me, since the roads through the hilly interior were poorly marked, if at all. I tried to memorize landmarks for the return drive, but my mind kept wandering to what I might learn from Colonel Stanley Grandy.

With the top down on the Jeep, Nanny sat back and enjoyed the wind blowing through her hair. The light brown of her complexion, along with what I guessed were subtle European features, made it clear that the past few hundred years had included family departures from her Maroon origins—no surprise given the brutal battles in the seventeenth and eighteenth centuries. I guessed her age to be close to my own, mid-thirties. Clearly she was perceptive, intellectual, strong, a community leader, and highly attractive in a nondeliberate way. What did she know about me beyond what had been included in Last Resort's application for the Port Royal project? Did she know e-Antiquity's history?

I swallowed. She was a professor of archaeology at one of the top schools in the Caribbean. Albeit far in the past, my failures were nearly as well documented as my successes. She had to know.

Her cell phone rang. She began a lengthy discussion with the person on the other end, speaking in local patois—Ashanti, I guessed, one of the African dialects still in use amongst the Maroons. I couldn't understand a word she was saying, so while she talked I steered the Jeep with my right hand, took my own cell phone out of my shirt pocket, and hit the speed dial.

"Mr. Buck, how did your talk go with that fine-looking professor?" Johnny's voice had a giggle to its cadence.

"Good, we're headed now to meet the Maroon elder who wanted to see me."

"Moore Town?"

"Right."

"You know about that place? The history of the Windward Maroons? They was some badass warriors, mon—"

"Listen, I have something I want you to do." I could hear Nanny still chattering away on her phone. "We need to file for another dive permit with JNHT—"

"What's that you say?"

"Not for salvage. To photograph the underwater Port Royal ruins—a few hundred yards to the west of SCG's westward boundary."

A long silence followed. "Photograph?"

"Right. Use Professor Adou's name as our sponsor. File that, then follow up with the people we were going to rent boats from. We only need a few, but I'm not sure for how long. Get a monthlong contract with a termination clause."

"I'm confused, mon. What kind of boats we need for photography? How many people? And how we make any money doing that?"

I explained we needed dive boats and not to share with anyone not on the application that we'd be doing a photographic survey.

Since Johnny still sounded confused and doubtful, I said, "If all goes well, it could lead to another salvage opportunity." That cheered him right up.

"You got me plenty curious now, Mr. Buck, but I like the sound of it."

"I'd like the boats ready ASAP. Nanny—um, Professor Adou—thought we could get a permit pretty fast." I gave him the name she'd mentioned.

"Nanny, huh? You work quick, mon." The giggle was back, then it vanished and I got Johnny's business voice. "I'll have the paperwork filed today and the deal cut on the boats by this time tomorrow. Guess this means I'm back on the payroll, too?"

"With a 1 percent finders' fee on anything we're allowed to keep if this turns into a salvage operation."

We hung up. Nanny, no longer on her phone, was staring at me.

"You work quickly, Buck." It was the second time I'd heard that in less than three minutes. "And confidently, too."

The balance of the drive was filled with switchbacks as we climbed through mountainous terrain above the Wild Cane River toward Moore Town. The view below was of green rolling hills that led to more mountainous terrain, steeped in mist and low clouds with the silver reflection of the river curving through it. The Maroon's successes against the far greater numbers of heavily armed Spanish and British pursuers in the late 1600s and early 1700s had been thanks to their better understanding of the landscape, superior vantage points, ahead-of-their time camouflage, fearless courage, and an unquenchable desire to maintain their freedom. As we drove through the same hills now, I imagined the guerilla warfare that rained down upon the Europeans until finally the land that now comprises Moore Town was ceded to the Maroons. The person who signed that land grant was none other than the general who led the campaign against their oppressors—Nanny, Mother of us all.

"Almost there," Nanny Adou said.

If she was an actual descendent of the original Nanny, then she was clearly more than just an academic. I sensed a predator's glint in her eyes, and while I didn't think it was geared toward me—I had nothing of value for her or the Maroons—the anticipation was as palpable as the humidity in the open vehicle.

The roads were little better than dirt tracks at this point—breathtaking views, but steep and without guardrails to prevent a hapless vehicle from driving off the sharp-edged cliff into the river valley below. While the vegetation was scrubby and thick on the uphill side of the road, the occasional breaks in the trees revealed picturesque overlooks.

A fit of anxiety produced a sweat bloom in my armpits. I was driving blindly into a village with a history of barbaric assaults on opposition. If somebody decided I was the enemy, I was well and truly screwed. On the other hand, if they wanted to work *with* me, it would significantly enhance my position and prospects in Jamaica.

We drove slowly up the dirt road past a group of men I guessed to be in their twenties. When they spotted me their expressions turned hard. One noticed Nanny. His eyes opened wide and he elbowed his friend as we drove past.

"Anything I should know about Colonel Grandy or the people of Moore Town before we get there?" I said.

Nanny gave me a long glance before offering a small smile.

"They don't trust strangers here. And the colonel is old, prefers to speak in Ashanti. He'll speak English for you and will seem charming, but he'll be judging your every word and movement."

I swallowed. "He asked to see *me*—"

"But he knows you're a treasure hunter, so he'll expect the worst." She looked away as she said that last part. I suddenly felt as if the dirt kicked up by our tires had coated my skin.

Or maybe I just felt dirty from the inside out.

We rounded the corner and the small village came into view. Houses were spread around the hills in a haphazard fashion. I spotted a flagpole surrounded by a fence, then a small blue building with an image of a woman's face painted on one side, the same face from the $500 bill. A landscape of the valley was painted on the other side. I glanced from the painted face to Nanny and back. She smiled. I saw no resemblance other than the notable glint in her eyes.

"The house in the middle there, with the red roof, is where we're going. Park down in the square."

Now came the familiar adrenaline rush, that buzz I always got when closing in on a lead.

I turned the Jeep off and Nanny looked hard into my eyes.

"Don't screw this up, Buck Reilly."

11

INSIDE THE HOUSE IT WAS DARK AND SMELLED OF SMOKE AND BOILING VEGETA-bles. The living room was neat, with sturdy, well-used furniture. There were paintings and photos on the walls, images from the countryside and what I presumed to be family.

Nanny called out in a dialect I couldn't follow—whether it was an announcement or a familiar greeting, I wasn't sure.

"Back here," a male voice said in English.

We turned a corner into a kitchen, void of contemporary conveniences but suited to the needs of the local lifestyle and cuisine. The colonel's eyes lit when he saw Nanny only to narrow at the sight of me behind her. He brushed his palms down his blue denim shirt and stepped forward.

"Colonel Grandy, meet Buck Reilly from e-Antiquity."

I extended my hand. "Actually, my company is now called Last Resort Charter and Salvage."

He shrugged. "Sounds desperate."

The colonel didn't fit what I'd expected. Short hair, lighter skinned, wearing a brown baseball hat and a scruffy week's worth of stubble. I wasn't sure of his age, given his slight frame, but he could be anywhere from his late fifties to early seventies. He was tall, too. I'd made a fortune reading people back in the heyday of e-Antiquity, and I didn't need Nanny's description to peg the colonel as distrustful and wary.

I reminded myself that he'd contacted me, not the other way around.

"You offered 75 percent of anything you recovered at Port Royal to the museum," he said.

"Excuse me?" I said.

"Your offer to dig up Port Royal. It included 75 percent of anything of value you found for the museum. You forget already?"

"That was a sealed bid."

"Ha! You funny, Buck Reilly. This is Jamaica, not Washington, D.C. We know things here. And your bid wasn't enough."

I bit my lip, unsure how to respond.

"And what did SCG International offer?"

He laughed and I saw he was missing a few of his molars.

"They offer 50 percent to the government—"

"What!"

He smiled and glanced at Nanny. There was no trace of humor on her face.

"But they offer up-front cash of $200,000 U.S. dollars. Since the government think it unlikely that anyone find anything out there—plus the winner had to restore some old sunken building—they take the cash."

The sight of me with my mouth hanging open was enough for Nanny to crack a smile, albeit briefly. I wasn't sure how to proceed, so I pressed my lips together, shrugged my shoulders, and waited. The colonel nodded and said something to Nanny, who nodded back.

"Come, let's sit," he said. "My feet hurt."

Next to the kitchen was a small square folding table with some mismatched wood chairs. They looked old, as old as Moore Town itself for all I knew. He pulled a pack of cigarettes from his breast pocket and offered me one, which I declined. He lit one with a blue plastic lighter.

"That treasure is ours, not the government's. And anyway, 75 percent still not enough." His eyes narrowed as smoke wafted up from his nostrils.

His statement intimated that there *was* a treasure. I sat forward.

"Why's that?"

He blew smoke out hard. "Many of Henry Morgan's men were freed slaves, Maroons. They could fight like hell, and Morgan had been a reasonable man, lieutenant governor of Jamaica in the end, and treated men like men, not property." He took a long drag on the cigarette. "Some of those Maroons helped Morgan hide what he took from Panama."

I saw certainty in his eyes, and a hot flash danced on my nerve endings.

"Morgan trusted us, our ancestors, and we want our share. You didn't bribe nobody, and I don't think it's because you're a fool. I think you might be one-a them rare, recovering greed addicts who'd rather lose than get dirty again."

I glanced at Nanny—her face was impassive. She'd be a hell of a poker player. I sat back in the wood chair, which creaked loudly.

"And given that Jack Dodson was once my partner and is now my sworn enemy, I'd do anything to prevent them from finding something of value."

The vision of Heather on Jack's boat had me wince.

"So you think about it, Buck Reilly. You tell Nanny what you willing to give up to get the Morgan treasure, then we talk again." He stubbed out his cigarette in a clean ashtray and sat back in his chair.

"You know where it is?" I said. "The Morgan treasure?"

"Ha! We know that, why'n the hell I'd be talking to you?" He shook his head and shot Nanny a look. "No, we have a lot of old papers from back then, from the men who helped Morgan, they mention details we want you to help us figure out if we can agree on terms. That's what we need you for."

The colonel stood, followed by Nanny, then me. My mind was reeling. What could their information be—and where might the treasure be? Certainly not in Port Royal.

I followed them toward the door. Before the colonel opened it, he turned back to face me.

"Time is important here. These other people looking in Port Royal getting plenty frustrated. They might start throwing money around, maybe somebody talk." His old dark eyes bored into mine. "Is it worth 10 percent of whatever is recovered for us to confide in you?"

"Ten percent wouldn't even cover—wait! How could I negotiate if I don't have any details? Is the treasure supposed to be underwater? Buried somewhere—"

"We won't tell you nothing until we have an agreement, plain and simple." He turned toward Nanny. "Take him back up to Oracabessa." With that he pulled the door open.

We stepped into the sun, which was blinding after being in his dark house—

A sudden burst of noise caught me off guard. A large man had started yelling something—in an African dialect and at the top of his voice—at the colonel and Nanny, while pointing to me.

The colonel flung his wrists at the man and hissed something back in the same dialect—just as angrily but not as loud. Nanny stepped toward the man and yelled at him. The man, who was muscular and not much older than thirty, had a sneer on his lips that exposed crooked teeth. Again he pointed at me.

"And you got no business here! Stay out of our history. And you two"— this for the colonel and Nanny—"don't you tell the likes of him nothing!"

Other people peered up and down the dirt road at us. The colonel, to his credit, shook his head and spoke in a low tone, first in the dialect, then English.

"You go ahead now, you don't want no trouble. And you don't tell me how to run our business."

The man looked into each of our faces, finishing with mine.

"None of you got no right to the history." His voice had lowered to a growl. He punctuated his statement with another hard glance at each of us, then turned and walked away, slowly.

"Pay no attention to him." But the colonel shuddered, which alarmed me.

Whatever I had walked into here felt thick with danger. It was also far more intriguing—and promising—than the old letter that had directed us toward Port Royal.

Hot damn.

12

THE SUN SET THIRTY MINUTES BEFORE WE MADE IT BACK TO GOLDENEYE.
Nanny turned down my offer to return her to her car at the Trident—
she said she'd arranged a dinner for tonight at the resort, and a friend from
Port Antonio would be coming to take her back afterwards.

My questions about the man who had verbally attacked us were met
with assurances that all was fine. She never mentioned the man's name, but
she did say he was from Accompong in the Cockpit Country, the western
wilderness region of Jamaica.

"He's of the Leeward Maroons," she said, "and there have been peri-
odic . . . tensions between the Windward and Leeward factions."

"Weren't all Maroons escaped slaves that fought and defeated Spanish
and British colonists? What's the issue?"

"Jamaicans never forget, Buck. And Maroons never forgive."

"Forgive what?"

She shifted in her seat. The darkness hid her expression, but I hadn't
been able to read her all day anyway. Hell, the only time I could ever read
her was when she narrowed her eyes or smiled.

"At the tail end of the Maroon independence wars, the Leewards had
negotiated a peaceful ceasefire with the British before the Windwards had.
They then began to work with the British to hunt down Spaniards and
terrify them, often kill them. The British used them to scare and repel the
Spanish, and it worked."

I waited, but she didn't elaborate.

"How did that create a divide with the Windwards?" I said.

She looked straight at me, and while the darkness hid most of her features, I saw her eyes narrow.

"Because they also helped the British to hunt down Windward Maroons. Only a few opportunists, really, bounty hunters, but it was Maroons selling out other Maroons."

I could easily imagine some, especially elders, who would still resent those betrayals, even though they happened three hundred years ago.

"Are you really convinced Henry Morgan had a stash of treasure? Most historians have concluded that he was a straight-up privateer, operating on the orders of the British government. My research at e-Antiquity, however, was less conclusive. Aside, of course, from when he was recalled to London to face trial for his attack on Spanish Panama, which unwittingly coincided with a ceasefire between the countries."

"Yes, but he was pardoned, knighted, and returned to Jamaica as the lieutenant governor."

"Right, so when did he stash the treasure? You mentioned Panama, but could it have been after he sacked Portobello?" I said.

"His most successful siege," she said. "Silver pesos, gold coins, silver bars, and several chests of silver-plated goods. At the time it was worth 250,000 pesos—of course, that's millions today."

"But all of the valuables were fully accounted for by officials who had accompanied them on the voyage. So then came his attack on Maracaibo."

Now I could see her smile. "That was perhaps the most brilliant strategy and attack he employed."

"Going in at night?" I said.

"That, and his using logs on ships to make it look like he had additional cannons. And loading his troops on unarmed merchant ships and ferrying them to shore at night, where they emptied the enemy's coffers and slipped past the long guns of the fort by drifting without sail during the same night."

"How much did he bring back from Maracaibo?"

"Same mix of valuables, but only half the value. Estimates were 125,000 pesos."

I smiled, glanced over, and saw she was smiling too. The connection between archaeologists, whether for-profit or not, was undeniable. But never had I known such an attractive, and yes, sexy professor of archaeology. I wondered what she was thinking.

"Sir Henry's fleet was larger at Maracaibo, so the share per man was much less," she said. "Sir Henry used his shares to buy over eight hundred acres of land to add to his holdings in the parish of Clarendon—it's still called the Morgan Valley."

"Maybe that's what he did with whatever treasure he stole, buy land—"

"That's not it."

I was again struck by her certainty, just like the colonel's. Confident that the treasure existed, just not sure exactly where it was.

"That leaves Panama, Morgan's last major campaign."

She nodded and let out a sigh.

"Again, an amazing strategy—a flawless attack spoiled by a lucky Spanish sentry. Nearly a thousand men sailed with Morgan—"

"Not to mention a hundred and seventy five treasure-hauling mules."

"I'm impressed," she said. "No wonder you were such a good treasure hunter."

My lips tugged in a tight smile. Information is power in any business, but detail is crucial when hunting antiquities.

She said, "My favorite detail of his assault on Panama was that they sailed their fleet as far as they could go up the Chagres River to avoid the fort and embattlements. But when they ran out of depth, they continued on in dozens of hand-carved canoes."

"Amazing forethought, I agree. Were the canoes carved in Jamaica?"

She shook her head. "Isla Vaca, off what's now Haiti. Morgan commenced all his campaigns by gathering his privateers at Isla Vaca."

Could that be where he dropped off some of the treasure? I kept that thought to myself, and instantly felt guilty for it.

"After all that planning and effort," Nanny said, "they only walked away with thirty thousand pesos."

"There were no shortage of doubters that thought Morgan stashed the brunt of the wealth somewhere—"

"His own crewman accused him of stealing from them," she said. "The shares per person that they brought home were nominal."

We turned off the main road to the coastal road, now only a few miles from GoldenEye. The time had flown by during the drive and I truly enjoyed the connection, formed from shared knowledge, mutual interest, and our physical proximity for most of the day.

I didn't want the day to end. I put out of mind for now the bizarre non-negotiation about whatever might be found if we ended up working together.

"And you said former slaves sailed with Morgan's fleet?"

"Full-shared privateers, just like the rest." She paused. "Historic archives state that over a hundred former slaves sailed with him to Panama."

"And that was what, 1681? Long before the Maroon wars, so 'former' slaves wouldn't have been recognized by true government officials, correct?"

She glanced over at me. "Morgan was no fool, they were Maroon warriors. The best fighters in the Caribbean."

Some facts clicked together in my mind. Maroon warriors wouldn't just be mercenaries, they might have also been Morgan's strategists.

Another dime dropped.

That explained why Colonel Grandy, Nanny, and even that asshole that chewed us out were so convinced about the treasure's existence.

They had *solid* insider's knowledge—real evidence—not just a hunch or Maroon legend.

"Listen, Nanny, I'm interested—very interested—in working with you on this project. You and the colonel approached me for good reason— nobody has found more missing antiquities in the past decade than me. But truth be told, I'm broke. Lost everything. Maybe I've learned from past mistakes, and I want to do things right, but I can't afford to be taken advantage of, even for a good cause."

I stretched my fingers on the steering wheel.

"I understand, Buck." Nanny was now looking straight ahead. "Nobody's trying to take advantage of you, but as Stanley—Colonel Grandy—said, if we're successful in finding something of value, we want it to be for the Jamaican people—not the government, not for treasure hunters. And we have reason to believe the treasure could be substantial."

It didn't sound like their demanding 90 percent was for self-enrichment. But what did that platitude about helping the Jamaican people mean? Helping them how? And not letting the government get any? Well, that was pure fantasy—unless the treasure wasn't in Jamaica.

She, or the colonel, possessed secret information I could help them resolve. If that led to the treasure, would 10 percent for me be fair? I swallowed. Depending on the value of the find, that could still be a hell of a lot of money, and without the overhead of mucking around out in the submerged ruins of Port Royal.

Just how reformed was I?

13

DINNER WAS AN HOUR AWAY AND I'D BEEN INVITED LAST-MINUTE, SO NANNY and I went our separate ways, then met in the bar at Bizot.

"Blackwell Rum on the rocks for me," I said just as she showed up.

"I'll have a club soda, please," she told the bartender.

"That's all?" he said.

"Add a twist of lime."

I spotted Chris Blackwell coming across the patio, a study in confidence. Since Nanny's back was to him, she didn't see him catch my eye and hold a finger to his lips. He snuck up behind her and slowly held his hands in front of her eyes.

A smile big enough to show all those perfectly straight, perfectly white teeth spread across her face. She took his wrists, stood, then spun between his arms and placed them around her in a move that would make a ballerina proud. They hugged and giggled like schoolchildren.

"Here I thought I'd scare you," he said.

"You might have, if I hadn't been here with a man like Buck Reilly. Can't imagine feeling unsafe with him around."

Chris pumped his eyebrows at me and I felt my cheeks heat up. Then he stepped back and took her in. Nanny looked as fresh now as she had when arriving at Trident this morning.

"Where's your friend?" he said.

"Should be here any—"

A roar sounded over our heads. I turned to see a sleek green helicopter settle onto an island just in front of the beach.

"Speak of the devil," Chris said.

Nanny slapped him on the shoulder. I hadn't asked but was suddenly very curious—who was joining us, and what was his or her relationship with Nanny?

Moments later a stocky man in a suit and tie emerged from the darkness and moved toward us at a steady pace. I glanced at Nanny—who, of course, could read my face like a book.

"Michael Portland, owner of the Trident," she said.

"Half the world," Chris said under his breath.

Michael Portland—the first Jamaican-born billionaire. Last I heard most of his enterprise was based in the United States.

We all stood as he approached.

Hugs for Nanny and Chris, then he turned his sharp eyes toward me.

"You must be Buck Reilly."

I stuck my hand out. I'd known other billionaires—hell, I was pretty damned sure Harry Greenbaum was one—and had once been worth tens of millions myself, so wealth didn't intimidate me. But I usually came more prepared when meeting them.

Chris ushered us up the beach to a private dining room where waiters stood at the ready. Champagne waited on ice, candles provided intimate circles of light in the otherwise dark space. Chris's and Michael's small talk about the resort business led to forward-looking assessments of how Jamaica might benefit from new laws legalizing marijuana in the U.S. I was just happy the conversation hadn't focused on me.

I caught Nanny watching me. She immediately looked away, then looked back a second later with a smile. We'd shared a connection during the ride, or so I thought. And just now in that moment I'd gotten a new look—an intimate look?

"So, Buck," Michael said. "Or do you still go by *King* Buck?"

If I had a dollar for every time someone used that line on me, I'd be a billionaire too, but I let it go.

"It's just Buck these days."

"Consider yourself lucky your opponent was selected to dig in the mud and stabilize sunken structures," Michael said.

"Couldn't agree more," I said. "Are you interested in missing treasure, Michael?"

He pressed his lips together. His eyes were jovial when chatting amongst friends, but he was always ready to pounce, that much I could see. You don't become a billionaire by being passive.

"I'm interested in fairness for the Jamaican people. Too many of our national treasures have been squandered by civil servants who may mean well or more likely may be trying to line their pockets—let's call it 'aggressive *touristization*.' It may provide some immediate benefits, but if not done thoughtfully it will hurt this country for generations to come."

I nodded.

"I know what you proposed in your application for the Port Royal farce," he said. "It would have been good for Jamaica—but less so for you." He paused and leaned closer. "Did you let your competitor outbid you?"

A laugh tickled my lips. "Do you really think I'm that calculating, Michael?"

"Given everything I'd heard about your past? Possibly." He smiled. "It's how I would have played it."

"Seems like our sealed bids must have been printed in the *Jamaican Gleaner*."

"Nanny and the colonel shared with you that our interest is for the Jamaican people—"

"Not self-enrichment?"

He smiled, and I immediately felt foolish.

"Do you think I need the money?" he said back. "I've already provided millions to help the Jamaican people, but this is different. This is our *history*. Using treasure from those who brought our forefathers here for something positive would be unlike any subsidy—ever. Can you imagine the sensation? The pride? The catharsis?"

Each of them stared at me intently. There was no sympathy on Nanny's face, and it hit me that we were picking up where we'd left off with Colonel Grandy—except the qualifications of the negotiators had elevated significantly.

I puckered my lips and pressed them between my teeth. If this was poker, I didn't even have a face card.

"If there was more in-depth information on the Morgan legacy than what led to the Port Royal excavation," Nanny said, "and if we were willing to share it with you—"

"But for only a fraction," Michael said.

"I'm going to speak with the chef," Chris said. He sauntered back toward the kitchen.

"Since I have no idea what you're talking about, or whether it would infringe on the permit already issued to Jack—that is, SCG International—"

"It doesn't infringe on what they're doing," Nanny said.

"We can handle the government and Heritage people," Michael said. "They will ultimately see the logic in this effort."

With my elbows on the table, I pressed my palms together and held them against my chin. Butterflies—hell, vampire bats—swirled in my stomach. Clearly they were convinced that whatever information they had was significant. But even with the aid of the intelligent and beautiful professor from the University of the West Indies, they hadn't been able to piece it together. They needed me.

"In all my years of working with governments, museums, or universities, we never accepted less than 25 percent for our efforts—"

"Weren't you listening to me?" Michael said.

"I don't even know what information you have."

"And you won't."

A deep breath filled my lungs. I was rusty at this. Facing off against a world-class billionaire negotiator like Michael Portland was futile. Time to tack.

"So what's it worth to you?"

"Only a small—"

I held up a hand. "To have King Buck, as you called me, on your team, connecting shreds of clues to discover long-lost antiquities and who-knows-how-valuable treasure? As one of my favorite philosophers once said, '15 percent of nothing is nothing.' Is that what you want, nothing?"

A wave of cold sweat ran over my brow. Why did I have to use that quote? I'd just dropped myself to 15 percent—thanks, Jimmy.

Michael shared a long look with Nanny before turning back to me. The candlelight reflected in his eyes like small fires. Maroons practiced ancient African Obeah, and Queen Nanny was a chieftainess and priestess as well as a revolutionary leader. Was Michael also of Maroon descent?

I looked up into the dark rafters of the ceiling, seeking to break the stare. Here I am at GoldenEye, former home of Ian Fleming—

Fleming.

Bond, James Bond.

I sat up straight. "You can shake me, but you can't stir me. I have partners, too. The cost of these efforts is huge, as are the risks, so if you can't agree to—"

"Ten percent, Reilly. We'll cover all the expenses. You'll get our information. *And* a cut of the treasure your former partner, Jack Dodson, and his crass partner Rostenkowski, have wasted a fortune digging for in the harbor."

I swallowed. Jack and Gunner.

Heather.

I tried to swallow again, but my throat had gone dry.

Michael and Nanny broke into smiles and I realized I'd nodded, accepting their offer. He extended his hand. At first my grip was soft, but then I clamped down and his eyes popped wide.

Fuck you, Jack. I promised revenge, and I meant it.

Another wave of cold sweat blew over me. Harry Greenbaum would kill me. I'd had to beg him to agree on 25 percent for the Port Royal project.

At 10 percent, this had better be one hell of a find.

Michael clapped his hands and two waiters rushed over, one carrying a tray of fresh seafood, the other two more bottles of champagne—Dom Pérignon, of course.

Nanny stood. While I was focused on what I'd tell Harry, she bent down to kiss my cheek. I found my face squarely in the low cut of her blouse for a moment before she straightened up.

Treasure comes in many forms.

14

THE NIGHT HAD RUN LONG, AND FEELING A BIT LIKE A HIRED HAND, I FINALLY said my goodbyes. The sound of Michael Portland's helicopter departing shortly thereafter allowed me to rest easy. In my champagne and rum-induced fog, I fantasized about Nanny entering my villa, but as I drifted into sleep I remembered she'd said a friend was taking her back to the Trident. No doubt she'd left with Michael.

A morning swim around the lagoon helped clear my head, and when I sat down at the restaurant to order breakfast I was surprised that a note came with my coffee. It had a familiar scent that made me smile.

I tore open the sealed envelope.

Buck,

Meet me at the grotto under the bridge at 10:00.
I have something to show you.

N.

I folded the letter and placed it back in the envelope. Images of Bond girls stepping out of the Caribbean onto white sand beaches ran through my head—

I glanced at my watch. Ten o'clock on the dot.

I wrapped my towel over my shoulders, left the coffee on the table, and headed down the stairs to where the sporting equipment was kept. No one was in the grotto, or so I thought.

Nanny stepped out from behind a wall of coral, the light reflecting off the water and dancing over her bare legs. She was wearing a swimsuit, and what I'd imagined about her figure yesterday wasn't nearly as alluring as the reality in front of me now.

She stepped into the light, carrying a plastic case. Without a word she nodded for me to follow and led me to a quiet picnic table on the edge of the water sports area.

"Sleep well?" she said.

"My mind was playing tricks on me at first, but I slept fine," I said. "How was the night flight?"

She shook her head. "I stayed here last night."

"Then why meet at this grotto instead of one of our rooms?"

Her eyes narrowed. "It seemed prudent."

She didn't want anybody to see me visiting her? Again I took in her supple body. She didn't trust us alone together?

I glanced at the plastic case. It was waterproof and looked heavy. She must have seen the crease in my brow.

"Michael brought it with him last night." She grabbed the two clasps that held the case shut, then looked up at me. "I take it you're still committed to what we discussed at dinner?"

"More than ever. What have you got?"

Inside the case were several archival sleeves filled with various notes, drawings, even a small leather-bound diary. A tingle ran down my arms and into my fingertips. She laid everything out on the table: I counted seven documents, including the diary. I put my finger gently on top of that one.

"Henry Morgan's last diary," she said. "Only a few pages filled, but there are some important passages that mention the name Njoni, one of his most trusted privateer associates. A Maroon—"

"Whoa," I said. "Back up."

"What is it?"

"Njoni was the author of the letter that led to the Port Royal salvage effort. He said the treasure had been buried under the Jamison House—"

"Right, but *this* evidence leads us to conclude that was a ruse planned by Morgan to protect the treasure."

My heart was racing. Pieces connected and hung in the air. What was true, what was a lie? Were we just seeing what we wanted to see? Always a concern in the hunt for antiquities, often a fatal mistake.

"And the rest?" I bent down to look at the sketches on bark or preserved parchment. My gaze stopped at a crude drawing on yellowed paper. It was too faded to determine the subject—all that remained visible were some curved lines. Which could be anything.

"Back in the day, I'd have these documents appraised for period and authenticity," I said.

"They're authentic, don't worry."

I stood up and looked into her eyes. She didn't flinch.

"You're a professor of archaeology," I said. "Why do you need me? I don't even understand the language on some of these—Ashanti, I presume?"

"That, and Akan. Just because we can read the language doesn't mean we know how to tie this material together and figure out what it refers to."

She took a deep breath. The sun through the trees caught her light brown eyes as she looked into mine.

She picked up the diary and removed it from the sleeve. As it opened, the pages moved around—they weren't bound or fastened, just loose. She scanned through a few and pulled a couple out. One page was stained with what looked like old wine, the next was clean. She held the stained one up for me.

"The ink is seriously faded." I leaned closer. The name Panama jumped off the page. I wished I at least had a magnifying glass.

I pointed to the page, a word that looked like "Njoni."

Nanny nodded.

I scanned down further and while the language was virtually impossible to read given the faded ink, old English, and what almost seemed like code, a number jumped off the page: 100,000 pesos.

My finger stopped there.

"Exactly," Nanny said.

"100,000 pesos in the late 1600s would be worth . . ." I tried to calculate. "Tens of millions today."

"Ten percent of that's not bad, Buck."

Her words stung. People always assumed I'd only been after money, but I liked to think it was more the hunt, the historic value of the antiquities, and most of all the thrill of finding what no other man had been able to unearth for centuries that really drove me.

Nanny must have read my thoughts.

"I didn't mean—"

"I'm used to it. Lots of stereotypes in this world, and a treasure hunter's pretty easy to pigeonhole."

"Your contributions to connecting missing links of world civilization are extremely valuable, Buck." She placed her arm on my bicep and squeezed. "Don't sell yourself short."

I leaned closer to the table, and she let go of my arm.

"So what have you deduced from all this?" I said.

"Morgan was sailing around Jamaica, coming across the northern coast—"

"He should have been coming from the southwest."

"May have been a storm, or the winds may have driven them there, we're not sure," she said. "Anyway, the diary refers to putting several canoes to shore near Port Antonio, in the dead of night."

"The Rio Grande?"

"Could be. Njoni was known throughout the island, but after Morgan's death, his heirs were more closely associated with the Leeward Maroons."

Some people were walking over the bridge toward us, so Nanny gently scooped up the archival sleeves and placed them back in the box, which I could see had locking clasps. She closed and spun the numeric dials.

"Now what?" I said.

"I suggest we return to Moore Town and sort through these papers with Stanley."

I dug my keys out of my pocket. "No time like the present."

She smiled. "I'll go get dressed."

"I'll get my Jeep."

So
Many
Rising

15

AFTER AN HOUR OF THE NINETY-MINUTE DRIVE FROM GOLDENEYE TO PORT Antonio, I was gripping the steering wheel so tight my neck ached. The same battered brown car had been traveling at the same distance behind us for too long now. When I sped up, it sped up. If I slowed down, it slowed down.

I kept my eye on the rearview mirror.

"Is this the only road to Port Antonio?"

"The A4 is the fastest road," Nanny said. "Why?"

"Just curious."

"Some roads cut in toward the coast more, but this is the most direct."

Given the value of the documents she'd shown me, it was possible she or Colonel Grandy or even Michael Portland might have someone shadowing us.

We passed through several small villages and so did the brown shitbox. Nanny hadn't once questioned my silence or my continual glances in the rearview mirror, and if she'd noticed we were being followed, she kept it to herself.

We finally passed over the Rio Grande River, drove into Port Antonio, and turned left toward the Errol Flynn Marina. "Where are you going?" she said.

"I want to stop in the ship's store for something."

I kept my eye on the rearview and counted to myself . . . fifteen, sixteen, seventeen, eighteen . . . there's the shitbox.

"Ship's store?"

I nodded.

Ship's store was an exaggeration, but there was a small marine supply and provisions store I hoped would have what I was looking for. Besides, the turn allowed me a chance to see who was in—

Where had the little brown car gone?

"You want me to come with you?" she said.

I was half in, half out of the Jeep, looking back over my shoulder.

"No, you should probably stay here with the documents. And call the colonel and tell him we're on our way."

"Oh, right. Good point."

Still no sign of the shitbox, so I entered the store. Just past a small selection of nautical charts I found a small magnifying glass and held it up to peer through. Satisfied, I took it to the counter and paid in cash—I was still a couple years away from being eligible for a credit card after my personal bankruptcy.

A pang of guilt stopped me in my tracks. I stared at my phone a long moment, then hit one of my saved numbers.

A familiar British voice answered on the third ring.

"Buck Reilly? I've been worried your silence meant you were in trouble, dear boy." True to his paternal role in my life, Harry Greenbaum knew how to simultaneously express concern and impose guilt.

"Sorry, Harry. It's been nip and tuck back here to say the least."

"Here meaning Jamaica." He paused. "Correct me if I'm wrong, but weren't you admonished to avoid Port Royal under penalty of law?"

"It's a long story, hopefully one we'll enjoy sharing over rum and a cigar, but bottom line is I was lured back to Jamaica by a direct heir to the Maroon legacy, and through her contacts we've gained new information that cast an entirely different light on the situation."

The sound of Harry's heavy breathing might have signaled excitement, but it was more likely that his advanced age and increasing weight were causing respiratory challenges.

"I just wanted to let you know I'm back on the hunt with fresh insight, and . . . it may be of far greater value than we'd originally projected."

"Excellent news, Buck. I knew I backed the right horse. Do keep me apprised, won't you?"

I promised to call again when I knew more and rang off.

Heading back to the Jeep I saw the A4 was shitbox-free, and off we went along the north coast, doubling back toward the Rio Grande.

"Get what you wanted?" Nanny said.

I handed her the little bag.

"Ah, smart," she said when she looked inside.

"Did you speak with Colonel Grandy?" I said.

"He'll meet us up river."

My head snapped to the right—I thought I'd seen the shitbox again, but there was no vehicle in sight. If it *had* been following us, they'd either anticipated where we were going or given up. I drove on and ignored the mirrors, focusing instead on the road ahead.

Once the main shipping port for the banana trade, the mouth of the Rio Grande was an eighth of a mile wide. I tried to imagine what it had looked like hundreds of years ago when there was nothing here but river and tropical foliage. Only natives who knew the dense mountain ranges and the river itself would risk travel at night by canoe into that black wilderness, especially if those canoes were laden with silver, gold, and other valuables. Maroons? That made sense. Or possibly even Taino Indians, but Nanny hadn't mentioned them.

I'd seen signs at the Errol Flynn Marina for boat rentals, but we wanted to travel silently. Another hour into the lush, steep contours of the green backcountry passed as Nanny guided me over unmarked roads to Berridale.

"The rafting camp is another two miles south," she said.

"Good thing we have the Jeep."

These mountains and the mass acreage of wilderness helped me appreciate how the Maroons had so successfully avoided the Spanish, then British troops that pursued them. The sheer size of the forest, combined with their skill in battle, made the Maroons as invincible as the Mujahideen of Afghanistan.

I steered the Jeep onto a narrow trail and pulled up out of sight.

"What are you doing?" Nanny said.

"Let's take a closer look at those archives before we meet with the colonel."

I opened the Jeep's tailgate, and Nanny spread out the archival sleeves. Using my new magnifying glass and the Notes application on my phone, I jotted down what information I could read. Nanny translated some of the old African writing, and we gradually pieced together something significant: the men who'd spirited away "goods" from Morgan's ship noted paddling against the current toward what we assumed eventually became known as Moore Town.

"Look at this." Nanny pointed at text under the magnifying glass I was holding. "Talks about seeing a flash—or maybe reflection—on the Great Mountain at dawn. It must mean Blue Mountain."

"How can you tell?" I held my arms wide. "There's a hell of a lot of big mountains around here."

"But Great Mountain is how the Blue Mountain Peak was known to Maroons in those times."

I smiled at Nanny. "Nice to have an accomplished professor of archaeology who speaks the ancient dialects on the team," I said.

It didn't take us long to finish reviewing the drawings, notes, and Henry Morgan's brief diary, and we were only on the road south another mile before reaching an outfitter who rented traditional bamboo rafts. I locked the Jeep, hoping it would be there when we returned. The advertised course was nearly seven miles downriver, ending at St. Margaret's. Our plan was to float past the confluence of this river, more a tributary, and the Rio Grande—on which we'd paddle upriver toward Moore Town to meet Colonel Grandy. If men had taken treasure off Morgan's ship by canoe and gone upriver, where were they headed? I hoped we'd find a clue of some sort by retracing their steps.

Taking a bamboo raft against the current on the mighty Rio Grande, though?

At least I'd have a paddle.

16

NANNY WAS ARRANGING FOR THE RAFT WHEN MY CELL PHONE RANG. I SAW Johnny Blake's name on the screen.

"Tell me something good," I said.

"We got the permit, mon, for photography only, but we got it."

I pumped my fist. The impromptu plan was coming together.

"What about the boats?"

"The rental people got boats, but what kind you want?"

Damn. I couldn't be in two places at once. Then I came up with an idea. "Let me call you back about the boats, Johnny. Pick up the permit, though."

"You still with the professor?"

"We're going to take a raft up the Rio Grande, following a lead."

"Yeah, mon, sound good."

Nanny was still inside the rental hut when I disconnected the call. Since my measly percentage didn't include expenses, I was off the hook as far as paying for anything on this trip. I scrolled through my few saved numbers until I found the one I wanted and hit send.

"Well, well, well, how's the Jamaican beach bum?"

"Are there beaches here?" I said. "I've been too busy to sit on my ass."

"What happened to your rock star buddy?" Ray said. "Thought you'd be fending off groupies by now."

"Thom's a country singer, Ray."

I heard him sigh.

"Let me guess," he said, "you're not just calling to brag about the babes in Kingston?"

"Even better. I'm calling with good news. You being my best friend—"

"One of your only friends is more like it."

Ray meant no malice, but the truth of his statement cut to the bone. I swallowed.

"Just kidding, Buck. Gosh, you know I—"

"I forgive you, and anyway, you'll feel like shit in a second."

"Why's that?"

"Because there's a plane ticket to Jamaica with your name on it waiting at the main counter there at EYW," I said.

Silence.

"Still with me, Ray?"

"What kind of trouble are you in now?"

"Trouble? Hell, I'm going to cut you in on something big—not to mention the beautiful babes in Kingston you mentioned—and all I get are insults and innuendos?"

"You never call me from one of your exotic trips if you're not in trouble—is it the Beauty?" His voice turned cold. "Have you hurt her?"

Ray and I had different perspectives on the 1946 Grumman Goose we'd repatriated from the bowels of a Cuban tobacco farm a few years ago. I thought of the fresh bullet holes in her wings and winced.

"As a matter of fact, we do need to patch a couple holes—above the waterline, mind you—but that's not why I invited you. I need your piloting skills while I'm pursuing something that could make you some nice money."

"Except it never seems to end up that way, Buck—and what do you mean patch some holes? What happened?"

I saw Nanny wrapping up the raft rental.

"Use the Last Resort credit card number and get on down here," I said. "Tomorrow, preferably. Call me when you land in Kingston. You're going to love this place." Nanny walked toward me. "And the women *are* beautiful."

She must have heard me, because she smiled.

"What about the holes in the plane, Buck? Tell me they're not bullet holes—"

"Nothing sketchy, just flying the Beast and babysitting her. Tomorrow. Economy class. Thanks, buddy, see you then."

"But—"

I hit the end button and turned to Nanny.

"All set?"

"Who are you telling lies to now?" she said.

"That was my friend Ray Floyd. He's my airplane mechanic in Key West." And one of the few people I could count on.

"Is he coming to help us look for Morgan's booty?"

"Indirectly, but don't say booty in front of Ray or he'll get distracted."

Nanny tipped her head back and laughed.

"We're all set here," she said. "It could take a couple hours to get to Moore Town, but they said the current's mild today, so maybe less. Do you really think you can paddle upriver against it?"

"I'll be fine, don't worry. If Morgan really did entrust treasure to his Maroon allies, we need to try and figure out what they might have done with it. You know the landscape pretty well?"

"A little, but I'm a university professor, not a Maroon warrior."

"Well, that's why we asked Colonel Grandy to meet us, right?"

Nanny wasn't looking at me. My heart sank.

"You did talk to him, right?"

"Yes . . . but he'll most likely be sending someone else." She clutched her hands together.

"What's wrong?"

She took in a deep breath and dropped her hands down to the side.

"He said he fell and got hurt, but I think someone may have attacked him."

I froze, the bamboo pole in my hand, just about to launch the raft.

"Attacked? Like maybe that asshole from yesterday who cussed us out?"

She shook her head. "I don't know, Buck. Maybe. Anyway, the colonel might be sending another trusted person along."

"You soft-pedaled that guy yesterday," I said. "Who was he?"

She frowned. "His name's Cuffee. A hothead, obviously, but I've never heard anyone say that he's violent—"

"Let me tell you, it's better to recognize danger and prepare for it than to pretend everything's fine." I paused. "And Jamaica does have a reputation for gang violence, so—"

Her eyes flared. "Maroons are *not* gangs—"

"No, but they all may not be just Maroons, either."

"I've survived thirty-four years on my own and don't need—"

I took her shoulders and squeezed them.

"I'm sorry if that came out wrong. That's just me thinking out loud, trying to prepare myself in case something *does* happen."

She took a deep breath, but the expression on her face was taut, not fearful. It made me like her even more. Strong women have that effect on me.

"Provided you can make it upriver against the current," she said.

"Only one way to find out."

WE SET OFF DOWN THE TRIBUTARY TOWARD THE RIO GRANDE. MY MIND was back on the notes we'd transcribed and Nanny's mention of the Blue Mountain peak at dawn. I hoped the flash was something more tangible than the green flash you're supposed to see at sunset over the ocean. While it may happen, it's damned rare, and we needed better odds than that.

Mountains loomed on both sides of the river, and myriad shades of green seemed to swirl beneath the clouds and mist that enveloped them. At the confluence of the Rio Grande I steered us right, upriver into the current. As I did, brown water slapped over the front of the raft, which was only a few inches above the water's surface.

"I feel like Cleopatra on the Nile." Nanny was seated behind me, her bare legs—runner's legs—now wet, as were her dark shorts.

Our conversation trailed off as I poled deeper into the water against the strong current. Thirty minutes of that and my shoulders and lower back started to ache and lock up. I often used a stand-up paddleboard out behind Louie's Backyard in Key West—in fact, using a SUP had become my favorite form of exercise since my basketball group broke up. But obviously there was a big difference between the aqua dynamics of a SUP board and large sections of bamboo strapped together. Not to mention paddling against the current of a mighty river. The sweat rolled off every exposed surface of my skin and soaked my shirt.

"That's the Blue Mountain peak over there." Nanny pointed up to our right, where a dark mountain thrust up high above the others around it. The peak wasn't close, even though its presence dominated the horizon.

"Are there trails from the Rio Grande that lead to it?" I said.

"Several, but only a couple go all the way to the mountain."

"Would Njoni, if it was him, have abandoned the river and headed toward the mountain, or continued on to Moore Town?"

"Hard to say, but climbing is very rough going from here. While the climb is still significant from Moore Town, it's an easier course."

If what Nanny said was accurate, they might have paddled all the way to Moore Town and hiked up the mountain from there rather than disembark here. Either way, my paddling up the river now helped me envision what Njoni and presumably others had seen and possibly done.

I studied the foothills that led to Blue Mountain. Maybe they didn't climb the peak at all—maybe they just used it, and the flash the notes referred to, as a reference point. Nanny deduced this to mean a flash *on* the mountain, but that seemed odd to me. Could it mean from *atop* the mountain instead?

From a distance came the sound of an outboard motor. We hadn't seen any boats since turning into the current toward Moore Town, but there had been several underpowered rental boats circling around when we reached the Rio Grande. The deeper rumble coming up behind us sounded like the larger, more powerful boats I heard in Key West Harbor that raced out to grab anchored buoys and fish for tarpon.

When the engine sound became a roar, a flat-bottomed skiff rounded the corner of the curve we'd just navigated.

We were in a fairly narrow section of river. I glanced back and lifted the pole to make sure the driver saw us. All I could see of him was the top of his head—black hair—over the center console. The banks of the river here were the closest of any place we'd passed yet but opened up in another fifty yards—and he was hauling ass, carving his way from side to side like a slalom skier.

The boat swerved toward us, now fifty feet away—I swung the pole high.

"Hey! Watch out!"

"What's happening, Buck?"

"Get down!"

If he didn't change course in seconds—

"Buck!"

"Jump!"

Just as I yelled and leapt to the opposite side from the boat's path, the driver changed course. As I splashed into dark water I caught a glimpse of a dreadlocked male driver in dark glasses who never, ever reduced speed.

"Bastard!" I yelled as the speedboat disappeared around the next bend. Then I pulled myself back up on the raft.

To my surprise, Nanny was lying on her back, hanging onto both sides, the plastic bag with the case of archives inside it clenched in her teeth. The raft lifted up and crashed down hard in the wake of the damn powerboat.

"You okay?" I said.

"Just great."

With the bag still between her teeth, her voice was a hiss, which even in the wake of nearly getting killed made me laugh out loud. She rolled to her side, spit the bag onto the deck and started laughing herself. We were both totally soaked, my T-shirt plastered to me like a thick layer of skin. She edged up on her elbows, and the way her wet white shirt clung to the curve of her breasts inspired another James Bond moment: I pictured opening credits with silhouetted beauties swimming or dancing.

As if reading my mind, she sat up and peeled her shirt over her head, revealing a frilly, full bra.

"No sense in wearing wet clothing." Her gaze hung on me, and as if on signal, I peeled my shirt off. She allowed her eyes a quick glance at my abs, recently enhanced through frequent swimming and SUP boarding, then spun to face forward and draped her wet shirt over her knees.

"Now mush, Reilly, we have an appointment."

I stood, the bamboo pole again in my hand. I was in front of her, so she couldn't see my smile.

"Yes, my queen."

17

A VISION OF CUFFEE, THE LEEWARD MAROON FROM YESTERDAY, FILLED MY mind as I pushed the bamboo pole deep into the dark water. I hadn't gotten a clear look at the boat driver, and dreadlocks in Jamaica were like goatees in the States, so there was no way I could tell he'd been behind the wheel. Still, someone had attacked Colonel Stanley last night, and the fire in Cuffee's eyes yesterday looked lethal. But then he hadn't mentioned treasure—only told us to stay away from "the history."

It took another hour to reach the rendezvous point a mile downriver from Moore Town, a gap where the road we'd driven yesterday veered close to the riverbank. An old Ford pickup was parked in the shade, smoke rising from the open driver's window.

"Good, they waited for us," Nanny said. "That trip took longer than I thought it would."

She climbed off the raft, pulled her half-dry shirt back over her head, and balled her fists on her hips as she looked up the steep, heavily eroded embankment toward the truck.

I dropped the pole on the bank. When I started to pull the raft ashore, the muscles in my lower back seized.

"Oof!"

I was bent over, my right hand clutching my back, convinced I would never again stand up straight in this world.

Without a word Nanny stepped behind me, placed her left hand on my left shoulder, and began to knead the palm of her right hand into my lower back. It sent an excruciating shock wave up my spine—but through the pain, the sensation of her warm, strong hand kneading my muscles created a wave of sensuous joy.

"That was hard work coming upriver," she said. "I never even offered to help."

"You're helping now." My voice was almost a whisper.

Nanny kept kneading. And kneading.

And the pain in my lower back had eased. I didn't want her to stop—

A horn honked above us. Nanny dropped her hands, and we both looked up. A man—no, a woman—standing next to a truck had reached in to press the horn.

"Any better, Buck?" Nanny was now facing me.

There was genuine concern mixed with an expression of discovery that made her seem both confident and vulnerable. Our eyes held for a long moment.

"Much," I said.

Slowly, and with tolerable pain, I stood up—just as the horn sounded again. We began hiking up the steep bank, Nanny holding the plastic bag of records in one hand. She slipped—I caught her free hand to help pull her up, but she shook her head. Maybe she wanted to spare my back, maybe she was embarrassed since I'd hurt it doing all the work that got us here. And that body of hers was strong—she was on her feet in no time.

We soon stepped onto the flat ground of the dirt road. There, at the top, a gnarled, ancient woman with a massive blunt in her hand was waiting for us.

"What you doing, girly?" She hacked out a laugh that sounded more like a cough.

Nanny marched forward. She hesitated, then reached out and hugged the old woman.

"Ms. Tarrah, meet Buck Reilly."

The woman—she had to be a hundred years old—looked me up and down. I hurried to put my shirt back on.

"The pleasure is mine," she said. Then, to Nanny, "He the treasure hunter the signs mentioned?"

Nanny cut me a side-glance, then looked back to Ms. Tarrah.

"Buck is helping us solve the mystery of the ancient papers."

The woman's laugh rattled out until she paused to take another lungful of the monster spliff. I braced myself to reject the offer to partake, but it never came. Granny wasn't planning to share, God bless her.

"Buck has some ideas we wanted to discuss with the colonel—how is he?"

"Busted up good." Ms. Tarrah frowned and the endless wrinkles of her face bunched together. Putting her age at one hundred suddenly seemed a conservative estimate.

"Any idea who—"

Nanny grabbed my arm, gave it a subtle squeeze, and I shut my mouth.

"Can we lay the papers out on the bed of your truck?" she said.

We did just that. Ms. Tarrah's truck, a once blue late 60s Ford as battered as they come, had a surprisingly clean bed, and Nanny carefully spread each paper out. Damned lucky they hadn't been lost to the river when that crazed boat driver ran us down. Had it been intentional? My natural paranoia had escalated since yesterday.

"You're right to be afraid."

I looked up. Tarrah was staring straight at me.

"Excuse me?"

"People will kill for these papers. Many have died through the years to protect them." She paused, then turned to Nanny. "Need to be careful."

"We will," Nanny said. "Buck's idea was that we should follow the path the men may have taken after leaving Morgan's ship. Seems far-fetched, but that's why we're here—"

"No. You here to see me, because I've known you'd be coming."

I pressed my teeth together. Nanny glanced over her shoulder and mouthed "Obeah."

I'd already figured that out. Along with the ancient Ashanti and African languages the last vestiges of Maroons sought to keep alive, some continued to practice the beliefs their forefathers brought with them from Mother Africa. A tingle tickled my arms.

The old woman smiled, her teeth brown but still in place. She turned to the papers spread out on the truck bed.

"My eyes aren't so good—"

I pulled the magnifying glass from my pocket. She laughed and nodded, then bent over the papers, most of which were incomprehensible to me. Her quick review of Morgan's journal made me think she'd studied it before. She stopped near the sudden conclusion of loose notes and glanced up, then shoved everything back in its plastic case. She had paused over the page that referred to the flash at dawn on Blue Mountain's peak.

She confirmed that there was an old legend—from the days the Taino Indians had Jamaica to themselves—about magic in the mountain, and specifically a cross that marked what she referred to as the site of a deep evil. She looked from Nanny to me.

"We been using fear to our advantage ever since we was dragged out of Africa."

The tingle in my arms shot across my shoulders. Watching me, the old woman cackled—I felt like she could see it.

"We need to go up there tonight, to the mountain, and wait for sunrise," I said.

Nanny looked at her watch, then at me. "I've been there at dawn and there was no flash on the mountain."

"Doesn't matter, it's all we have to work with," I said. "And think about this. What if the flash is visible *from* the peak, not *on* the peak?"

Nanny squinted her eyes for a second then popped them wide. "We never—" She glanced at her watch. "It's almost three o'clock now. . ." Her eyes narrowed. "We'll need a guide. And a vehicle."

"Use my truck," Tarrah said. "I get out in Moore Town and Stephen can take you there tonight."

Adrenaline was pumping so much energy through my body I didn't care how much it hurt from the trip upriver. A nighttime hike to the 7,400-foot high Blue Mountain peak would knock my already kicked ass out, but if it led to a clue about Morgan's stash, my legs and back would just have to suck it up.

18

Moore Town was far enough from the water that the river wasn't visible, so I had no idea if the speedboat that nearly swamped us was here or not. Nanny had gone to check on the Colonel and get his thoughts on the materials. She returned with a jug of water and a backpack.

"Chicken sandwiches and flashlights," she said. Stephen, waiting by the truck, was Tarrah's great grandson and looked to be around my age. He had a serious-looking face with a turned-down mouth, short hair, and short stature—maybe five foot six.

"Stephen, thanks for guiding us tonight." Nanny gave him a brief hug, but even that didn't soften his expression.

"Going to be cold tonight, maybe wet, too," he said.

"How long does it take to hike to the peak?" I said.

"Normally about seven hours."

"*Seven?*"

"We got Granny's truck."

I glanced at Nanny, unsure how far we could drive and what impact that would have on the time. I wanted to get moving and cover as much of the distance in daylight as possible—especially if we were driving the old truck along hiking trails. There were no roads that led to the Blue Mountain peak.

"Did the Colonel have any ideas on the flash?" I said.

Nanny shook her head. "He's heavily sedated."

"That bad?"

She sighed. "Afraid so."

I wanted to know how far we could drive and what impact that would have on the time, but Stephen's lips were pinched tight. For whatever reason, nobody wanted to talk about what had happened to the colonel.

And so we climbed inside the truck, which had roll-up windows, no radio, and an ashtray full of gray powder that stank. I dumped that out the window, not wanting to smell it for the next several hours.

Stephen drove. Nanny sat in the middle, but with her legs on the passenger side due to the transmission being a four-on-the-floor standard shift. The road out of Moore Town was gravel—dirt, really—and it only got worse as we crossed the river and began a treacherous journey through dense forest, part of the heavily contoured topography.

After a couple hours in, I wondered whether we could have gone faster on mountain bikes—we were averaging maybe fifteen miles per hour. But then we began a steady ascent, which the old Ford handled admirably. We straddled streams and passed perilously close to a steep drop-off—a slide six inches to the right and we'd have plunged hundreds of feet to a rocky demise.

Nanny was calm, occasionally speaking to Stephen in one of the African dialects. She patted me on the leg every so often and asked if I was okay. I wasn't, but I'd never admit it to her. I had no aversion to precarious travel—hell, anyone who'd ridden in Betty or the Beast could tell you that—but I preferred being in control of the situation. Ceding that to Stephen had me squirming in my seat.

The mass of the mountain filled the windshield. If I leaned forward I could see sky, but only just. The light faded quickly since we were on the eastern side, and the old truck's headlights were weak. When the boulders, cliffs, and sinkholes finally forced us off-trail, Stephen pulled into a relatively flat place and turned off the engine.

"Can't drive no more."

"How much further to the peak?"

He glanced down at the odometer. "Maybe two hours, walking."

"We'll stop for rest," Nanny said. "Let's light a fire."

Using the flashlights, we collected dry wood and sticks. The temperature had already dropped ten degrees, and a chill crept through my tired bones. No sooner did we dump the wood in a pile than it started to rain. We kicked the wood underneath the truck, got back inside the cab, and waited.

The jerk-chicken sandwiches were amazing. I could have eaten all three myself, but at least one was enough to stop the cramp in my stomach. Forty-five minutes later, the clouds parted and a canopy of bright stars lit the sky.

"It's been a while since I've been in such a remote location," I said.

"The Blue Mountain range is nearly two hundred thousand square acres," Nanny said.

"Big for a Caribbean island."

I got out of the truck, retrieved the wood—mostly dry—and made a teepee of sticks. My watch read 10:09. The note in Morgan's journal referred to a flash that could only be seen at sunrise, so we'd need to commence the hike around three o'clock a.m. in order to reach the peak in time.

Nanny pulled out an old newspaper from her bag that helped me start the fire. Before long we had a nice blaze going. We refrained from discussing the purpose of our trip in front of Stephen, which left only the basics.

"No, I've never married," she said. "You?"

"Yeah, briefly."

"That bad, huh?" Nanny said. "You look like you just drank one of Ms. Tarrah's teas."

"Worse." I sat forward on the rock we shared—Stephen was on the other side of the fire, sleeping on the open ground. "So what drove you to archaeology?"

"History, of course—the history of my people." Nanny's white teeth were bright in the firelight. "My studies and interests are exclusively focused on the last five hundred years of Jamaican history."

"You're the perfect person to solve Morgan's archives. But I'm sure you've tried many times. What makes you think this'll be different?"

"You, Buck Reilly. A fresh perspective from someone who has unearthed antiquities others failed to find. We . . . *I* am counting on you to help us see something we've overlooked—and your idea about the flash being seen *from* the peak rather than *on* the peak could be just that spark we needed."

I took a deep breath, partly grateful, partly proud, and partly afraid of failing. It would take more than one clue to solve this mystery.

"That being the case, I suggest we get some sleep." It was nearly midnight.

We crawled into the bed of the pickup truck. Nanny had a light blanket in that apparently bottomless bag of hers.

"We can use each other's body heat to keep warm," she said as she rolled onto her side.

I was cold, but I hesitated.

"Don't be shy, Buck Reilly. Spoon me, I'm cold too."

I lay down, slid close, and pressed my body against hers. She pulled the blanket up over us—I was anything but cold now. I tried to think of the day's events, the archives, the flash at sunrise, anything to take my mind off the fact that I was pressed against the beautiful professor. Instead, my mind rewound to the moment I fell off the raft but she hung on, how calm she was, how she pulled her shirt off without any hesitation.

Beautiful, smart, *and* confident.

Her breathing settled into the slow rhythm of slumber. She was clearly not distracted by the heat between our bodies—or the involuntary reaction it caused in mine. I backed my hips away but kept our shoulders pressed tight, closed my eyes, and started counting backwards from one hundred.

Somewhere around -263, I lost count.

19

A SHARP TUG ON MY FOOT LAUNCHED ME UPRIGHT INTO DARKNESS. I SAW stars blurred overhead, a dark figure crouched by my feet—

"Hey!" I said.

Something stirred next to me.

"What's wrong?" Nanny.

"Time to go," Stephen said.

I lay back down, my heart still thumping. Good grief.

I'd been dreaming, something about Jack and Heather, with Gunner laughing in the background. The remaining fluorescence on my watch indicated—probably—2:45. Once out of the truck bed I stretched, which hurt less than I expected. Nanny climbed out after me and stuffed the blanket back into her bag. The few hours of sleep helped, but I was jumpy from the sudden reveille.

"Got to go," Stephen said.

We all turned on flashlights and moved in single file, with me bringing up the rear. Night sounds carried on the cold predawn breeze. Heavy mists and low clouds blocked most of the sky and swirled through valleys below, distorting my depth perception to the point that—

Damn. If the fog blocked our view of the valley, the freezing night behind us and rough climb ahead of us would be for nothing.

"You okay back there?" Nanny said.

"Still waking up. So you've done this before?"

"Many times. I grew up in Moore Town—we did this hike and sunrise ceremony at least once a year."

Looking for the flash? No wonder she seemed so sure of foot. I stayed close to her and Stephen until my senses adjusted to the ambient light and the tempo of their movement. The path was narrow but well worn. The ascent sharpened, and in places we needed both hands to climb up steep rock slopes, taking turns shining flashlights on the rocks to allow each other to see.

"We're behind schedule," Stephen said. "Need to take a more direct path."

"Jacob's Ladder?" Nanny said.

All I heard from our guide was a grunt.

Time passed with no conversation. All our concentration was focused on placing one foot in above the other. I grabbed hold of dark rocks and hauled myself up. My lungs were burning as we crested a ridge.

All of a sudden there was a floor of misty gray below us. Stephen and Nanny had stopped.

"We're here," Nanny said.

"What about the fog? Will that clear? How will we see whatever it is we're looking for?"

Stephen gave me a look. "Patience."

It was now 5:20. A ribbon of pink seared the eastern horizon behind us.

"According to the notes, the flash or reflection takes place on the north side—or north *of* the peak," Nanny said. "Morgan's raid of Panama took place in January of 1671 and he returned to Jamaica a couple months later. It's May now, so there should be a slight difference in the position of the sun."

"North is that way." Stephen pointed to our right, so we settled in to watch in that general direction.

I felt like I had as a little boy on Christmas Eve, staring out my bedroom window hoping to glimpse Santa's sleigh. More than once I was certain I had, only realizing when I was older that it had just been airplane traffic.

The cold made the minutes drag, but as the sun rose above the gray band on the horizon, the clouds to the north parted to reveal a valley with other peaks rising in all directions. Nanny pressed against me and I felt her shivering.

"Sorry," she said.

"Since you've come here before and not seen any flash on the mountain, let's each focus on different sections of the valley," I said. "Increase the odds that one of us will spot a flash, if there is one."

The sun rose slowly. Long shadows reached out and gradually shrank back toward the northern slope of the Blue Mountain peak. The scenery and height, or maybe the altitude, took my breath away. Nanny's teeth gradually stopped chattering. And then—just when I thought the sun was high enough that we'd either missed whatever we were supposed to see or there wasn't anything to see—her hand shot forward.

"There!"

Stephen and I turned to see her arm was outstretched downward toward a sparkle of pearly light.

"I see it!"

If you weren't searching for it, you might never notice the flash—or was it a reflection? Didn't look like one—more of a radiance than a reflection. And whatever it was, based on the distance from here, it had to be about the size of a Frisbee.

"Must be over near the crossroads," Stephen said.

"Crossroads? Like we could drive the truck down there?" I said.

His long glance made me feel foolish.

"No, where many trails intersect. It looks to be close to that place."

"Didn't Tarrah mention some cross of evil" I said. Nanny and Stephen looked at each other with raised eyebrows.

"Then let's go down from here," she said.

The descent was easier than the climb had been, especially once we picked up a hidden trail a third of the way down the peak. "We're in the heart of the Maroon region from the time before the peace treaty had been signed," Nanny said.

I studied the shadows and imagined how the Maroon warriors had moved through the hills like silent sentinels, dispatching any Spaniard or Brit foolish enough to come hunting them.

Stephen stopped suddenly and held his hand up. His gaze was fixed further east, and he squinted as he studied the ridgeline to our right.

"I thought I heard something."

"Like what?" I said.

He didn't answer, just stood there a few minutes before continuing down the trail. Nanny and I shrugged and followed after him.

The Blue Mountain range was lush. I'd once heard the country was 98 percent green, which right now felt 100 percent accurate. There was no sign of civilization anywhere in sight. Only countless hills, many green and rounded so they looked like rows of broccoli with their heads all standing up straight. The environment literally hadn't changed for hundreds, if not thousands of years. The light churning mist and old growth landscape made me half expect an ancient Maroon to pounce on us.

The angle of descent eased. I could see nothing but the trees and shrubs pressing in on us, yet the narrow trail continued. I bit off the urge to ask if Stephen knew where, exactly, we were going.

After another twenty minutes, I had my answer.

20

THE CROSSROADS CONSISTED OF TWO TRAILS INTERSECTING AT ROUGH RIGHT angles. Otherwise unmarked, the trails themselves had narrowed to dirt lines that looked as if they were now used only by animals, with vegetation encroaching from the sides.

"The crossroads were once a location where Windward and Leeward Maroons met to share information on their strategies, their numbers, their victories and losses," Nanny said.

"You've been here?"

"It's a sacred spot, Buck. Once prohibited to all but the leaders, scouts, and warriors who had killed the most enemies."

I liked the sound of "prohibited." That could easily mean a place with low traffic, exactly the kind of location you'd want to hide items of value. Could it be the cross of evil that Tarrah had mentioned?

"Can you tell where the reflection was coming from?" I said.

Stephen glanced from Nanny to me.

"I have an idea." He again turned his eyes toward her and waited until she gave a discreet nod. "Come."

He stepped forward into the wedge of land between the two far trails. He pushed through some thick brush until he stopped at a flat rock wall that led straight up.

Dead end.

The gray rock surface was coated in moss, lichen, vines, roots. It was impenetrable, an impasse.

"Now what?" I said.

Stephen again looked at Nanny, who looked sullen. After a five-count, I stepped forward.

"Let me see the archive material again."

Nanny swung the pack off her shoulder and took her time removing the plastic case that held the old documents—which the shade of the woods would have made it impossible to read without the flashlight. I shuffled through them until I found the one that had led us here, alluding to the *flash at dawn*. The next page had what appeared to be water or age stains, and under the glare of the LED light I saw the faint, mysterious illustrations—only a few lines: curved, angled and parallel. The next page was much cleaner and had ancient writing on it that Nanny had previously deciphered as someone's biography.

I held the drawing up for both of them to see, a sense of frustration blooming inside me.

"These sketches mean anything to you?"

Stephen immediately turned to Nanny, whose eyes revealed nothing. Then she looked at my face.

"My guess is Taino petroglyphs," she said.

"Taino Indians were here long before the Spanish—and certainly the British, or Maroons," I said. "What would they have to do with . . ."

I turned to face the rock wall, turned back to look at them. Stephen nodded. I glanced at the wall again, then bent over and started searching the forest floor until I found a flat, sharp rock.

I began to scrape moss off the face of the wall. Irritated that they just watched me, I continued scraping until the edge of the rock caught in a groove.

Nanny stepped closer.

Now, more gently, I peeled away the loose green material until I had uncovered an image. An ancient petroglyph of what looked like a telephone pole with three crossbars on top. What the heck?

I had researched many a Taino site, but since they hadn't been much for hoarding precious metals or stones, they'd been of minimal interest. They had inhabited much of the Caribbean at one time but had pretty much died out—slaughtered by more aggressive tribes or done in by the diseases Europeans brought to the islands.

"This mean anything to you?"

Nanny leaned closer and after a quick look shook her head.

"And that flash we saw? The woods would cover this petroglyph, and any others on here. Something higher up must have caused the flash."

Stephen pointed up the sheer rock wall. I tilted my head back—there! I could see a narrow natural shelf bathed in morning light but also coated in fauna of the moist woodland. Leaves, vines, and lichen hung off the shelf.

"So?"

"There's a natural chunk of quartz above that shelf that has attracted people for eons," Nanny said. "More petroglyphs, too. But we never connected the quartz to the flash from Blue Mountain."

"*Eons?*" If the area was that well trampled, the odds of us finding anything here seemed slim. And if they already knew about the quartz and the petroglyphs, why had Nanny and Stephen waited until we were here to mention them, even if they didn't get the connection? Maybe it was all the silent, significant glances they kept giving each other, but I was getting more than a little agitated.

I glanced straight up—there was no direct climbing route to the ledge—then walked forward around the corner of the wall. There were crevices and enough exposed jagged edges for a climb, so I started up.

"Be careful, Buck," Nanny said. "No way to get you out of here if you fall and break something."

Her voice already had a distant sound as curiosity drove me up the wall like a spider monkey. I zigged and zagged my way toward the southeastern-facing shelf. The final several feet required me to grab hold of the rock outcropping and pull myself up. The rocks dug into my fingers—my arms shook, my face scraped against the damp wall—

"Buck?"

With my arms still shaking, I finally hauled myself onto the shelf and pushed my back against the wall, taking a moment to catch my breath. My feet dangled some twenty-five feet above Nanny and Stephen. She looked frightened, and even Stephen was staring up at me with his mouth open.

A big exhale nearly caused me to slip off the front of what was not that big a ledge. I edged sideways—carefully—and spotted a dinner-plate-sized chunk of rose quartz embedded in the wall and surrounded by matte-black rock, which accounted for the beacon that had caught the sunlight. So much for its being Morgan's stash site.

"What do you see?" Nanny called up.

"You mean you haven't been up here before?"

"No . . ."

"You didn't seem very excited about the petroglyphs."

"Of course I was. Why else would we have come down here?"

Stephen said nothing.

I pulled the sharp flat rock from my pocket and started scraping at the moss, which peeled off like dried wallpaper. I could make out what looked like a curved edge. I scraped at it—then another, and another. After several minutes I'd uncovered a carving—several carvings–of symbols. They were circular and oval and all connected.

"What have you found?" Stephen said.

"I don't know."

My voice must not have carried, because Nanny called up with the same question. From my breast pocket I removed a pencil and piece of paper and tried to copy the symbols as accurately as I could. I dug at the moss around them in a wide radius but uncovered nothing else.

Satisfied I'd found everything there was to find, I reversed course and dropped below the shelf. My fingers caught the edge and I hung until my right foot caught a toehold on the edge that allowed me to reach around, grab an indentation in the wall, and swing over until I could shimmy my way down.

Ideas ricocheted around my mind, drawing on past experiences with Mayan and other wall carvings.

"Buck!"

BOOM!

Gunshot?

My ass slipped, everything spun, my shoulder bounced off rock—sharp pain, then a branch cracked, pine needles brushed past my face, my shirt ripped—

THUD!

I hit the ground and saw stars through the pain.

I lay there a moment, taking a quick inventory. Nothing felt broken, but blood flowed from multiple gashes. The sketch of the wall carving was clutched in my hand. Looking straight up at the massive pine tree I'd careened through, I saw broken branches that had softened my fall.

"What you got there, Reilly?"

No way!

I turned to face the only man on Jamaica likely to be shooting at me.

21

"**W**HAT THE HELL ARE YOU DOING HERE?" MY VOICE SOUNDED LIKE I'D just reached puberty. "You shot at me *again*, you son of a bitch."

Gunner stood over me. There were two men behind him—big men—and both of them were holding shotguns.

He laughed that hyena-pitched cackle I'd learned to loathe, his small square teeth and his blue mirrored sunglasses catching the light.

"Not yet we haven't."

"Are you following us?"

"We're just hunting, Reilly." He paused, his double entendre floating in the air. "Hogs. You seen any?"

He reached down and yanked the sketch out of my hand.

"Hey!" I rolled onto my knee and stood up.

"You okay, Buck?" Nanny's voice came from behind them.

"What the hell kind of drawing's this?"

"How come you're not out in Port Royal, Gunner? You run out of brewer's vats?"

He ignored me, the sketch still held up to his face. Then he lowered it.

"The question is, Reilly, what are *you* doing out here—with her?"

Nanny had walked around them and now stood next to me. Her face was hard. Stephen was nowhere in sight. I focused on one of Gunner's associates—Cuffee, the enraged Maroon from Moore Town.

"You!" I said. "Did you beat up Colonel Stanley?"

Gunner cackled again. "You know Cuffee? Small island, ain't it?"

"It's actually a pretty big island, Gunner, so I'll ask you again, what the hell are you doing here? What do you want?"

Gunner was not above having us shot and leaving us here for animals to devour. Armed or not, he was too big for me to overpower alone, and with three of them?

"We won the rights to salvage Morgan's treasure," he said. "Sure feels like you're trespassing on our claim."

I nearly laughed. Gunner sounded like he was in an old Western.

"You were awarded the right to dig in a specific location at Port Royal."

"Maybe you need to update yourself on our rights."

That caught me off guard. Had they somehow obtained broader rights related to Morgan? I'd never heard of anything other than a specific location being protected—

"And what's this little honey doing with you, anyway?" He nodded toward Nanny.

"Not that it's any of your business, but she and Stephen are my guides. I hired them to take me up to see the sunrise from Blue Mountain, but you already know that, since you've obviously been following us."

"Sunrise, my ass." His mouth tightened to a thin line. "Miss Nanny Adou here, *Professor* Nanny Adou, from the Archaeology Department at the University of West Indies, was on the review and award committee that gave me and Dodson the contract for Port Royal."

My breathing stopped.

"So I'll ask you again, what the hell are you two doing out here together?"

My head spun toward Nanny so hard my neck cracked.

"You were on the award committee?"

She looked away.

Gunner's cackle broke the silence again.

"Looks like she's playing both sides against the middle, Reilly." He laughed again. "Your luck with women ain't too good here in Jamaica, is it? Must of been a kick in the balls, seeing your ex-wife and Dodson—"

I flung myself at Gunner, catching him off guard and driving him hard into the bushes. We fell, me on top of him.

He squealed, dug his hands into my ribcage—instant pain—and flung me aside.

All the wind whooshed out of my lungs. I rolled to my right and stood up. Gunner's goons—Cuffee and the other one—held their guns on me, but I didn't care.

"Son of a bitch, Reilly!" Gunner rolled over and I saw he'd landed on a large rock. He held his back and got slowly to his feet, his sunglasses knocked askew, his eyes black and livid. "You'll pay for that!"

"Stop it!" Nanny stepped between us. "A lot of people know we're here, and Stephen has already informed the authorities."

All eyes followed the finger she pointed to where Stephen held up his phone.

Gunner swung back to face us, his jaw trembling and his square teeth pressed together, then stepped as close as he dared to Nanny.

"We're not done with you, either, woman. If you're double-crossing us, you'll be sorry, count on it. That treasure belongs to us and the Leeward Maroons. Step back and mind your own business."

Gunner held my sketch up, then shoved it into his breast pocket.

"And whatever the hell this shit drawing is, it's no concern of yours. We got the legal rights to everything related to Morgan, Reilly. Not that I can't handle you myself, but maybe I'll wait until we drag your ass through court again first."

He walked over to where I'd scraped the moss off the rock wall and used his phone to take pictures of the other petroglyphs. Once finished, he looked from face to face.

"Now back the fuck off. And that includes you, *Professor.*"

Gunner, Cuffee, and the other large Jamaican disappeared into the woods. I turned toward Nanny, my eyes pinched.

"What the hell's going on here?"

22

"**W**HY DIDN'T YOU TELL ME YOU WERE ON THE SELECTION COMMITTEE?**"
Hurt mixed with anger made my voice sound shrill. I didn't care.

"Why does it matter?" Nanny said.

Stephen had already started back up the trail. I couldn't believe we had to climb the damn mountain all over again, but we headed off. Slowly.

"The difference is whether I can trust you or not, and obviously I can't."

"Trust me for what, exactly? Haven't I been helping you? I could have given this information to those other men but I didn't. Jamaica's been the victim of plunder and abuse for hundreds of years, now we're supposed to help one group of American treasure hunters over the other? What if Dodson's team finds a clue that might—"

"*You* called *me*! I'd given up and gone home—*and* I've agreed to give up 90 percent of anything we find, never mind the remaining 10 percent might cost me my life, as you just witnessed. I can't operate on half-truths and lies, so if there's any other surprises around the corner, you need to tell me now."

"I did call you, Buck, because I convinced Stanley you could help, and I was right—you connected the clue about the flash to the petroglyphs."

The angle of ascent had increased to the point that my breath was already coming in shorter bursts, which pretty much tabled our discussion for the time being. Clouds enveloped the peak above us. Where had Gunner gone?

Based on his direction, he could have taken one of the other three paths that led to the crossroads. Did one of them lead to the Rio Grande? Would Njoni have carried the goods through here?

Nanny hadn't apologized, and she hadn't asked me what I'd found on the ledge. I couldn't tell if she already knew or just didn't care. But now that I'd made the connection, would they try to proceed without me? Seemed unlikely, but still . . .

We stopped for a drink of water from a spring.

"Can I see the archive again?"

Nanny paused, then swung the backpack off her shoulder. Good thing Stephen had hidden her precious archives in the bushes back on the trail after Gunner fired that shot.

She removed the document from the plastic case and handed it over.

"What do you think the circles from the petroglyph could mean?" she said.

My shoulders dropped. "So you already knew what was up there?"

She scowled. "I saw the paper when that lunatic ripped it from your hand."

I stared at her for a long time, but she never flinched. Sucks when you trust someone, then find out they haven't been straight up. From that point on you never know when to believe them. Can never really trust them again. My ex-wife came to mind. Gunner rubbed my nose in that, too, the prick.

The faint drawings didn't offer anything further.

"Can I see the rest?"

She opened up the box and handed it to me. I flipped slowly through pages in their archival sleeves, but there was nothing like the circular images from the petroglyph. Could have been totally unconnected. The Blue Mountain range was three hundred square miles—the odds of our finding anything here were infinitesimal. Yet we had found the flash at dawn, and the quartz crystal that produced it.

I shuffled through the loose diary pages, then fanned through them.

They got increasingly darker and stained toward the end, with a wine or bloodstain seeping through the last few pages—then the next page was clean. No stains, no writing, nothing.

As if some pages were missing.

I glanced up at Nanny, who was looking away.

Dammit.

"Keep it." I dropped the notebook into the plastic container and set off up the trail at a fast clip. I soon felt Stephen's eyes on my back as I went and could hear him and Nanny walking behind me, but nobody said a word during the rest of the two-hour hike.

If Nanny was holding out on me, this whole search was pointless. She must be analyzing the information on her own. She was a professor of archaeology, after all—what did I expect? Just another kind of treasure hunter. And based on what she'd said about people plundering Jamaica for hundreds of years, she'd apparently heaped me in with that lot. I'd let her beauty, background, knowledge—and, dammit, her compliments—sucker me into thinking I was a valued member of their team.

Cuffee's statement about Morgan's treasure belonging to the Leeward Maroons was another interesting revelation. Thanks to the peace treaties they'd individually signed with the British, both the Windward and Leeward Maroons had what amounted to sovereign territory within Jamaica. Even if I found something, if it was within those territories they could stiff me on my 10 percent.

It took a couple of hours to crest Blue Mountain and hike back to the truck. I arrived about fifteen minutes ahead of Nanny and Stephen, and I was sitting in the truck bed when they showed up. Although it was bumpy as hell, I stayed there with my back against the cab as Stephen drove us slowly back to Moore Town, then to where we'd left the bamboo raft.

Stephen stopped the truck but didn't turn it off. I jumped out of the truck bed. Nanny's window was down, but she made no move to get out.

"I'm staying in Moore Town tonight," she said.

To try and piece together the drawing of the circles that nearly got me killed? Or mull over any other clues she'd withheld from me?

"I'll take the raft back to my Jeep."

"Where are you going next?" she said.

Crap. I just remembered I'd pissed away five hundred dollars for Ray Floyd to fly down here.

"My friend Ray's probably already on-island. He's meeting me back at GoldenEye. I'm not sure how long we'll be there."

She turned to look out the windshield of the truck.

"I *am* sorry, Buck. I didn't think of it as lying to you." She turned back to face me. "Have you considered that maybe I wanted them to be searching underwater, knowing nothing was there, so I could work with you to focus on a search I thought was a lot more likely?"

I bit my lip. It was an appealing explanation, it even made sense. Or made her a creative liar. I thought back to Morgan's loosely bound diary, to the stained pages suddenly turning clean. That felt like another half-truth. Who knew what else she was holding back?

"See you around."

I walked down the steep hill toward the raft I'd beached on the riverbank, my quads burning from all the mountain climbing. I didn't look back as I waded into the cold water and climbed up onto the raft. Now going with the current, I rounded a bend a few minutes later, and the truck, Stephen, and Nanny all disappeared.

So much for Morgan's treasure.

So much for the beautiful Nanny Adou.

23

IT WAS DARK BY THE TIME I MADE IT BACK TO GOLDENEYE. I WANTED NOTHING more than to collapse on the bed in my villa and sleep for a year, but on the floor under my door was a note.

My back hurt when I bent over to get it, sore from the ping-pong between branches when I fell off the shelf at the crossroads, not to mention poling the raft up and down rivers. I touched my ribs on the right side and winced. Gunner had dug his fingers between them like he was grabbing a twelve-pack of beer.

With the note under my arm, I took ice from the bucket, dropped it in a glass, and doused it with some of the complimentary Blackwell Rum. I then stepped outside and dropped into the chaise longue overlooking the blue lagoon. After a slurp of rum, I peeled open the note.

> *I'm in the bar.*
> *This place is amazing!*
>
> *Ray*

I smiled. Ray's enthusiasm would lighten my mood. And I needed to get my mind off Nanny more than I needed sleep.

After a quick shower and an inspection of my bruises and gashes, including one on my cheek that prevented me from shaving, I pulled on some blue linen slacks and a white linen shirt, then used my fingers to comb back my shoulder-length hair.

The bar was crowded. I found Ray on the corner, sitting with Johnny Blake, both drinking rum punches. I hoped they weren't putting them on my tab.

"Buck!" Ray said. "This place is gorgeous!"

He was dressed in cargo shorts and a red Hawaiian shirt, no different than if he'd been at the private aviation terminal in Key West. I smiled. Ray was always true to himself.

And he always came when I called for help.

"Wait until you see the Ian Fleming suite," I said. "We can take a peek if it's not rented."

"I can't wait—you seen the lounge with those old pictures of Fleming and Sean Connery?"

Johnny Blake shook his head. He could care less about Ian Fleming or any of the history surrounding GoldenEye. He was here for a purpose he would soon learn had been turned upside down. After ordering a Black and Stormy, I decided not to burst his bubble just yet. And Ray had no clue what was going on.

"Should have brought Lenny down too, Buck. He'd get a kick out of all this."

Lenny Jackson, friend and former bartender at Blue Heaven, nephew of Reverend Willy Peebles, was now on the ballot for his second term on Key West's city council. His initial success had surprised no one more than me. Not that I didn't believe in his abilities, but his blunt approach to issues could have easily killed his political career. Fortunately for the people of Key West, it had done the opposite.

"I know," I said. "Knee deep in elections when he could be getting in trouble with us."

"Us? You mean *your* trouble, my friend. I'm only here to make sure the Beast is safe, and to bail you out of jail if need be."

"All this happy reunion shit's gonna make me cry," Johnny said. "I ain't heard from you since you went rafting with the lovely professor yesterday, mon. What's the news?"

Ray's eyebrows lifted.

"Fair enough," I said. "But first, what's the status of our logistics?"

Johnny drank from his rum, then smiled big.

"All set, mon. The boat's ready to go in the morning. The charter company got to have a month's payment up-front—let your friend Greenbaum know I put that on his credit card."

"Harry Greenbaum is in on this?" Ray said.

"Deeper by the minute."

Johnny reached into the breast pocket of his tunic-style white shirt.

"And right here's the permit."

Ray asked to see it, and he handed it over.

"'Permit for photographic survey of underwater portions of Port Royal?'" Ray said. "What the heck?"

Johnny grinned. "That should distract the hell out of your boy Dodson. The coordinates are exactly an eighth of a mile to the west of their dive site—far enough so they can't really see what we're doing, close enough to drive them crazy."

Gunner's warning from earlier today rang in my ears. Screw him.

"Wait a minute," Ray said. "This is for a dive site next to Dodson and that trigger-happy lunatic Gunner? Buck, no way—"

"Relax, Ray." I waved to the bartender and pointed to their empty glasses. "They have observers from the Jamaican National Heritage Trust on-site to monitor the restoration of everything they uncover—"

"That guy nearly killed me—both of us—and you're telling me to relax?"

"You'll be fine—"

"What do you mean *I'll* be fine?" Ray threw up his hands. "Where will you be?"

I hesitated. Given my falling out with Nanny, I didn't really have a plan anymore. Messing with Dodson would be fun as hell, but it wasn't worth putting Ray in harm's way. Still, Johnny wouldn't stick around if there were no payday, and I might need him.

I sipped my rum.

"Buck?" Ray said. "I hope you're not setting me up as some kind of decoy here."

Which is exactly what I'd planned on doing, but now I wasn't so sure. I took a guzzle of rum at the realization that doing it would make me a card-carrying asshole.

A friend not to be trusted?

"What about the professor, Buck?" Not Mr. Buck. Johnny's respect for me was waning along with my own.

"She has some detailed information about Morgan that's never come to light," I said.

His eyes lit up. "Serious?"

"Yeah, but . . ." I was about to say that Nanny couldn't be trusted when I spotted a tall woman in a short, tight, low-cut dress in the distance, walking barefoot up the beach toward the bar.

"But what?" Johnny said.

The woman pushed her hair back from her face as she climbed the steps, paused, bent down to put her heels back on, and stepped onto the patio. She zeroed in on me and headed toward us. She was dressed to the nines, and I was sure every head turned to watch her approach.

"Buck?" Ray said.

"You can ask her yourself, guys." I leaned forward and lowered my voice to a whisper. "Just don't mention the boats, okay?"

Ray's eyes shot open.

Nanny stepped into the middle of our threesome, right up between Ray and Johnny, put a hand on each of their chests, and pushed them back a bit. She then leaned forward and kissed me on the cheek.

"Makes sense that this was where Ian Fleming lived," she said. "You gentlemen look straight out of a James Bond movie."

"Good guys or bad guys?" Ray muttered.

"I never thanked you for your brilliance today, Buck. I came here to do that, properly."

24

NANNY WAS CHARMING TO ALL THREE OF US. SHE PULLED UP A WHITE WOODEN barstool next to me, while Ray and Johnny stood facing us. Ray had that loopy grin he got around pretty women who were being nice to him.

Conversation was light, and neither Nanny nor I mentioned Blue Mountains, petroglyphs, or Gunner with his goons and guns. Johnny chewed on his lip and held his arms crossed, Ray leaned against one of the columns plastered with old rock star photos and stared unabashed at Nanny. I caught myself doing the same thing a couple times. I'd thought her attractive since the moment I met her, but tonight she looked like a Jamaican Halle Berry with longer hair.

Movie star looks and university professor brains.

The nerve endings in my back sprang to life when she ran one of her fingers across my shoulder blade. I cut a glance toward her, a hopeless attempt to be nonchalant, and we caught each other's eyes for a moment. She slowly raised the eyebrow over her right eye. I swallowed, still wondering what she meant about thanking me *properly*.

"I need to get back to Kingston tonight, get the boats going bright and early," Johnny said. "And if I drink any more rum, that won't be happening."

"Boats?" Nanny said.

"I'll explain later."

Ray cocked his head toward me and raised a brow.

"Okay, Johnny. Thanks for getting that rolling. We'll see you some time tomorrow."

He held his fist forward and we all gave him gentle fist bumps. Nanny seemed to get a kick out of this greeting, typical for many Jamaicans, especially Rastas. As Johnny left, Ray excused himself and headed toward the men's room.

"To say I'm surprised to see you here would be an understatement," I said.

She studied my face. I wasn't smiling.

"I meant what I said, that I came to thank you. And to apologize."

"You could have sent me a text."

She glanced in both directions and leaned closer.

"Cuffee, the crazy one who was with your, ah, friend today, is stirring up trouble in Cockpit Country."

"What's that supposed to mean?"

"The Leeward Maroons are thriving, more than our small community in Moore Town. Moore Town used to be the center of Maroon heritage, but now the Leewards in Accompong aren't just clinging to the past—they're setting their own agenda for the future. They—"

I held up a hand, palm out.

"Whoa. What does that have to do with—"

"Cuffee's trying to challenge our possession of the Morgan documents."

My eyes and lips narrowed—involuntarily, but Nanny stiffened.

"I *am* sorry, Buck. I meant what I told you—I wanted Dodson out on the water in Port Royal so I could work with you on this. And yes, I'm not proud of it, but I lied to the committee to make that happen. Nobody thinks he has a prayer of finding anything of value, and Jamaica gets an historic structure salvaged at someone else's expense—"

"And treasure hunters are considered rogues?"

A flush of color bloomed in her cheeks.

"Didn't I call you right after you left Jamaica? You kept blowing me off—"

"Nanny, I get everything you've said, but you've been holding out on me. If I can't trust you—"

"You *can* trust me."

"How am I supposed to—"

"Stanley refused to share all the information until you'd proven yourself capable. You did that in the mountains." She inhaled a deep breath. "But you're right. I did withhold some pages from Morgan's diary—"

"I knew it!" I pounded my fist on the bar.

"Which I brought here with me tonight."

Ours eyes locked. My mind opened like a flower.

What else could be in the archives? Would it connect the circular petroglyphs we'd discovered this morning? Provide a meaningful clue to the treasure? And why was Nanny so dolled up for an apology?

She hadn't told me what was in the papers she'd withheld yet, so I needed to play this out.

"To answer the question I'm sure you're wondering," she said, "Morgan's documents don't specifically say anything about the petroglyphs you found today."

I sagged. Both at what she'd just said and because it wasn't the only thing I'd been wondering.

"But it does have some detailed statements about Isla Vaca, among other things."

"You need to fill in the blanks here if you expect me to stay involved," I said. "You mentioned Isla Vaca before, is that the same as Île à Vache off Haiti?"

"Haiti, yes."

"Haiti, you say?" Ray had returned from the men's room but neither of us had noticed him walk up. "I'm not going to Haiti, Buck." Ray held his palms up toward me and shook them. "You know how I feel about voodoo."

"Relax, will you? I have no plans to go to Haiti, and I need you out with Johnny anyway." I checked my watch. It had been a very long day, and I still wasn't sure what the night might hold, but if Nanny had come clean, and still wanted us to work together, we'd have a busy morning ahead.

I promised to explain my plan to Ray at an early breakfast. He sauntered off to the Lagoon villa we were sharing, and I turned back to Nanny.

"When do I get to see the pages?"

She cocked her head slightly to the side, tugging up on the deep V neck of her dress.

"Well now, Mr. Bond, you do work fast, don't you?"

I felt my face flush.

She laughed. "The pages are back in the Ian Fleming suite—Chris let me use it for the night. Would you like to come have a look?"

My turn to smirk. "Well now, Moneypenny, I'd love to."

I stood and held up my arm, which she took. We made our way across the beach, over the illuminated bridge, and on to the very private Ian Fleming suite.

25

WHEN WE ARRIVED AT THE WELL-APPOINTED SUITE, NANNY AND I STUDIED the Morgan archives together with increasing excitement. The missing pages added some details about Morgan's Maroon associates, mentioning Akim, who had sailed with him, and Njoni his son, and noted a date that had been in the future—in fact, after Morgan died. The assumption was that this future date was for a meeting. Other details showed what I assumed to be some type of code:

$$III = III \wedge III \ 0$$

Could this be some type of map code we had no context to unravel? If we could get a better bearing on the macro of where the stash might be located, maybe it could help us with the micro of details to locate it.

This information calmed my concerns about Nanny—to the point that I said we deserved a moonlight swim on the private beach.

"Don't fall," I said a few minutes later. "There are a dozen steps and they're steep."

"And the stone is sharp," Nanny said.

The moon cast a brilliant glow on the private beach below, along with the white-capped waves crashing against it. I stepped from the stone landing onto the still warm sand, the champagne flutes in my left hand clinking against one another. I placed them on the ledge and filled them.

I stood up and held out a flute to Nanny. Instead of reaching for it she grasped the knot on her robe, twisted it, and let the batik print fabric fall to the beach. She turned, and the moonlight that filtered through the sea grape trees cast her breasts into silhouette.

"After we go swimming," she said—then stepped into the water. No swimsuit, no hesitation, no modesty.

I put the glass down, removed my trunks and robe, laid them next to the champagne bottle, and followed her in. The water was warm, but the night air was cool, so I stayed under except for my head as I caught up to her.

I pulled her into my arms. The warmth of her skin encouraged me to press her body against mine—with predictable effects.

Waves rocked us to and fro and we wound up rolling slowly across the surf-swept beach, moonlight reflecting off our wet skin, her chest lifting quickly with each breath as we kissed and allowed our fingers to explore one another, stroking, kneading, clutching.

A slight shriek escaped her parted lips, the sound lost on the breeze but not on me as I held her tight, thrusting, rocking her beneath the water, my shudders matching hers, until we both let our limbs fall flat and we drifted into the shallow water that lapped at our spent bodies. After a moment, when a larger wave lifted us for a second or two, she rolled on top of me and buried her face in my neck. I shivered.

"Apology accepted?"

"Almost," I said.

Her laugh carried through the stone cavern around the beach.

I WAS GRADUALLY AWAKENED BY THE SOUND OF WAVES BEATING ON THE beach. The same beach in the framed black and white photograph on the wall of Ian Fleming in dark trousers and a white shirt with a woman behind him holding a rake. The same beach where Nanny and I had walked into the surf and made love last night.

Dawn had just broken, and the sky through the open curtains was a swirl of pinks and oranges. Nanny was spooning me, and the warmth between our bodies was incendiary. Her arm being draped over me, I studied her hand—fingers long and graceful, nails smooth without polish, skin brown against my tanned chest. The empty champagne bottle sat on the night-stand, one flute half full and the other lying on its side.

After our moonlight swim we'd beat a sandy return to Mr. Fleming's former villa, where a hot shower led to a complete and thorough atonement. After which Nanny had promised there would be no more half-truths or omissions—all known facts would be in the open. While tempered by my usual paranoia, I believed she had been sincere.

The digital clock surprised me—I was supposed to meet Ray in ten minutes. I started to roll toward the side of the bed. Nanny flinched, then wrapped her arm tight around my chest.

"Where do you think you're going, Mr. Reilly?" Her low, half-asleep voice was incredibly sexy.

I rolled back to face her. Our lips brushed—I felt my whiskers rub against her cheek. She didn't complain.

"Ray's waiting in the restaurant," I said.

She let out a short breath, her eyes wide for a moment, then half lidded. "Can you be a little late?"

I lowered my lips to her cheek, then down to her throat.

"I can be a *lot* late."

My lips continued down to the darker brown circle of her areola and nipple, which tightened at the touch of my tongue.

Sorry, Ray.

26

B REAKFAST WAS HURRIED, AND WHILE RAY DIDN'T ASK WHY I WAS LATE HE
grunted and mumbled something about me and women. As for me?
Once Nanny shared that the colonel had been responsible for her holding
out on me and we viewed the missing pages, my evening with her had been
beyond words, not a single one of which I was going to share with anybody.

My cell phone rang—Johnny.

"How's it going?" I said.

"Like clockwork, mon. What else you expect from Johnny Blake?"

"That's why you get paid the big bucks."

"Very funny, Mr. Buck. But yes, I do hope to get the big bucks you
mention, and if this charade helps make them happen, I will perform like
Denzel Washington for you."

"You have the boats?"

"A fishing boat with salon—very nice old Viking. A work barge with
enclosed bridge, two center console fishing boats, and a small tugboat
for the barge. All fueled up, captains at the helm, just need your word to
proceed."

Ray's eyebrows lifted at the smile on my face.

"Then go ahead and have your JNHT contact alert his counterpart on
Dodson's crew. Once that's done, proceed with caution." I remembered the
bullet holes in the Beast's wing—crap! Ray hadn't seen them yet. "Just be
careful, Johnny. These guys are very protective of their turf."

"Well, they not found shit, so maybe not so worried anymore." He laughed and I could almost see his bright smile at the other end of the line.

"And make sure to alert the Coast Guard station there at Port Royal, too. Don't need them firing practice rounds toward our boats—we do have insurance, right?"

Johnny confirmed he'd paid extra for insurance and we disconnected.

Ray shook his head. "Even you have to admit this is one of your crazier schemes, Buck."

"If it works, it'll be great. If not, we'll still be a burr under their saddle." An expensive burr, to say the least. Harry Greenbaum would definitely not be happy if that turned out to be the case, which reminded me that I really needed to update him on our progress. I winced. I'd been hoping to have more news of tangible progress.

McGyver, Chris Blackwell's friend and driver, got us in ten minutes to Ian Fleming Airport, where the Beast was tied down. A big, friendly man, he laughed when I asked if his real name was McGyver.

"Plenty rock stars call me McGyver, so you can too." His smile was so infectious it gave me confidence that the day—this trip—might actually work out.

Once inside the barbed wire compound, I suggested that Ray go do the preflight inspection of the Beast while I filed the flight plan.

"Aren't we just going to Kingston?"

"Water landing, Ray? Let's not get shot at like Buffett did."

"Oh yeah. 'Jamaica Mistaica.'" He scowled. "Is this going to be—"

"That's why I'm filing the flight plan. It'll all be fine, don't worry."

He headed off for the Beast while I went into the pilot's lounge. I looked at my area chart, pulled out one that covered a broader territory, used the computer to check weather, scratched some notes. I peeked in on the airport manager and told him what I had planned. He wasn't happy—in fact he tried hard to discourage me—but in the end he sighed and said he'd make the necessary phone calls.

With my flight bag over my shoulder I left the terminal and walked to the Beast. Ray was scurrying around, making animated gestures at the wing. I took in a deep breath. It was a miracle Ray Floyd was still my friend after all I'd put him through, but I was convinced he secretly enjoyed the fly-by-the-edge-of-our-seat trips he sometimes took with me—not that he'd ever admit it.

"These *are* bullet holes!" He glared at me. "You said they weren't!"

"I said I wasn't sure—"

"How can you not be sure? Either someone shot at you or they didn't."

"Jack Dodson thought I was there to poach his dive site—"

"Which is exactly what he'll think again with your mini-flotilla heading out there!"

"Which is why I filed our flight plan coming in from the west. We'll land nearly a quarter mile away from them, Ray. Relax, I've got it all figured."

Ray turned away and continued to apply the patching material to the wing. Although it was temporary, it would keep out water, which could lead to corrosion—or worse, throw off our center of gravity.

"Got it all figured, my ass." He'd muttered it to himself, but I heard it.

I ignored him and climbed inside the open hatch.

"Hello, girl," I said. "Ready for some fun?"

Once Ray was aboard, we completed the preflight check, then cranked up the ancient twin Pratt & Whitney 450 horsepower Wasp Junior engines. I checked the elevator trim tabs, the rudder, and the wing flaps—no warning lights lit. Satisfied, we taxied out to the end of the runway. I pressed the throttles forward and we hurtled ahead to the east. Once airborne we continued east and climbed to seven thousand feet.

"Don't we need to vector south?" Ray pointed his thumb back over his shoulder. "Kingston's back that way."

"Yeah, but first we're going further east."

I pressed my lips together to stop a smile.

I could hear Ray breathing heavily inside my headset. The eastern tip of Jamaica appeared ahead of us.

"How much further east?"

I cleared my throat. "Two hundred and four miles, to be exact."

"Fucking Haiti? *You said we weren't going to Haiti!* You know I don't do voodoo, Buck—"

"Calm down, will you? We're not going to Haiti, we're going to—"

"Isla Vaca, which is in Haitian waters, so yes, we are going to Haiti."

"I'm not planning to land."

"*Unless?*"

"Well, if we see something of interest—"

"Interest? Like what?"

I reached into my pocket, pulled out another sketch—this one from memory—of the petroglyphs I'd seen up above the shelf on the rock wall at the crossroads, and handed it to Ray.

"Looks like someone drew the Olympic symbol when they were drunk."

"That may be related to Morgan's hidden treasure, missing since his death in 1688."

"What are these, crop circles? Did aliens hide Morgan's treasure?" Ray was studying the drawings.

"Maroons *were* aliens back in those days. They certainly didn't want to be here. But that petroglyph was probably carved by Taino Indians long before, so I'm not sure of the connection or significance. That's why this is just an aerial research trip."

We closed the distance in forty minutes. I alerted Air Traffic Control that we'd be flying low altitude over Isla Vaca and held my breath.

Permission was granted. I exhaled and mentally thanked the airport manager back at Ian Fleming.

We flew low with the banana-shaped island on our port side. As I studied the landscape I explained that this was where Henry Morgan used to have all his privateers gather before they commenced one of his strategically planned invasions. I'd slowed the plane to 125 knots, but on my first pass only saw a high peak, a large pond, some nice beaches, resorts, and a lot of flat area covered with mangroves.

When I flew back around and Ray studied the island from the starboard side, he noted some large boulders and cliffs above a beach.

"Those big rocks could sort of replicate these circles," he said. "But I don't know."

Good point. But if Morgan had buried his booty under large rocks, he'd had a *lot* of help. I flew back around so I could see what Ray had described. There was a beautiful deserted beach that led straight to a massive rock cliff with five large boulders at its base, right on the water's edge. From the aerial perspective, it was the only thing we'd seen with any resemblance to the petroglyph.

"How's the water look?"

"Shallow—look how light blue it is," Ray said.

"And consistent, so it must be sandy."

He sighed. "You're landing, aren't you."

I vectored directly south a few miles, then banked back around. Ray went through the water-landing checklist as I reduced power, and about a half mile out I settled the Beast into the light chop. Water splashed in all directions as we continued toward the white beach ahead, and within minutes we felt the sensation of the plane's bow settling onto the sand. I added thrust to get us up a little further, then cut the engines. Ray hopped out the front hatch and started setting anchors.

I climbed through the back hatch and jumped into the water, which soaked my shorts and orange fishing shirt. The short slog through the warm water led me to the beach, where Ray stood with his hands on his hips.

"Let's make this quick," he said.

"Unless we find something."

We walked to the end of the beach and searched for signs of—well, anything.

A distant rumble sounded overhead. Ray heard it the same time I did.

"Police?" he said. "Already? There an airport on this island?"

"No, that sounds like . . ."

My stomach sank. "Ray, hide in those bushes—quick!"

He scurried into some scrubby brush and I walked down to where the beach and rock wall met the water.

A plane flew low, just over the waterline—the roar of the twin engines made me cover my ears. The plane banked hard to the south, and all I could see was the dove-gray of her belly and the floats that hung from under each wing.

"Hi, Betty," I said.

She circled back around, even lower this time, and I caught a flash of Gunner giving me the finger from the starboard window. Jack must be at the helm.

Was Heather on board? I didn't see any other faces as they blew by.

"Breaks my heart to see you with those assholes, girl." I sighed. "I meant that for you, Betty, not Heather."

They continued east and I heard her change course and turn back around to the west. They didn't buzz me again, no doubt satisfied they knew where I was. They were clearly focused on my efforts at this point, having dug up nothing of value at Port Royal.

But how did they know we were here?

Had they seen my boats yet?

Would that blow their minds?

Hopefully.

Ray rejoined me and we silently resumed our search—he knew better than to mention Betty's name.

When we reached the colossal boulders, I used my mask, snorkel and fins to check the waterline along them but found nothing—no underwater caves or anything that appeared to be man-made. I'd need a magnetometer to detect whether or not there was any gold or silver here, but my gut said there wasn't. Given that this was the only thing we'd spotted on the tiny island that resembled the petroglyph drawing, and since Morgan's diary hinted at treasure off-loaded near the Rio Grande, I concluded there was nothing of value here. But the process of elimination in itself was valuable.

We met back at the plane.

"Find anything?" I said.

"Sure, vast piles of flotsam, plastic bottles, trap floats, and junk in the bushes. On top of the hill was a road and wood stakes set by engineers for some big tourist development."

"Figures."

Nothing pristine lasts for long, even in Haiti.

There was no conversation on the flight back to Jamaica, but my mind was noisy with frustration, and not just because Isla Vaca had turned out to be a dud. The sight of Betty in the hands of Jack and Gunner was a fresh kick in the balls. No matter how many times I glimpsed my old plane—my sole possession after filing bankruptcy—it still hurt. How she'd been rebuilt I still didn't know, but she was as beautiful now as she'd ever been.

Even though she was no longer mine.

27

UPON REACHING JAMAICA WE BANKED DOWN OVER THE CENTRAL HIGHWAY that led from Ocho Rios to Kingston. My promise that we'd approach Port Royal from the opposite direction of Jack's dive site was as much for my peace of mind as Ray's. Gunner and his mercenaries had already fired on me once, and that was before they knew why I was here. After seeing him in the mountains yesterday, and with our boats parked on their perimeter today, I wouldn't be surprised if he fired a heat-seeking missile at us.

With both his hands on top of the instrument panel, Ray searched ahead of us for boats and debris.

"There are three, four, five boats anchored in a group ahead, one of them a barge."

"Sounds like Johnny. Can you see a larger group of boats a quarter mile or so further east?"

"Yeah, looks like—yeah, there's Betty anchored inside of them."

He glanced at me and I bit my lip. He didn't know Heather was over there too, or at least she had been. That could fray his nerves a bit more than this escapade already had. It certainly frayed mine.

The Beast set down in the two-foot seas, still a quarter mile out from our boats, and while we skipped and bounced, water blasting off the props, we quickly settled into a good pace on the step, aimed toward the Viking that Johnny had rented.

"Okay, let's switch positions," I said.

"What, while we're moving?"

"Part of the plan, Ray. I want them to think you're me—that's why I had you hide back at Isla Vaca, so they wouldn't see you."

"I thought you were just protecting me."

"And take your shirt off."

"Excuse me?"

I held the wheel with my knee and pulled my orange fishing shirt over my head. "They've seen me in this—"

"That's gonna be a little tight, Buck."

"It's an XL, you'll be fine."

He unbuttoned his red floral Hawaiian shirt and took it off, one arm after the other.

"Okay, let's switch."

I got up, leaning over—the Beast veered and dove awkwardly in the trough of a wave—

"Hang on!"

To his credit, Ray dove under my arm into the left seat and quickly got the plane back on course. I fell into the right seat, sat back up, and pushed the orange shirt over his head. He struggled to get each arm through the long sleeves while still guiding the plane. I dug in the storage panel under the starboard window and pulled out the sun mask and gloves I'd worn the day I confronted Jack.

"These too."

"Is that *blood*—"

"They're fishing gloves, Ray. You just had skin cancer, so you're trying to avoid the sun—"

"No I didn't—"

"Ray! Just play along."

He slowed the plane. Our boats were dead ahead, maybe a hundred yards off the bow. All our men, none of whom I'd met aside from Johnny, were standing on the deck of the Viking, staring and pointing at us. Good news—there was a small police boat out there too.

Well done, Johnny.

I took my binoculars from the storage bin, crouched low, and focused them past our boats and onto Jack's. His crew were also all facing toward us, no doubt curious about the new boats—and now another antique flying boat. Jack and Gunner wouldn't have told them anything, yet. The big difference between our two groups, aside from the number of people and craft, was that several of Jack's people held rifles and shotguns. I scanned from man to man—there!

Jack and Gunner stood in the middle of their men—Jack was waving his arm and pointing toward Gunner, whose mouth looked thin as a razor.

"Do they see us?" Ray said.

"They see us."

"Are they pissed?"

"They're pissed. Oh, yeah, they're pissed."

He let out a long sigh.

"Remember, Ray, both groups have representatives from the Jamaican National Heritage Trust on board. They'll force everybody to play by the rules—"

"If they haven't been tied up and gagged, you mean."

We taxied to the north of our boats to be in the wind's lee, and on the inside edge facing the harbor at Kingston. The Coast Guard base at the end of Port Royal was weather-beaten and dominated the waterfront there, but it also provided some sense of comfort—flimsy as it might be.

"Can you get the anchors ready?" he said.

"I'll get them ready, but you need to go through the bow and open the port side hatch to set them yourself. They need to think you're alone here."

"Seriously? That's a pain in the—"

"They have binoculars too, Ray. They see me and we're pissing in the wind."

I scrambled back into the cabin, popped open the rear storage door, and readied the stern anchor for him—all from my knees. Next I crawled back and up into the nose, then cleared the bow anchor too. The pitch of the engines made it clear Ray was in position.

"You all set?" I said.

"Yeah, sure, I'm set."

"Okay." I paused for two seconds. "Ready, go!"

Ray jumped up, scrambled under the instrument—

"Oww, crap!"

Everyone hits their head on that panel.

Cussing ensued, then I heard the bow hatch swing open. Ray grunted, I heard some shuffling, and he came crawling like a demon back through the hatch—I couldn't see his face because of the sun mask.

"You're doing great, Ray."

"Shut up!"

He climbed into the left seat, added reverse thrust and backed away from the anchor.

"Taut!" He jumped up again, climbed over me, and popped open the port hatch—nearly fell in the water, grumbling and talking to himself as he grabbed the Danforth anchor and tossed it out with a grunt. Once the rope went slack he started retrieving it, yanking every few feet until it went taut. He took in a deep breath—I could see the fabric on the sun mask suck inside his mouth.

"Better check the front anchor," I said.

"Shut up, Buck! God . . . darn it, how . . . do I . . . let you—"

"Save your breath, too."

As Ray passed me, the toe of his right foot kicked me in the shoulder.

"Did you do that on purpose?"

"I was aiming for your head!"

The sound of a motorboat approaching caught my attention. Could one of Jack's people be here this fast? He did have a couple of speedboats.

I scurried up into the flight deck and tried to hide, which wasn't easy. Ray backed out of the forward hatch.

"Hey! Can you let me by, please?"

"There's a boat coming," I said. "Fix your mask!"

He pulled the mask back down over his face and peered out the window.

"It's your guy Johnny."

"Okay, here's what we're going to do."

"About time," Ray said.

"An old-fashioned switcheroo. They'll think you're me out here on my new dive site, so they won't try and follow me around Jamaica anymore."

"That's it? How will you get out of here, then?"

"Once you've settled in on the boat and their attention wanes, I'll swim over and sneak onto one of the other boats. Johnny will drive it to shore."

"Better you than me," he said.

The motorboat idled up to the open hatch on the port side of the Beast.

"Yoo-hoo, anybody home?" Johnny said.

"Yeah, hang on, Johnny. Ray's going with you and I'm staying here. He'll explain it to you. But act like you never saw me."

He puckered his lips and scratched his head, all while keeping the boat straight in the press of the current.

"Okay," Ray said, "See you later—"

"One other thing, Ray." I paused. "Jack, Gunner, and those guys all have guns."

Ray froze.

"They'll be pissed and probably come over to see what the hell's going on. You just keep that mask on and let Johnny do the talking. You refuse to speak with them, because Dodson and my/your ex-wife are having an affair—"

"*What?*"

"She was on his boat the day I got here." I tried to keep my expression neutral. "Seems they'd been seeing each other since I was still married to her."

"Damn, Buck. Sorry, man."

"Plenty reason for you to give them the bird and stay inside that big cabin cruiser. Johnny will play the heavy—"

"Let's go," Johnny said. "I'm gonna smash this boat into the side of your plane in a minute, mon."

Ray hesitated, looking like a mummified fishing guide in the sun mask and gloves, then he nodded once, stepped outside, and slammed the hatch shut. A moment later the motorboat's engine revved and then faded into the distance, leaving only the sound of waves slapping against the hull of my ancient flying boat.

28

I WATCHED THROUGH THE BINOCULARS AS JACK AND GUNNER STOMPED AROUND the deck of their fancy Merritt yacht and yelled at some of their crewmen. As much money as he'd spent by now, with me here setting up another dive site, examining petroglyphs in the mountains, and flying to distant islands connected to Henry Morgan, Jack would be shitting glass by now.

Ray and Johnny arrived back at the Viking, tied off, and climbed aboard. Didn't help that Ray was four inches shorter than me and closer to twenty pounds heavier.

"Get below deck, Ray." I held my breath as he stopped to speak with some of the people on deck. He reached behind and scratched his ass.

"Don't ham it up trying to pretend you're me—stick to the plan!"

He finally waved to one of the other men on a boat and stepped down into the salon. Crap. Would Jack realize that wasn't me? I hoped their seeing me just an hour ago at Isla Vaca, in the same orange shirt, would be convincing enough.

Once an hour had passed and the afternoon sun had flattened, I cracked the port hatch open. The pull of the current had us facing away from both flotillas. Stripped down to my underwear, I edged outside and managed to hang on to the exterior handle. The fresh air and breeze were a relief to my stomach, a bit queasy after the constant rocking in the steady chop.

I pulled the hatch down, pushed it until it snapped, locked it, then hung the key on the chain around my neck and knifed into the cool water.

I did my best to keep most of my body submerged as I swam, trying to position myself so Jack's group couldn't see me as I approached my boats. My heart raced—if one of my own men or someone on the police boat saw me, they might sound an alarm. I had to trust that Johnny had told our people to keep their mouths shut.

Nobody even glanced my way as I did a very slow stroke right up to the speedboat, now tied up next to the big cabin cruiser. I swam to its stern and peeked around the corner toward Jack's boats. It was too far to be sure whether anyone was watching or not, so I swam to the middle of the boat, reached up to the dock bumper, then the side of the boat and pulled myself up and in, hoping the center console would block their view if they were watching. I lay flat, shivering in the shade, the sound of my heart throbbing in my ears.

An engine revved in the distance, and within moments it sounded as if somebody had shoved a boat's throttle, or throttles, into full speed and was coming this way.

Fast.

I scurried to the opposite side of the boat and lay flat against the gunwale closest to the direction of the approaching boat.

"The hell's going on?" I heard Johnny Blake on the deck of the cabin cruiser "You stay down there!"

I wasn't sure if he was talking to me or Ray, but hopefully both.

"Yo, mister Constable? Hello? Yeah, you! That boat is not welcome over here—they'll be trespassing, could be armed and dangerous!"

Good, Johnny, good.

I heard someone reply from the police boat, then it started up too. It sounded as if it pulled up to our cabin cruiser and was idling as the other boat got louder, closing the distance. Then the pitch of its engine changed as it slowed down—if not inside our survey area, damn close.

"Buck Reilly!"

Jack Dodson's voice.

"The hell you want, mon?" Johnny said.

"Tell Buck to get topside, I want to have a word with him."

"I don't think so, brother. He don't want to talk to none of you."

A megaphone crackled. "Stay on the other side of those buoys, or you will be trespassing!" Must be the constable.

"Buck, get your ass up here and face me!"

"I said to get back!" The constable's voice was louder.

"Don't be a pussy, Reilly! Get out here now—"

BOOM!

The crack of a pistol shot sounded. The air seized in my throat.

"Get back over that line between the buoys!" The constable's voice was so loud—and aggressive—it was half garbled as it came through the megaphone.

"Goddammit, Reilly, we have a blanket claim on Morgan's missing estate—we've spent a fortune out here digging up this sunken shithole thanks to the fucking letter you bought with our money. Now, you back off, or we'll get the government involved, and Gunner, well, I won't be able to control him!"

It had worked. They'd obviously seen Ray board the boat, which had driven Jack to come confront me.

Silence followed. He must have at least retreated behind the line to keep the constable from shooting him. I couldn't bring myself to smile, but hearing Jack on the brink of desperation loosed a perverse satisfaction that warmed my shivering body.

"Head on back to your dive site, Mr. Dodson," Johnny said. "Mr. Buck not interested in speaking with you, and no sense getting shot by Jamaica's finest."

Jack's motors revved.

"You'll regret this, Buck! You can count on that."

His engines again went straight into high gear, and the boat I was lying on bounced in his wake. I focused on my breathing and listened as I heard some muffled discussion from the cabin cruiser, then a door slammed shut.

"Thank you, Mr. Constable," Johnny said. "I'm going to run to town and would appreciate you keeping an eye on our boats here—and maybe let someone know I'm coming to shore in case those crazy bastards try to follow me."

There was no response, but a moment later Johnny appeared above me, high up on the deck of the Viking. He jumped, landing feet first on the front deck of the speedboat. He giggled as he walked past me, untied the two lines that connected this boat to our mother ship, then turned the keys to start the twin outboards. I watched him from the deck and found myself smiling as he pulled away.

As we added speed and distance, I belly-crawled back toward the helm. Undoubtedly every eye from both groups would be on him, so I just stayed flat.

"You'd make one hell of an actor, Johnny."

He cackled but put a hand over his wide grin.

"Your boy was pissed, mon." He shook his head. "Know you heard some of that, but you should of seen his eyes. They was wild, mon. Think he's some crazed, that one."

Lovely. If Jack seemed crazy, Gunner must look like Charles Manson by now.

The ride to the Kingston harbor took fifteen minutes. By the time we were there Johnny opened a hatch and tossed me a pair of cutoff jeans and a green Jamaica T-shirt. They were tight, but it was better than walking down the street in my briefs.

"You see anybody following us?" I said.

"No, mon, all clear. The dock's up ahead. You can hop out and I run over to the marina, get gas and some Red Stripe. Your friend Ray said he need a drink."

"Better get him some Blackwell Rum." I paused. "No ganja, though. Ray's too paranoid for that."

This time Johnny didn't cover his broad grin.

When the boat slowed to a crawl, I knew we were at the dock and I stood up just in time to see Nanny arrive at the end of the pier. She saw me and waved, her smile big and her eyes glowing.

"Damn, mon, someone look happy to see you."

The boat pulled up beside the dock, and by the time my feet landed on the wood planks Johnny was already in reverse and backing out.

"Thanks, Johnny. I'll be in touch."

"For sure, Mr. Buck."

With that he wheeled the boat hard to the left, gunned it, and lit out in a streak of white wake.

All was going according to plan. And when I turned around I was given an unforgettably warm welcome back to Kingston from Professor Nanny Adou.

Capture
Land

29

WE TOOK OFF IN THE JEEP AND FOLLOWED THE WATERFRONT. KINGSTON'S port was far from the most beautiful in the Caribbean—too many large cranes and piers for container ships. And I knew that much of the long history of this city wasn't kind to the near-million people who lived here.

I scanned the horizon but couldn't make out either group of boats at the sunken city of Port Royal. Hopefully Ray was hanging in there, sticking to the plan and lost in a haze of Jamaican beer in the Viking's salon.

Nanny hadn't said much since she'd picked me up. I decided not to mention my expedition out at Port Royal or Ray's and my trip to Isla Vaca.

"Where are we going?" I said.

"West."

We passed by the highway that led north into the mountains, but she continued west into the heart of Kingston.

"How did your research go?" I said. "Anything to follow up on from your visit to Moore Town?"

"I rereviewed all the archives—the originals are more legible than the copies I gave you." She adjusted her position in the driver's seat. "I talked with Stanley and some of the elders in Moore Town about the names of the people we think helped Morgan hide the treasure . . . They recognized some connections to modern Maroon families."

I turned to face her. "That's great. Did you speak with any of the descendents? Or did the colonel—is he feeling better?"

"Yes he is, and no, it's more complicated than just talking to the descendents." She was deadpan, no excitement at whatever connections they'd made.

"What's the problem?"

"That's why we're headed west. We need to go up into Cockpit Country and try to speak with leaders there."

"In Accompong?"

She nodded.

Uh-oh. The rest of the world wouldn't differentiate between the two groups of Maroons, but their history—enmity—ran deep, and that had already been thrown in our faces.

"You worried about Cuffee?"

She nodded again.

"Did the colonel ever confirm he was the one who beat him?"

"He said he thought it was a white man. My guess is it was the man with Cuffee yesterday—the one you fought with."

"Wouldn't surprise me," I said. "But the other people in Cockpit can't be as crazy as Cuffee and Gunner—right?"

"Henry Kujo is the leader there, but they're holding an election soon and that makes everyone a little crazy."

Nanny had said the Leewards were a flourishing community, so Henry Kujo would be a powerful man. Would Cuffee's claim to Morgan's treasure be something Kujo supported? Come to think of it, how valid a claim did the Leeward Maroons have?

"The people you spoke with today, what names did they recognize?" I said.

"Njoni—"

"Who wrote the phony letter," I said.

"Correct. His father, Akim, was legendary at the time because he was a fierce Windward Maroon warrior *and* because he was a black man and privateer sailing with one of the most famous men of the time, Captain Henry Morgan."

"Sounds fine so far."

Nanny turned left toward Spanish Town, and vehicles of all sizes passed us at high speed. A careful, slow driver, she didn't seem to notice.

"Njoni was essentially a scout fighting against the British, and part of his responsibilities was to communicate with other Maroons throughout the mountains, all over Jamaica."

"Okay, so?"

"So, he fell in love with a woman in the western end of the country and settled there—in what today is called Accompong."

"I figured it was something like that, but what's the significance?"

"Cuffee's a distant relative to Njoni and Akim."

I saw a sign for Treasure Beach ahead and momentarily lost my train of thought. That's where the *Sports Illustrated* swimsuit edition was being shot—where my ex-wife was purportedly modeling bikinis.

"Buck? You see the problem, yes?"

Unfortunately I did. "Njoni might have hid the loot, or booty, or treasure, or whatever you want to call it, and Cuffee is making noise in Accompong that it belongs to him, and the Leeward Maroons."

"Exactly."

So that's what had Nanny upset. A provenance, or title dispute. I'd battled many of them in my day and been successful more often than not. Sometimes it required making a deal, though. I said so to Nanny.

"Do you really think Cuffee and that barbarian he's working with would cut a fair and equitable deal?"

Good point. "Look, right now we have no idea whether there even *is* any treasure, and if there is, we have no idea where it might be. That being the case, I wouldn't get too worried about—"

"Two things," she said. "First, Cuffee has agitated the Leewards against us, so we can't really count on much assistance there. And second, the Obeah woman who met us at the river a couple days ago?"

"The two hundred-year-old one?"

"Be nice." Nanny took a deep breath. "She had a vision that we *do* find treasure."

I held my hands up. "Well, if you believe in that, sounds like everything will be fine."

That got me a hard look. "She also had a vision that someone is going to get killed."

I crossed my arms. Given the instability of Dodson, Gunner, Cuffee, and their crew, that particular prophecy didn't sound too far off the mark. I squirmed in my seat, now second-guessing my decision to leave Ray and the Beast out on the water. I didn't believe in black magic, but I'd seen enough cases where its practitioners were either able to manipulate events to meet their "visions" or were damned good speculators.

But for those who believed—which Nanny seemed to—nothing was more powerful.

"Okay, we need to be cautious, that's the bottom line."

She cut me a glance. Of course she knew that being cautious and hunting treasure were polar opposite.

My phone rang and the screen lit up. Johnny.

"Hey, everything okay?"

"No, mon, not really. I was on my way back out and that crazy bastard with the blue sunglasses near T-boned me—cut me off just inside the point of Port Royal—and one-a his men got a machine gun—"

"Did you stop?"

"Yeah, mon, no choice. He's, ah, on board now and wants to—"

There was loud static—

"What the fuck are you doing out here, Reilly? Haven't I warned your ass—"

I jerked forward in my seat. "Get off my boat, Gunner! I'll have the police there in—"

"Get off our site—"

"I'm not on your site! I have a separate permit—"

"How the hell did you get that? Who'd you bribe? Our permit's exclusive—"

"Get off the boat now, Gunner." I shot a quick look at Nanny, who was glancing back and forth from the road to me. "I'm signaling the police right now—hello! Constable?"

Nanny squinted and shook her head.

"This is your last warning, Reilly. Our divers will scuttle your boats one by one if you don't clear out—"

"One of the partners from SCG International—that group of boats over there—has one of my men captive and is making threats!"

My shout caused Nanny to swerve.

"We're leaving, Reilly, but I'm not messing around. You turned yourself into a serious irritation I got to get rid of. If you're smart you'll be out of my life before that happens."

The line went dead. I glanced at the screen.

"What was that all about?" Nanny said.

"Our friends out on the water don't like having company. They think I'm out there on one of the survey boats yelling to the police to protect us.

The phone rang again.

"You okay?" I said.

"Oh yeah, mon, peachy. Those some crazy bastards. They headed to shore now—you still at the dock?"

"No, we're headed up to Accompong. Keep out of their way, Johnny, and tell the constable what happened."

He bitched and moaned but promised to be vigilant. I was just glad Ray hadn't been there when Gunner came calling. I'd never hear the end of it.

"You're playing a dangerous game, Buck Reilly," Nanny said.

"Welcome to the treasure-hunting business."

Traffic slowed ahead of us. Large food trucks were parked along the side of the road, and there was loud music playing and crowds standing behind a fenced-off area. We were at Treasure Beach. I saw women in the distance—white women in bikinis—lounging around, coming in and out of white tents on the sand. There were a couple recreational vehicles parked down on the beach too. Would Thom Shepherd be there, shooting his video?

What if I saw Heather? My stomach did *not* like this thought.

"You want to stop for some food?" Nanny said.

"No! Please, just keep driving."

She gave me a double-take, but we kept going, slowly and methodically, until we turned north and followed a sign that said: Accompong 92 Km.

My stomach was no longer queasy. But I knew I'd rather face the descendents of every savage Maroon warrior in history than run into my ex-wife again.

30

Nanny had managed to arrange for Henry Kujo, the sitting Leeward Maroon leader, to meet us at a jerk stand just south of the town. She parked the Jeep beside the small yellow building, which had nearly been overtaken from behind by a dense wall of vegetation that looked as aggressive as kudzu. Once she turned the engine off, she rubbed her hands together, checked her hair in the mirror, rubbed her hands again—was that another shudder?

"You okay?"

"Not really." She again glanced at the mirror. "I'm a university professor, not a treasure hunter. That might have worked for Indiana Jones or you, but it's not for me." She ran a palm up one sleeve, then repeated the gesture with her other hand.

I studied her. Beautiful, intelligent, passionate, and yes, a university professor. But also a direct descendent of the "Mother of us all." That must come with immense pressure.

"So why are you doing this?" I said.

Her chest lifted with a long intake of breath. "Because I have to."

"What's that mean?"

"Between Dodson's group and the well-publicized competition between the two of you, the island is aware—entirely too aware—of the possibility of buried treasure."

I suddenly felt a tic in my right eyelid.

"The colonel and I feel responsible," she said, "to ensure that if there *is* a treasure—a direct link to the history of cooperation between Morgan and the Maroons—it will benefit all of the Jamaican people, not fall in the hands of—"

"Treasure hunters who seek personal gain or if not, personal aggrandizement. Nanny, we've already had this conversation."

She looked at my chest, unable to meet my eyes.

"What bothers me," she said, "is that I'm using my lineage to get meetings with people like Henry Kujo and Michael Portland—jeopardizing my career, my stature at the university that I've worked so hard to achieve . . . once word spreads of my involvement in this—"

"But you're not doing this for self-enrichment—"

"Nobody will believe that." She sighed. "Every meeting like this will erode my reputation—people will say I'm using my lineage for profit, exploiting the memory of the Mother of us all—" Another shudder.

I leaned over and wrapped my arm around her, pulling her in tight. She quivered like a kitten during its first visit to the veterinarian. When I stepped back she must have caught the glint in my eye, because her face brightened a bit.

"Let's play it like I'm the only one who's searching," I said. "Tell them you've imposed severe restrictions on me and you're just monitoring my activities."

A slow smile parted her lips.

"I'm certain I'll have to barter to get answers, so I doubt that will work. But thank you."

I leaned forward and gave her an unhurried kiss that made it clear I held no regrets from last night.

"Now," she said when we finally broke apart, "let's go—"

"One question," I said. "The separate treaties with the British, between the Leeward and Windward Maroons? How long was the gap?"

"It's not a piece of history our people are proud of, but it was relatively short-lived and it was later determined to be amongst only a few opportun-ists who acted as traitors. But . . . one of those hunters was Njoni."

Good Lord.

"Now let's go meet Mr. Kujo and see what we can learn, Buck."

31

INSIDE THE JERK STAND WAS AN OPEN KITCHEN WHERE THE COOK HUNCHED over a grill perched unsteadily above a fire. There were only four tables, and just one was occupied—an older man, distinguished, wearing a white shirt buttoned to the top and gray slacks. It took a second look to notice that the slacks were frayed at the hems above his nicely polished black loafers. Seated with him was a younger man with quick eyes. He saw us first and his lips moved as he whispered something under his breath.

Henry Kujo stood and turned to face us.

"Follow my lead," Nanny said.

She stepped forward in three long strides, her hand outstretched. Kujo's eyes softened at her approach and when he took her hand he pulled her close for a hug. They exchanged a fast couple sentences in the Jamaican patois I had yet to master, then she turned to hold a hand out to me.

"I'd like you to meet Buck Reilly, a once famous archaeologist from America."

Kujo and I shook, his grip lighter than I expected.

"I recall reading about you in the *Gleaner* not too long ago. Seems you were here in Jamaica to excavate part of Port Royal."

"Fortunately, I did not prevail in that effort, as the search has been fruitless for the winning bidder."

Kujo turned to a younger man at his side. "This is my aide, Clayton Perkins."

"Pleasure to meet you, Nanny." Clayton's keen eyes had turned to her even while giving my hand a firm shake.

Kujo was tall, lean, and had light gray eyes that seemed to disappear as you stared into them. Clayton was short, muscular, and wore a blue tie with his light green short-sleeved shirt. He also sported remarkably detailed brown wingtip shoes. He seemed to inflate when he saw me checking them out.

"Nanny, it's been far too long since we've seen you here in Accompong," Kujo said. "When was it, Maroon Festival maybe three years ago? Come, let's sit."

"Something like that, Henry. My duties at the university seem to increase on a monthly basis, along with my involvement with JNHT."

"And still no husband or children?" Kujo cut a glance toward me.

Nanny dodged his questions with ones of her own—checking up on known family members and elders. Then the two of them compared notes on the waning interest of today's youth in the history older Maroons identified with to their core.

"Tell me what brings you here to Accompong? Have you come to endorse my reelection?"

Kujo's broad smile left me certain his statement was only partially in jest. And I'd come to recognize Nanny's quick squirms, one of which manifested now via a shift in her seat from one side to the other.

"I generally stay out of politics, Henry." The conversation we were about to engage in hung as heavily as soot in the jerk-thick air. "But I may be persuaded to speak out on your behalf."

He reached over and took one of her hands in both of his.

"Thank you, my dear. That would be valuable indeed. Now tell me, what can Clayton and I do for you today?" His eyes shot over at me for a moment.

I sat forward. "I'd asked the archaeology—"

"Buck, please, let me," Nanny said. "As you're aware, Mr. Reilly was here in Jamaica for archaeological purposes—"

"You mean treasure hunting," Clayton said.

"Clayton, show respect," Kujo said.

The aide's eyes did not relent as he stared at me.

"As I was saying," Nanny said. "Mr. Reilly's expertise came to my attention during the Port Royal process, and we at the university recognized that this treasure hunt, as you referred to it, would not subside once it had begun. And so we appealed to Mr. Reilly to assist us in locating the missing archives—"

So I've heard," Kujo said.

"What's his cut?" Clayton said.

Kujo let the question hang.

Nanny hesitated, in over her head already. I sat back.

"The opportunity to assist the Jamaican people to locate such a material piece of their national history was immediately attractive to me," I said. "In past efforts like these in Mexico, Panama, and Colombia—"

"What's your cut?"

I glanced at Nanny who gave me a slight nod. I said, "The equivalent of 10 percent—"

"Ha! I figured," Clayton said.

"Mr. Reilly's experience and knowledge is priceless in this effort. His application at Port Royal originally sought 25 percent, so his 'cut,' as you put it, represents a substantial reduction—"

"We estimate the treasure's worth to be fifty million U.S.—that's five million to *Mr.* Reilly." His eyes glistened now.

"That's enough, Clayton."

Had Clayton just acknowledged the treasure existed? I sat forward as my heart upshifted.

"So you're confident the treasure does exist?" I said.

"Not at all." Kujo raised his palms as if to settle the runaway speculation. "But assuming just for a moment that it does, then Clayton has raised a valid point."

I looked directly into Clayton's eyes.

"But assuming—as is far more likely—that the treasure *doesn't* exist,"

"Then 10 percent of nothing is nothing."

"That's not what Cuffee—"

"Let's listen to what our guests have to say, Clayton." Kujo's stare now bore like lasers into his assistant's eyes.

Nanny turned to look directly at Clayton.

"And whatever might be found," Nanny said, "our interest here is preserving Jamaican heritage. If the winning bidders find what they seek, they will get 50 percent—"

"A travesty," Kujo said.

"Agreed, but nobody believed there was any chance for their success. We considered it an opportunity to have a major underwater structure restored and stabilized at their expense."

An uncomfortable silence fell over the table. The restaurateur approached with a tray of jerked chicken, and to my disappointment, Clayton waved him off.

"Our goal," Nanny said, "is—"

"Excuse me, but who exactly is *our*?" Kujo said.

Nanny again shifted in her seat. "Members of the community interested in preserving—"

"Not the university?"

"No. They have agreed to my taking a leave of absence to pursue the effort. Now listen, Henry, much of anything found would be enshrined in the National Maritime Museum in Kingston—neutral ground for all parties. And depending upon *what* is found—"

"If anything's found," Kujo said.

Nanny continued. "The majority would be used to the benefit of the Jamaican people in a social program—"

"Don't forget about King Buck's 10 percent," Clayton said.

Nanny ignored him. "The reason I'm here is to ask if you have any knowledge about the Morgan legacy as it relates to our ancestors who split their time on both sides of the country."

I was watching Kujo's face. A flicker registered in his eyes.

"I've only heard the same legends and rumors we've all been told for generations," he said.

"And those have been based on warriors from Cockpit who had been with Morgan—"

"Not originally, Clayton," Nanny said. "Historical documents and records tell a different story."

 "Not according to—"

"Clayton!" Kujo's voice was sharp. "Don't be a fool arguing history with one of Jamaica's most acclaimed historians. Who lived where and when is not the point here. I understand what Nanny has alluded to. And given what happened to Stanley Grandy—which I was sickened to hear—it *is* a valid problem."

I sat quickly forward, Clayton's mention of Cuffee on my lips—but Nanny's not-so-subtle headshake caused me to lean back again.

For a long moment we all seemed to be trying not to look at each other—until Nanny got Kujo's attention.

"Given what happened to Stanley, can you calm down some of the more aggressive members of your community, Henry?" she said.

Kujo frowned. "Are you insinuating that someone from here—"

Nanny sat bolt upright. "I'm not insinuating anything, but as we all know, the situation could unravel quickly into a free-for-all if we're not careful."

Kujo looked from her to me, then back. Clayton's lips were pursed.

"I will urge for calm amongst my community."

"Thank you, Henry. I—"

"*But*, if the treasure is found, we must have a say in what becomes of it." Kujo had transformed from an elderly gentlemen to a sharp-eyed negotiator in the blink of an eye.

Now we all stared at one another.

"No chicken?" the proprietor said.

"No!" everyone except me said at once.

32

THE ROAD BACK TO THE SOUTHEAST WAS UNMARKED FOR MUCH OF THE WAY
and had potholes that nearly jarred the fillings from my molars. Nanny
hadn't said a word since we left the jerk shack, but my mind had been
whirling. Now, fifteen minutes later, I heard a long, long sigh.

"That went worse than I expected," she said.

"Depends on how you look at it," I said. "They seem certain there *is* a
treasure. When Clayton—that little prick—mentioned Cuffee, I thought
Kujo was going to backhand him. I was ready to punch the smug smile off
his face before he let that drop."

She giggled. "I'd have helped."

"Their mention of a fifty million dollar value is the same figure other
archaeologists and treasure hunters have speculated," I said. "And my 10
percent? Clayton being pissed about it is only relevant if he thinks it exists
and we might find it."

We continued on without talking, Nanny driving uncharacteristically
fast now that the road had improved. Dwellings began to appear.

"I'm convinced that there's a treasure now, but know what my one
disappointment was?" I said.

She glanced toward me. "No idea."

"I really wish we'd gotten some of that jerk chicken."

A flicker of a smile. "There's a good place up ahead."

The area was mountainous, its peaks smaller and more conical than the Blue Mountains—classic karst topography. This was the landscape that had helped the Leeward Maroon warriors avoid capture as guerilla fighters.

In a valley where two steep mountains met was a small village, just a few miles south of Albert Town. Smoke rose from behind a wooden structure not unlike the one where we'd met Kujo, though the wood exterior was faded rather than smartly painted.

"This restaurant's been here as long as I can remember. And there's an outfitter out back that leads hiking and camping trips into Cockpit Country from here."

"I'm starving," I said.

While we waited for our food I noticed a pair of old hand-carved canoes hanging from massive limbs on seriously massive trees—the trunks had to be six feet across.

I ate some excellent jerk chicken, and Nanny had a yam cooked in tinfoil over an open fire, along with some fresh bananas and sweetsop. Nobody paid us much attention, which was fine with me. Once done, we dumped our trash in a bin.

I followed Nanny out the door. A black truck was now parked between the Jeep and us.

Nanny stumbled—whoa! There were three men in front of her, and one grabbed her by the arm—

"Hey!" I yelled as I dove for him.

"Buck!" Nanny shrieked.

The man who had her arm was big—they all were. I clamped onto his forearm—he released her.

"Run!" I yelled.

The men gathered around me. One came in with his arms wide—a jab to his face and his lower lip exploded in a burst of blood. He dropped to his knees. I recognized none of them.

Nanny stood frozen, having run ten feet and stopped.

"Buck!"

The man to my left dove for my waist—dreadlocks jumped into the air and bounced off my chest as he caromed into me. I rabbit-punched the back of his head, then chopped down on his neck. His momentum and size forced me to backstep. I chopped again but missed. I saw a work boot swing up behind my right leg—

WHAP!

Something hit the side of my head. Bright lights erupted . . . swirled . . . Then there was no light at all.

THE SMELL OF BURNT MEAT CAUSED ME TO WAKE WITH A START.

I rolled over in loose dirt. Everything wobbled, and I had double vision—there were two of each canoe hanging from the branches. I closed my eyes and carefully touched the welt and gash on the right side of my skull—moist with blood.

I shook my head gently, hoping to clear it—all that did was make the distortion worse. But I made it to my knees before I puked: jerk chicken, sauce, blood.

Still on all fours I glanced around, my vision no longer double but really blurry, like staring through a car windshield in a driving rainstorm with no wipers. The Jeep was still there, but no men, no black truck, no Nanny Adou.

I knew there was no point in shouting.

"Nanny!" The shout echoed in my ears, the taste of bile soured in my mouth.

I got to my feet, staggered, then stood straight.

I stumbled toward the jerk stand and found the front door locked. No smoke billowed from the chimney.

I checked my watch but didn't know what time we'd gotten here, so I wasn't sure how long I'd been out. It was 3:25 now.

I made it to the Jeep, surprised to find the keys in the ignition.

Not surprised that Nanny was gone.

33

I DROVE SLOWLY IN A CROOKED LINE TOWARD ALBERT TOWN, MY VISION STILL blurry, the pain god-awful. The Jeep veered off the right shoulder, sideswiped a boulder, and bounced back out into the road. Talking to myself actually helped.

Have to get . . . to . . . Albert Town. That's where Nanny had us headed . . . so maybe . . . she'll be there.

I slowed the Jeep to a stop and sat in the middle of the road, trying to get my bearings. Movement on the left side gradually caught my blurry eye. I squinted.

A black and white goat stared at me, the only other living creature in sight.

I slowly depressed the accelerator and strained to see ahead. The last few miles felt endless, but I finally reached Albert Town's main drag: a series of squat homes and buildings pressed together with red roofs and green trees for backdrop. I drove through the town without seeing a vehicle remotely similar to the black truck.

Nausea again hit me like a stiff breeze. I crashed into the curb and scared a dog off the sidewalk before I jammed on the brakes and turned off the ignition.

My head pounded, and closing my eyes helped a little. I grabbed my backpack off the seat, got out, and staggered into a small restaurant where I collapsed onto a wooden chair.

"You there!" A woman came toward me. "No drunks in here—find somewhere else to—"

Her mouth dropped when she saw the side of my head. Blood had clotted in and matted my hair, and while I didn't think the gash was deep enough to need stitches I could imagine how it looked.

"Oh, mon, you hurt bad!"

My blurry vision made out a pink apron that didn't look big enough on a woman who looked to be in her late fifties. Eyes round with dark circles in the middle.

"Nanny, Mother of us all—they kidnapped her and beat me down when—"

She put a finger to her lips.

"Don't try to talk—come back here. Can you stand?"

I was fading in and out of consciousness, but I know she led me by the hand back into the kitchen, where an old man with a red, yellow, and black bandana tied around his head gawked at me. Behind the kitchen was a small room with a sink. She pulled over a chair for me and then, using an old cloth, proceeded to wash my scalp, very gently, with cool water.

Everything went swirly—but only until I felt my shoulder hit the floor.

WHEN I AWOKE IT WAS DARK OUTSIDE, ASSUMING THE ONE SMALL WINDOW opened to the outside. I lay on a couch, trying to sort out where I was— then I saw the sink with the rag draped over the basin.

Breathe deep. In and out.

Slowly, my eyes adjusted to the light. There was a small, low-watt lamp on a table next to the couch. Nobody else was in the small room—

Nanny. My heart skidded. Where was she?

I swung my left hand down the side of the couch and was relieved to find my backpack. According to my watch it was now 10:47. There was no sound coming from what I thought was the kitchen, which looked dark through the half-open door. Near it was a door shut with light showing underneath it. The woman and the cook, married I assumed, probably lived in there.

My vision had largely if not entirely cleared, and the head wound, though it was tender, wasn't as swollen. The really good news was that the orchestra of pain inside my head had quieted down to a snare drum.

I sat on the couch and started unzipping compartments in my backpack. I checked every one of them: no phone. Dammit. I didn't know who to call about Nanny. I must have told the woman here something about the kidnapping—had she alerted the authorities? I stood up to go ask her—

And swooned, just managing to fall backward onto the couch. The dizziness quickly subsided, and every sip I took of the cool water in the glass next to the lamp seemed to infuse me with strength. But no way was I up to driving these back roads in the dark to search for Nanny.

Inside the main pouch of my backpack was the envelope with the copies of the archives Nanny had given me, including the pages initially withheld. She'd had the originals with her, so her captors must have them now—

Hell with the treasure—where was Nanny? Who were the men? Was she safe? She was much more valuable to them alive than dead, but would they know that? I checked my watch again: 11:15. I needed to reach Colonel Grandy.

I checked my pants pockets—no phone.

I pulled the cushions off the couch—no phone.

Damn.

The sound of a door squeaking caused me to douse the light. The Jeep was parked out front, a dead giveaway to my whereabouts.

A moment later the door to the room opened slowly. My heart throbbed in my ears—what if it wasn't the woman? A large person moved through the darkness—were those dreadlocks? I coiled myself, ready to spring. An arm reached out toward my head—I grabbed it.

"Aggh!"

Something crashed to the floor and shattered.

A piercing screech—a woman. I let go of her arm, reached over, and switched on the light.

"Are you okay?" I said. "I'm so sorry!"

"Good God, mon, you frightened me."

She had her hair up in a flowing scarf and she was in a bathrobe. She stretched her arm for a minute. "I brought you some food. You feeling any better? You was talking crazy."

The shattered remains of a heaping pile of what smelled like curried chicken with rice and peas was splattered across the tile floor.

"Yes, thanks to you I do feel a little better."

"You go ahead and sleep there tonight. I'll, ah, make you some breakfast early. You'll be plenty hungry by then."

I swung my legs around and sat upright.

"Do you have a cell phone—or telephone? My friend and I were jumped—she was kidnapped. I need to call someone."

She stared at me for a long moment, no doubt trying to decide if I was still delirious.

"Yes, Charles, we got a wall phone."

Had I told her my name? She must have looked through my wallet when I was passed out. I couldn't blame her.

When I stood, a meteor shower lit up inside my head. She held my arm so I wouldn't fall, a maternal bend to her mouth and look in her eyes. Concern had the same expression the world over. She led me back through the darkness into the front room. A phone that looked like one my grandparents had in their kitchen—a circular dial model—was mounted to the wall.

Crap. I didn't know Colonel Grandy's phone number.

"Do you have a phone book?"

She clutched her hands in front of her and shook her head. Her eyes bugged out when I told her who I wanted to call, and after a moment spent convincing her I really did know Colonel Grandy, she called a friend, who led her to another friend, who had a relative in Moore Town.

Ten minutes later I dialed the colonel's number while my hostess hovered at my elbow, now a part of my drama.

After a dozen rings, a machine picked up. The recorded voice was fast and in the local patois that my mind was way too fogged to comprehend—but I understood the beep that followed the message.

"Colonel, er, Stanley, it's me, ah, Buck Reilly." I rattled on about Nanny being grabbed and implored him to call the police—another beep. The call had ended.

My hostess was staring at me. "And I thought you was talking nonsense."

Dizziness caused me to sway toward the wall. She grabbed me and again led me back to the couch in the back room.

"Will you call the police and tell them about Professor Nanny Adou being kidnapped?"

She hesitated. "Our police in Albert Town aren't real active this time of night. But I can leave a message, yes."

With that she extinguished the light and told me to rest.

It hit me that just last night I'd been skinny-dipping on Ian Fleming's private beach and making love to a beautiful woman in the small villa where he'd penned bestselling spy stories that became blockbuster movies. Nanny was possibly the smartest woman I'd ever known—not to mention the best educated and most complex.

But she had also been my Bond girl, and that made her being gone even worse.

I COULDN'T SLEEP, COULDN'T DRIVE, COULDN'T REACH ANYBODY—COULDN'T remember when I'd felt so useless. The only thing that might help me find Nanny was the copy of the archives she'd given me—if her captors were on the same trail, we'd be bound to run into one another at some point.

I turned the light back on and studied each page—all twelve of them—including the eight from the journal purportedly belonging to Morgan and the pages that had been missing. It all looked like chicken scratch.

There were notes from when Morgan was sent back to London to face trial, after he sacked Panama. Another page looked like a list of some type, but the ink was faded and the cursive letters poorly defined, nearly impossible to read. I was 100 percent certain of just four words and a date: "Port." "Boy." "Blue." "Settle." and "23, June, 1690."

I knew there were hints here. Piecing words and themes together provided a sense of secrets, coconspirators, a date—23, June, 1690—that happened to fall after Morgan's death, other references to the Rio Grande, the Blue Mountain peak and the flash at dawn, perhaps a boy of a trusted friend, and some other language I needed Nanny to transcribe—

Nanny.

My hostess was right. I needed rest. Pain—emotional and physical—had exhausted me. I switched off the light and my frustration and my worry and my thoughts, every one of them. My eyelids fluttered, and . . .

34

Dawn lit a fire under me and I was up and ready to go. Daylight showed my dormitory to be a small storeroom on the back of the kitchen.

There was a knock on the door. My hostess had prepared a callaloo omelet with Jamaican spices. She said she'd left a message for the local police last night and had not yet heard back. I inhaled the omelet along with fresh juice and a pitcher of water, all in less than five minutes after sitting down. Her eyes grew wider with each massive mouthful.

"I cook more—"

"No, thanks, really. I appreciate your kindness, but I've got to go find my friend." I suddenly realized I didn't even know the woman's name, but it seemed too late to ask. I offered a heartfelt thank-you for everything and a hug, grabbed my backpack, and left.

Now that my head was clear, the urgency of finding Nanny had me shaky and jumpy.

The Jeep was thirty yards down the street, and my face was flushed with embarrassment when I saw the front right wheel up on the curb and all the windows wide open. A small boy was squatted next to it on the sidewalk—staring at the door of the vehicle where I'd crashed into . . . whatever. Had Johnny obtained renter's insurance on my car, too?

"This your Jeep?" he said.

"I'm afraid so."

He nodded his head. "It's been buzzing."

Buzzing? Was there an alarm or—

Buzz, buzz, buzz.

My phone!

I pulled open the driver's door—*buzz*—where was it?

Buzz—on the floor under the seat!

I scooped it up—the battery indicator showed 3 percent.

"Hello?"

"Buck Reilly?" The voice was deep.

I leaned against the Jeep and saw the boy was still squatted and watching me.

"Who is this? Where's Nanny?"

What sounded like a growl had me pull the phone away from my ear.

"You were right, they got her." The growl, I realized, was a burst of emotion. "This is Stanley Grandy."

My throat seized at the news and the raw emotion in his voice. I opened my mouth and tried to speak.

"Buck? You there?"

I cleared my throat and realized I was standing on the curb next to the little boy. I sat inside the Jeep and closed the door, swallowing a couple times—

"We were south of Albert Town, three men jumped us—I fought, but they clubbed me, knocked me out."

"I know." His voice was steadier. "She told me—they called and put her on the phone to talk 'cause I wouldn't believe she was okay. Turned out she was fine, just madder than hell. "

"Did she say anything specific?"

"She did, but I didn't understand it. 'The answer's up in the air,' she said. I think they must have slapped her because the phone fell and they wouldn't let me talk to her again."

"The answer's up in the air? What the hell's that mean?"

"I don't know, Buck, that was all she said—"

"What did you ask her, Colonel—this is important!" I was practically screaming.

"I just asked if she was okay. Then she said that about the answer. I was hoping you'd know what it meant . . ."

"Was the caller the same man who attacked you?"

"Men, not man. I couldn't tell, but he had a Jamaican accent."

Silence gripped us both. I could hear wheezing, as if he'd been crying.

"At least she was okay. What do they want?"

A sniffle—he blew his nose. "Said she told them all about the clues you two been putting together. Said they wouldn't hurt her, as long as . . ." He blew his nose again. "As long as you find the treasure within forty-eight hours, turn it over to them, then get out of Jamaica by three o'clock p.m." His voice had dropped to a whisper, but I heard every insane word.

"Forty-eight hours? That's crazy! They can't possibly think—"

"He said they kill her if you—or we don't."

I swallowed hard. The forty-eight hour deadline was preposterous—they had to know I couldn't meet it. Did they just want me off-island?

"The men who attacked you, Colonel, what were *they* after?"

"It's Stanley, Buck. And they was after the Morgan history. Asked about what we had, what Nanny knew." He hesitated, but I knew what was coming. "And they ask about you."

"You recognize them?"

"I couldn't see them—came from behind and put a sack over my head while they were hitting me. But one could have been that damned Cuffee, and the other one was big—he squeezed me—whispered something to Cuffee, sounded white and American, couldn't tell for sure . . . What are you going to *do*, Buck? Can you see any way through the next two days that won't get Nanny killed? Any chance of doing what they asked?"

I closed my eyes for a minute, thinking hard.

"Number one, keep in mind that Nanny's worth a lot more to them alive than dead. Number two, we have a few clues that point toward the treasure but nothing definitive, and forty-eight hours is ludicrous. How are we supposed to communicate with them?"

"They'll be calling me back," he said. "I have men organized, talking to people all over Jamaica. We'll find her."

"That's number three. Good."

Provided she was still here. Her "up in the air" might mean they'd taken her somewhere else, maybe in Betty. Her kidnapping had to involve Gunner and Cuffee, given our confrontation at the crossroads near Blue Mountain.

"Keep your phone with you from now on, okay?"

I sat forward, the explanation of what happened on my lips, but I swallowed it.

"Will do, Colonel. I need to think about this, but I'll be in touch."

"We'll talk later, Buck. And for the last time, call me Stanley, please. We have even more in common now."

MY ORIGINAL PLAN HAD BEEN TO DRIVE BACK TO GOLDENEYE AND RALLY the troops through Chris Blackwell. Guilt caused a blast of acid reflux—that spicy callaloo omelet.

Why should I feel guilty? Hell, they'd all recruited me—Nanny, Stanley, everyone.

Why should I feel stupid?

The answer's up in the air.

The answer's up in the air?

The Jeep started right up. I drove forward and the front tire came down hard off the curb. I cut the wheel to the left—I'd also been parked on the wrong side of the road. The compass on the dashboard read south.

Time to head back to Port Royal.

35

THE DRIVE TOOK OVER TWO HOURS. MY HEAD STILL ACHED FROM GETTING pounded and from trying to figure out the meaning of Nanny's coded statement. Nothing resonated. That being the case, I considered my options: a full frontal on Jack's dive site, getting the police involved, the JNHT, Blackwell, or the other influential people who'd been interested in helping the Jamaican people rather than pursuing the Morgan treasure for their own purposes.

In the end, I had no choice. I had forty-eight hours—fewer now—to get some traction on this search.

I drove along the industrial waterfront of Kingston and it struck me that I'd driven right past Treasure Beach. I couldn't recall if I'd seen any trailers from the photo shoot—where was Thom Shepherd? The question was instantly replaced by more important ones.

Would Heather know what Jack was up to?

For that matter, would Jack know what Gunner was up to?

Could the kidnappers be totally unconnected to them? Say, Cuffee and friends?

It was unlikely that Jack and Gunner knew Cuffee before they showed up on Jamaica six months ago. In fact, Cuffee probably contacted them, to negotiate or demand a cut in exchange for cooperation or peaceful coexistence. Gunner would embrace him or kill him, had that been his approach, but they appeared to be bats of the same guano pile, so more likely the former.

A stiff wind rocked the Jeep, and I looked out to the water. White caps the size of sand dunes rocked the harbor, and out toward the horizon the waves seemed closer together, virtually a single white jagged line.

Crap. They must be getting pounded out on the dive site.

I stepped harder on the gas pedal and shot around traffic. The remaining ten minutes was focused on driving. When I whipped the Jeep into the same parking spot where Nanny had picked me up yesterday, Johnny Blake was already there, chatting up a girl of maybe seventeen. She had her hands on her hips and was nodding. He was smiling—until he saw me, at which point he walked away from her without another word.

We met halfway between the Jeep and the boat.

"Let's go, Johnny. I need to get out to the dive site, now."

"Got it, boss."

He had to jog to keep up with me—I pushed the boat off the beach and Johnny hopped in the water after me as I waded out deeper before we jumped aboard.

"What's going on, Mr. Buck? You find something?" His brown forehead was knit tight. "You don't look excited-happy—look more excited-pissed off."

At the center console, I turned the two keys and started the twin engines.

"Sit up on the bow, I'll drive."

"Rough out here, mon—"

Water launched over the transom as I backed the boat out too fast. Rather than slowing, I spun the wheel to swing the bow around—then jammed the gears into forward and maxed the throttle. Johnny, thrown backwards, sat down hard on the ice chest in front of the console.

Rough water began an immediate assault that had us fighting our way through every wave. Johnny came back to stand by my side, the water too rough for him to be on the bow. The sound of the props screaming sounded each time we shot airborne over the waves, only to pound down into the trough again and again with a fiberglass-rattling slam. We both stood, our knees bent to absorb the shock, huddled to avoid the water splashing over the bow.

Why did I always feel like fate was testing me, one shit grenade after another? Was the universe trying to see how much I could take before I imploded?

Just when the conditions didn't seem like they could get any worse, we passed around the outer edge of the Coast Guard base at Port Royal, where several of their ships sat idle in port. The waves intensified. Our speed didn't help—the bow dove into a wave and water exploded over our heads.

Jack's flotilla was intact on their site. Betty was there too, her wings bobbing like a seesaw in the surf. They hadn't given up, or at least they hadn't reduced their presence here. Past them was our smaller group of boats, lifting on waves, each at a different rhythm. The Beast was there too, her wings rolling wildly.

Sorry, girl. Not the best day for a flying boat to be anchored out here.

We took a wide berth around Jack and I could see men with binoculars trained upon us, others holding weapons.

"Not hiding this time?" Johnny said. "So much for Ray's costume."

"They know I'm not there."

With our boats in sight, I reduced power and chose a careful path toward the Viking, which was also bobbing in what I estimated to be three-foot seas. As we wove in between one of our smaller boats and the tug, I couldn't help doing the math on this enterprise: nearly fifty thousand dollars at this point. Harry Greenbaum—damn, I owed him an update.

Johnny threw the line to the mate on the deck of the Viking. He missed, and the line fell back in the water. Johnny pulled it up quick, coiled it, bent down, and threw it underhand—this time the mate snagged it out of the air and wrapped it around a stern cleat.

Now Johnny pulled us close, and I killed the engines. With both boats rocking violently it wasn't an easy or graceful jump onto the Viking, but I made it.

"Ray?" I called when I reached the hatch and proceeded down the steps. "You down here?"

His head popped up from a bunk on the starboard side—he looked green.

"Buck . . ."

"You ready to blow this roller coaster ride?"

His head dropped onto the pillow. "So . . . sick."

"Sorry, brother. Come on, let's get you out of here."

I helped him out of the bunk and his legs buckled when they hit the deck. When I wrapped my arm around him he looked at me, his eyes a bit watery but surprisingly sharp. He rallied and pushed my arm off.

"I'm on the first plane . . . out . . . of here."

"Get your shoes on, I'll grab your bag."

It was an effort, but Johnny got us shuttled out to the Beast, which was rollicking in the waves like a bucking bronco. Ray shot me an incredulous look, but I could tell his desire to get in the air, or at least back on land, exceeded his concern about the takeoff conditions. Once I got the hatch open and Ray inside to begin the preflight inspection, I turned back to Johnny Blake.

"Party's over, Johnny."

"What's that supposed to mean?"

"It means when the seas settle down, return all the boats to port, terminate the contracts, get the men paid and wrap this charade up."

His eyes cut to slits. "What did you and Nanny find?"

"Nothing yet. She's been taken hostage."

"Shit!" Johnny's brow wrinkled. "In exchange for what?"

"I have forty-eight hours to find the treasure and get out of Jamaica or they'll kill her."

He stood straight, rock steady on the pitching deck.

"The hell—you can make that?"

"Not even close."

I turned and tried to climb into the bouncing hatch, slipped, and my right leg slid into the cold water up to my balls. I pulled hard on the handle, my eyes laser focused on the boat slamming into the water. Johnny backed away.

I gained purchase and pulled myself inside.

Johnny cut in next to the Beast—

"Watch that wing!"

"You keep me posted!" Johnny yelled back. "I'm still a part of this—"

I waved once, then hauled on the anchor rope until it came free. I pulled it up so fast my arms burned, then dropped it on the deck and slammed the hatch shut. Just then the prop on the port engine turned and a backfire made me jump. Ray was sideways in the left seat—his complexion still slightly green—but he was working the controls to get the Beast going.

"Get the bow anchor," he said. "We're floating askew into the oncoming waves."

I dove down between the seats, barely avoided smashing my already aching skull on the bulkhead. I shimmied in until I could kneel and popped the bow hatch just enough to release the line attached to the anchor, which disappeared instantly—what's another $300 at this point?

The Beast shook as the starboard engine coughed to life. I felt the waves lift us up at an angle and slam the starboard wingtip into the water as Ray added thrust and jockeyed to get us positioned on the waves. On my knees, I tried to time my passage through the narrow hatch back into the cabin. We rolled from side to side as the plane lurched in motion, the flying boat anything but nimble. I was propelled forward, and my forehead hit the bulkhead—HARD. And yes, I saw stars. Dammit!

Icing on the concussion cake.

I baby-crawled out and gazed up at Ray, his lips pressed tight, color back in his cheeks, his eyes glancing from wingtip to wingtip, his feet shuffling on the pedals as his right hand pulled and pushed on the throttles—it almost made me smile. He was in the moment, no fear, no whining, no—

"Get your ass up here and get buckled in!"

I scurried out and into the right seat. "I take it you're up to this?"

He snorted but kept his attention on each indicator of potential danger, knowing how easily he could capsize us if he made the wrong move.

"You think I'd trust you to get us out of this mess? Ha! Now buckle up."

I followed orders, called out waves, and kept quiet a couple times when I felt myself about to question his moves—he had the helm, not me.

The wind whipped perpendicular to the waves, from the east, and Ray—massaging the throttles and flaps, crabbing forward to keep us from slamming too hard in the rough water—had us on a course toward the Coast Guard base. He was trying to make the lee of the wind, which the land might provide. There was still heavy water there, too, but it was a sound strategy—

A wave caught the port float, pulling us into the incoming whitecap—the port prop caught the water and tore at the ocean's surface.

Ray jumped up in the seat and leaned to the starboard side. I did the same, an effort more out of instinct than any practical value—the eight-thousand-pound Beast ignored our collective four-hundred-plus pounds. The float popped free when the wave passed and we dropped back down. Ray maneuvered us back east and added throttle—we slammed down but gained speed.

"We're surfing!" Ray yelled.

I watched the tachometers and speed indicators. He'd found an equilibrium that had us stable—land was close.

"Don't get too close to the Coast Guard, Ray—they'll shoot at us."

The Beast shimmied and shook and our speed increased steadily. Moments later we lifted off the water—the breeze blew hard over the land and caught us in sudden turbulence. We slammed back down—

The starboard wingtip dropped. I saw a burst of water shoot toward me. Ray jerked back on the wheel with one hand and pressed the throttles forward with the other, then banked hard to the north. We caught the wind just right and the Beast ascended steeply.

"What's with the goofy smile?" Ray's voice sounded inside my headset.

"Nice job."

"Shit, I probably have more hours in this old bird than you do," he said.

"Given your maniacal tinkering to keep her running, that's probably right."

I grinned. Ray's work was invaluable, and he knew it. I liked to bust his balls anyway.

"Where the hell are we going?" he said. "Key West, I hope."

"Not yet. Take her back to Ian Fleming. We still have work to do."

"You have any luck yet? Aside from with—"

"Nanny was kidnapped."

"What?" He whipped around to face me.

"We have two days to find the treasure, hand it over, and get out of Jamaica, or they say they'll kill her."

He was staring at me as if I'd just said the craziest thing he'd ever heard. Which it probably was. Then he lifted his chin.

"So what are we going to do, Buck?"

"Find *this* damned treasure—or flush the kidnappers out in the process and find Nanny ourselves."

36

WE FLEW AS LOW AS AIR TRAFFIC CONTROL WOULD ALLOW, FIRST UP THE western mountain range that led to the Cockpit Country, then in a pattern around Albert Town and Accompong. Nanny's coded clue—to her whereabouts? To the treasure's whereabouts—went around and around on a loop in my brain.

The answer's up in the air.

The answer's up in the air.

What the hell that meant, I had no idea.

Just as we'd done at Isla Vaca, Ray and I searched for circular formations that might resemble the petroglyph from the Blue Mountain crossing. From this altitude it was hard to see much detail, though we'd both spotted several caves, small contiguous ponds, sinkholes, and even adjacent hilltops that had some similarity to the carving.

"How would the people who carved those rocks hundreds of years ago know what any of this looked like from the sky?" Ray said.

A smart question, but those circles and ovals were all I had to go on. We requested and were granted permission to vector toward Oracabessa, where we landed at Ian Fleming International Airport. As Ray shut the Beast down, I placed a couple phone calls and came up with a quick strategy.

"The wheels are turning," I said when Ray joined me on the tarmac.

He ignored me and tied down the wings, no doubt irritated that I'd done nothing to assist. When the fuel jockey appeared, Ray wasted no time asking them to top off the tanks. He was ready to go home, and he didn't want anything to delay our departure.

I got it, but I wasn't going anywhere until Nanny was free.

When he finished we walked inside and waited in the pilot's lounge for our ride.

"What's with Johnny Blake?" Ray said.

"What do you mean?"

"He was a flaming asshole out on the water."

That didn't sound like Johnny. "How so?"

"Grumpy, yelling at the men—shouted at me when I wanted to get some fresh air. Spent most of the time on his cell phone."

I remembered him flirting with the girl on the beach. "Talking to women?"

Ray scowled. "I don't know, he was whispering off in the corner. He looked upset about something."

"I have no idea. I've known him for a couple years—he sold me the letter that led to the Port Royal fiasco." I smiled. "Cost Dodson a few million by now."

"Well, he's a weird dude. Gave me the creeps."

"Johnny's looking for a big payout. Who knows, could be living above his means and broke like the rest of us—"

A horn sounded. When I glanced out the window I saw the Land Rover, McGyver waiting beside it, his smile a momentary relief given all that had happened in the past couple days.

"Buck Reilly, what's up, big boss?"

"Nice to see you, McGyver. Let's head back to GoldenEye. I'm expecting some visitors at Bizot in an hour or so."

After we loaded up he offered us Blackwell Rum punches from his cooler, which both Ray and I declined for different reasons. As we entered the gate of the resort I was crushed that I'd left here with Nanny and was returning without her.

Cymanthia greeted us at the front desk and said we could stay in Villa 001 tonight, which only had one bed, and informed us the resort was totally full tomorrow night. Villa 001 was directly adjacent to the Ian Fleming Villa.

Ray claimed the bed and I took the couch in the villa's living area. While he disappeared to take an outdoor shower under a banyan tree, I sat in the sun and laid out each of the archives, just like I'd done with Nanny a few days ago. I grabbed a notepad and pen and started listing open questions:

Njoni, son of Akim, friend of Morgan, wrote the Port Royal letter for misdirection. Had moved to the Leeward Windward region. Had he brought the treasure there to hide on Morgan's behalf?

Morgan's notes indicated they might have dropped "cargo," which I assumed meant treasure, near Port Antonio and up the Rio Grande. But where did they go from there? The elders in Moore Town had no idea.

Blue Mountain: the reference about the flash at dawn from the peak on Blue Mountain led to wall carvings that might go back as far as the Taino Indians. But what did they represent?

When Morgan returned from London after being arrested for attacking Panama, he had retired as a privateer and officiated over pirate hangings at Port Royal. Why? To get rid of the competition and disgruntled former crew members? Did they know he'd hidden something?

A future meeting had been set for 23 June 1690, but Morgan had died before that date.

One of the pages that had chicken scratch on it might very well be a map. But what did these symbols mean?

III =III ^III 0

Assuming it referred to the treasure, what fuck did *the answer's up in the air* mean?

"WHAT ARE YOU DOING?" RAY WAS WEARING A RED BATIK PRINT BATHROBE that sent an immediate shiver through me—it was the same color and pattern as the one Nanny had worn for our moonlight swim. "You okay?"

I walked Ray through my list of questions and his curiosity quickly overcame his anger from being left in the dark for so long.

"Hello?" A voice rang from up the path leading to the villa.

My heart leapt. I scurried to collect the archives—

"Buck, are you there?"

Chris Blackwell walked around the corner of the villa, hesitated when he saw Ray in the robe, and gave me a long look—no glint in his eye now. I waved him forward and let the archives remain in the pile atop the table. I introduced Chris to Ray, whom I referred to as my friend and expert aviation mechanic from Key West. Ray stared in awe at Chris. Probably accustomed to that reaction, Chris smiled and patted Ray on the shoulder, since he'd been too surprised to grasp Chris's outstretched hand.

"Awful news about Nanny," Chris said. "Stanley told me about her captors' demands.

We held a long glance, but I could read nothing in his expression.

"I'm doing my best," I said.

He nodded.

"Nanny needs you, Buck. You have to do whatever necessary to find her. And the Jamaican people need you. If that lost wealth falls into the hands of modern-day privateers . . ."

"Why do the Jamaican people need us to find it?" Ray said.

I turned to face him. "Our agreement is that 90 percent of whatever is found will be used for the Jamaican people—as determined *by* the people, not the government."

"Education is the answer, the greatest benefit for the greatest number," Chris said. "The school systems here are fine, but the geographic diversity makes it too difficult for many to actually get to school, and there's been a flight off-island of the most educated—"

"Hold on," Ray said. "I'm confused, what does the missing treasure have to do with education?"

"iPads," Chris said. "That's an important part of the answer. Get them into every home and connected to an educational program, something like Kahn Academy, taught in the patois the children and their families will understand. We'd be looking at a huge increase in literacy and opportunity, also a reduction in domestic violence—" Chris swallowed and crossed his arms. "Most important, Nanny's life depends on your finding that bloody treasure. Her rescue is all that matters now."

"*If* there's a treasure," I said, "and *if* we find it in a day and a half. And what about the authorities?"

"There's a full-on manhunt, including those boats out at Port Royal, but they've found nothing." Chris looked at our pile of papers and notes. "What have you learned at this point?"

After I'd gone over everything I knew or had guessed so far, he shook his head.

"All of this is wonderful, very nice work." He actually started rocking back and forth on his feet as he spoke. "But you've missed something, Buck."

I crossed my arms. "I'm sure I have, but what are you talking about?"

"Firefly." He was smiling, and the glint was back in his eyes.

"Noel Coward's house?" Ray said.

"Quite," Chris said. "But hundreds of years before that, it was one of Henry Morgan's prime observation points on the north coast. He, or his lieutenants, spent a lot of time there. The old stone building he had built upon the promontory still exists."

"Do you know when the building was built?" I said.

Chris nodded. "Not long after Henry returned from Panama."

Damn! "Why am I only now hearing about this?"

"It's been picked over dozens of times by professional and amateur archaeologists," Chris said, "so nobody believes there's treasure there, but it's one of the few remaining buildings known to have been erected by Morgan. McGyver's still here, I'll ask him to run you over to Port Maria while there's still light."

I checked my watch. "If we left now . . . Colonel Stanley, Professor Keith, and I don't know who else is coming to meet us at Bizot—"

"I'll feed them and keep them around until you return," Chris said.

I turned to Ray. "Firefly it is."

37

McGyver made the trip to Firefly at breakneck speed when I told him it closed at 6:00 p.m., twenty minutes from now. Once we turned off the main road, we zigged and zagged our way up through a residential community overrun with foliage until we reached the top. There, a square stone building stood at the back of a broad green lawn that led to a cliff. From here I could tell it overlooked an amazing seascape.

A tall woman in a long dress stepped down from the back patio, waving her arms and pointing to her watch.

"Trouble?" I said.

"No problem, mon." McGyver got out of the truck and called out, "Nancy!" Then gave her a quick hug, turned back to the Land Rover, and waved us forward.

Ray and I jumped out.

McGyver explained we were on a quick recon mission, would only be a few minutes, and didn't need to enter the Coward estate, which we saw up the hill to our left. It was an old white two-story house that in the fading light looked as if its better days were well past.

I began a quick walk around the property. There were some large partially exposed boulders poking up from the lawn between the Coward residence and the square stone building.

McGyver was keeping up with me.

"Mr. Blackwell's mother used to attend parties here with Ian Fleming and Noel Coward," he said.

"Are there any other structures or facilities here that we should study—Coward's house is too new—is there anything the same age as that old stone building?"

"You got Coward's grave over there." McGyver pointed back toward the water. The top of a white in-ground crypt, the size of a small coffin, rested alone on the edge of the manicured lawn.

"Too new. Any other buried structures or tunnels?"

He put his hands on his hips and thought for a moment.

"Got the concrete pool—all covered over." He pointed up toward Coward's residence. "Never saw it be used."

"I've got to leave soon!" Nancy shouted up from the stone building.

My watch showed 6:15. We were pressing our luck.

"Let's go check out the stone building."

We jogged down to where Nancy stood by the back patio, tapping her right foot against the concrete floor.

"Do you know how long the pool's been covered up?" I said.

Nancy shook her head. "Maybe thirty years."

I wondered whether it could have been longer, and whether there was a pool there at all.

"What's inside this stone building?" I said.

"A bar," she said.

"Perfect," Ray said.

Nancy didn't smile.

Past the heavy wooden door was a small room with a brick fireplace, and just as Nancy had said, a freestanding bar that looked like it had been built in the 1950s.

"Is this original?" I pointed toward the fireplace, its floor covered with dusty old conch shells.

She nodded.

"Do you know what year the house was built?"

She glanced at McGyver, then shook her head.

I reached in my pocket. "I'm sorry, we'll be glad to pay for the tour—and we'll only be another few minutes."

Her expression softened when she took the money.

"I'll go check the back room," Ray said.

The shelves in this one displayed bottles, small figurines, clay pots, tools, and other items I assumed to be antiques.

"Anything in particular you're looking for?" Nancy said.

Ray walked out from the back room and shook his head.

"We're not really sure," I said. "But—do you have a piece of paper and a pen?"

She went behind the bar and passed over a yellowed cocktail napkin and a pencil. I took it and sketched out my best recollection of the petroglyphs I'd found at the Blue Mountain crossing. I felt foolish handing it to her, but a long shot was better than no shot.

"Have you ever seen anything like that around here? Maybe a rock formation, or some holes, or even—"

Her eyes opened so wide I stopped midsentence.

"There's a drawing like this—a carving, really. Nobody's ever known what it meant. We just assumed it was an old vandal—"

"Where?"

My voice was so loud she jumped.

"I'm sorry," I said, "the meaning of that series of shapes is urgent. Can you show me the carving? Is it outside?"

She lifted her hand and pointed toward the brick fireplace. All I saw were the conch shells, the red bricks, junk, old candlesticks, a dark wood mantelpiece—

"She's pointing toward the mantle, Buck," Ray said.

I stepped closer—we all did.

"There's an odd series of circles—ovals, really—carved into the wood. They've been there forever." She touched the far left corner of the mantle. The wood was only six inches wide.

Gradually I was able to make out images—dust-filled and faint, but clear indents just the same.

I leaned closer.

"Ray, bring that lamp over here and plug it in!" I pointed toward an old table lamp on top of the bar.

He plugged it into a wall outlet, took off the shade, then handed it to me as I studied the carvings. The scale was smaller, but with the light aimed at them I could see that the shape was exactly the same.

I blew at the thick dust, sneezed, and got simultaneous bless-you's from McGyver and Nancy.

Ray handed me a fireplace tool with a small broom on the end. After repeated brushing, the dust was clear and the light revealed more than just the oval and circle shapes—a sideways V was carved into the wood on the left side of the ovals. The sideways V, which was jagged but distinct, seemed familiar—

Of course!

I fumbled the lamp, but caught it before it hit the ground.

"What? Did you see something?" Ray said.

Everyone leaned in close.

The outside line appeared to be the configuration of the western coast of Jamaica. The line started somewhere between Ocho Rios and Montego Bay—in fact, there was a series of scrapings where Montego Bay would have been—then veered out to the left through what today is Negril but back then would have been desolate, curved down to the south and to the east by Treasure Beach, then down again and faded out as it headed toward what would have been the approximate location of Spanish Town.

I took a deep breath.

"Does it mean something to you?" Nancy said.

I took another deep breath. "Yes, but I'm not sure what. It does resemble the petroglyph."

"It's a mirror image," Ray said.

I shot him a look and he pursed his lips.

"Even if it is, I still don't know what it means."

Nancy's shoulders dropped and she looked at her watch. I pulled my phone from my pocket and took a couple photos of the faint carving, with flash and without. The circles were roughly two-thirds to the north, and in the center of what I estimated to be the western third of the Jamaican land mass. Could Morgan have carved this as a reminder of something?

Or maybe someone else carved it as a message to him?

The shock I'd felt upon recognizing the circles had been replaced with an adrenaline shot from the new information. If these circles indicated the location of something, the location had just become a hell of a lot clearer even if—

The sound of Nancy clearing her throat broke my spell.

I thanked her and tipped her an additional $20. When we stepped outside I saw it was dark. She followed us out and turned to lock the door.

"Have you seen those circles and ovals anywhere else here at Firefly?" I said.

"No, just there. Like I said, we always figured it was some old vandalism." She paused. "If you find out what it means, I would love to know." She smiled. "We can add the information to the tour if it's anything worthwhile."

My smile caused her to stop in her tracks.

"If I find out, you will too."

38

THE BAR AT BIZOT WAS PACKED WITH HAPPY VACATIONERS, COUPLES WITH their noses pressed together over candlelight, and our small group of five men in the back of the bar beside the oceanfront yoga platform. We were huddled close for quiet conversation, not that anyone could hear us over the party atmosphere of Bizot's Rum Night. I was on my second Black and Stormy, and it was all I could do not to knock it back in one long gulp.

Ray sat next to me, his lips pressed tight and his brow bulging. Across from us was Colonel Stanley, along with Keith Quao, Maroon elder and university professor who'd sat in on the committee meeting when the Port Royal project was awarded to Jack, flanking him on one side. On Stanley's other side was a younger, bulkier man named Pierce. He hadn't said much, and I assumed he was a bodyguard for the older men. We'd planned the meeting prior to Ray's and my trip to Firefly, but the news of finding the same pattern of circles and ovals within what appeared to be a map of western Jamaica had led to much speculation on what the symbols represented and its location. The common assumption was that they reflected either sinkholes or caves.

"If they's sinkholes, we got no chance of finding that pattern," Keith said.

"Don't be so negative," Stanley said.

"Negative? That whole part of the island is constantly sinking! There's new holes all the time, you can't even map them—"

"It's probably caves," I said. "I can't imagine anyone would hide valuables in a sinkhole."

"Oh, there are plenty of sinkholes that produce new caves and all kinds of tunnels," Keith said. "Fools get lost bad in those things all the time."

"And what about caves?" Ray said.

I winced, already knowing the answer.

"The Jamaican Caves Organization estimates there's over a thousand caves on this island," Keith said. "You going to check every damned one?"

"That's enough, Keith." Stanley glanced at his watch. I'd looked at mine just a moment before—we had barely forty hours left. "We all want to find Nanny, but we need to use the information Buck's found, not tear it apart."

Keith grumbled under his breath, and though I was more optimistic by nature—hell, you had to be in the treasure-hunting business—I was equally overwhelmed by the number of potential stash sites.

"Those old petroglyphs at Blue Mountain crossing are Taino Indian, no doubt," Keith said. "Maroons coexisted with the Tainos, and they certainly shared the same trails through the mountains. For different purposes, of course, but they could have easily shared information on the meanings of carvings, whether they be for gods, hunting grounds, or hidey-holes."

Since when was "hidey-holes" an archaeological term? Keith had been Nanny's stand-in at the committee hearing so she could avoid the spotlight, and as I recalled she thought of him as something of a buffoon. But at the moment he was our resident expert, and you could be a buffoon and still know your field.

Keith said, "My feeling is we should start at Green Grotto Cave, the best-known Taino cave—"

"It's too far northeast, Keith," Stanley said.

"You're an archaeologist now?" Keith said.

I spotted people from neighboring tables glancing in our direction. I held my palms up.

"Gentlemen, please, let's not attract attention."

Ray leaned closer to me. "A *thousand* caves?" He rolled his eyes.

"The police haven't had a single lead," Stanley said. "Nobody on the whole damn island's seen her. It's unbelievable given that everyone *knows* her."

The answer's up in the air. Could they have flown her off-island? A thought struck me. What about the big rocks at Isla Vaca where I'd been searching when Jack and Gunner flew over?

When I mentioned that, Stanley said he had contacts in Haiti who would know people at Isla Vaca—he'd have them go check the area in the morning.

"But Green Grotto Cave is so overrun with tourists, it's hard to imagine it being a hiding place for anything," Keith said. Apparently he was the type to debate with himself out loud.

"I'm convinced the symbols represent caves in Cockpit Country," I said. "The Tainos were very active in that region in their heyday, and it's where Njoni settled after leaving Moore Town. If he hid the booty, there's a good chance it would have been around there."

"If he *had* the booty, why wouldn't he have taken it for himself?" Keith said.

I leaned forward and kept my voice low, hoping Keith, especially, would do the same.

"Among the notes in Morgan's diary was a date, 23 June 1690. The rest was faded, but it was right after the mention of a friend's son. Good chance that friend would have been Akim, father of Njoni, and my guess is the date was set for a future meeting when Morgan's associates from the Panama raid would have given up on their accusations of him hiding the lion's share of plunder. Hell, he was only fifty-three years old when he died in 1688, so he could have easily planned a meeting for when he was fifty-five—"

"But what would have prevented Njoni from stealing it?" Ray said.

"Steal from Lieutenant Governor Henry Morgan, the most ruthless and cunning privateer in history?" I said. "Njoni would have been hunted down and flayed alive."

Everyone nodded.

"Besides, the plan must have been to cut him and his father in on the date they'd planned to meet—"

"What about the letter credited to Njoni?" Keith said. "The one that led to the offshore dig at Port Royal?"

I smiled. "Remember the date of the letter?"

Keith rubbed his nose between his thumb and index finger.

"Sometime in 1673 as I recall—"

"Right. We backtracked and confirmed that Morgan was still on trial in London for sacking Panama during the truce with Spain. Sure, he returned from London as the lieutenant governor, but when that letter was written he wasn't even on Jamaica."

"So?" Stanley said.

"So, I suspect Njoni forged the letter after Morgan's death to draw attention away from his former privateer colleagues, who were tearing all of Morgan's possessions to shreds searching for clues to the treasure."

"So why didn't Njoni collect after Morgan died?" Ray said.

"Now *that's* a good question," I said.

Keith leaned forward, a Cheshire cat smile on his face.

"If you're correct, Njoni never would have had the chance to grab the treasure at that point." He paused. "According to the records of the time, Njoni was arrested by the colonial government after presenting the letter, then shipped off to Nova Scotia with all the other Trelawney Maroons."

"Damn!" Ray said. "Weren't any cell phones for him to phone a friend in those days." Ray's smile was not reciprocated.

Silence fell over the table.

Keith's information filled in a major puzzle piece. If he was correct, then there might not have been anyone left who knew where Morgan's Panama treasure had been hidden.

"Cockpit Country's sure big," Stanley said.

"Right, but that's where Nanny and I were when she was grabbed—"

"I have an associate there who's a guide and spelunker—cave junkie," Keith said. "He's on the board of the Jamaican Cave Organization. I could get him to meet us—"

"Early tomorrow morning at the jerk shack just south of Accompong," I said. "That's where Nanny and I met with Kujo and his snarky little assistant, Clayton. If you superimpose the map from the Firefly mantelpiece over a modern map of Jamaica, it's somewhere in that vicinity."

Keith nodded. "I'll go along with it—"

"We don't have any choice," Stanley said.

"No, but based on the proximity to the north and south coast once you overlay that map, it could easily reflect a twenty-mile radius."

Stanley sighed. Ray, along with Pierce—who had yet to say a word—both stared at me. I read the questions in their eyes, and while I didn't have answers I did have a tickle in my stomach—the same tickle I felt the day before our expedition into the Guatemalan rainforest, the hunt that led to my largest archaeological find ever and precipitated my photo on the cover of the *Wall Street Journal.*

That detail soured the tickle, but I'd learned long ago to study the facts, tighten the circle, and go with my gut.

"A twenty-mile radius is damn good progress, now we just need some luck." We'd fly around the area again if we had to, but we'd start on the ground. Wheels and feet are a lot slower than propellers, but we needed to turn rocks over, not fly above them.

39

AFTER READING THE TEXT, I DIALED JOHNNY'S NUMBER. IT ONLY RANG ONCE.
"Damn, Mr. Buck, all hell busting loose out here."

"What's wrong?"

"The police crash your old friends Jack and Gunner, and after they left our neighbors start making all kinds of threats, shooting guns—they chased off their observer from JNHT. Our men are scared!"

I took a couple breaths. "You were supposed to have returned the boats by now, Johnny, that's costing me—"

"Been too damned rough, mon, worse than when you left yesterday— and the police come out here with an official from the Heritage Trust to ask about our license, too—"

"We never even did anything! Now pull anchor and get those boats—"

"You need to get back out here, mon. Too crazy for me. Police and crazed salvage hunters, unh-uh, no thank you."

"Okay, Johnny. I'll come out later, but we have some other things we have to do first. Get the constables to protect you."

I glanced at Ray in the Jeep's rearview mirror. He shook his head.

"Well, make it quick as you can, Mr. Buck. Not taking a bullet from these guys."

I hit end and put the phone in my breast pocket. Then gave Stanley the gist of what Johnny had said.

"I'm going to make some calls." He stepped outside with his cell phone, then slammed the door shut.

"What exactly did Johnny say?" Ray said.

"Problems out on the water. Says I better come quick."

"We really going through with this?"

"Yep." I popped the door open.

"Wish I had better shoes." But he stepped out with me.

Keith was there as were Pierce, the Rasta bodyguard/pack mule, and a trail guide for a local outfitter that Keith had arranged through his friend at the Jamaican Cave Organization. A pile of backpacks was heaped into the open bed of the guide's red pickup truck.

Since Keith had vouched for the guide's skill, reliability, and discretion, Stanley and I had agreed to show him the sketch of the circles and ovals. They weren't popular caves to explore, he said, but they were in the vicinity of some others he knew well. The guide was one of the top spelunkers in Jamaica—if the petroglyphs were indeed a series of caves, then this was our best shot.

"Are we ready?" I said.

"Lets take a look at the map." The guide unfolded a worn-looking map onto the opened gate of the pickup's bed and smoothed it gently with his palms. "We are here." He pointed to a spot on the two-lane road, just south of Accompong, near the jerk shack where Nanny and I had met Kujo and Clayton. "Based on the drawing you showed me, I think we follow this road." He dragged his finger up the main road and then to a dotted line and off sharply to the left. "We can drive a few miles into here." He tapped an area where there were some tight topographic lines. "We have to park vehicles there and hike to caves. Halfway up this mountain, on a plateau."

"Dear God." Ray's voice was a whisper behind me.

"There are many sinkholes and caves over all the area," the guide said. "So we need to be bloody careful so nobody breaks their neck or disappears for good."

Nobody said anything for a long moment.

"Is there a vantage point where we can visually survey the scene?" I asked.

He dragged his finger up to where the topographic lines formed tight concentric circles.

"Up here. You can see many of the formations from here."

Stanley chose that moment to walk around the Jeep to the back of the truck, his lips pursed. Our eyes caught.

"I'm going to keep digging," he said.

"Okay," I said, "let's load up."

Keith got inside the truck with the guide, the rest of us followed them in the Jeep. While trying to avoid potholes I pictured the guide's map in my head. The jerk shack was just ahead when the guide took a sharp turn to the left onto a dirt road. So much dust exploded into the air that I had to drop back to keep from being blinded.

The trail was so narrow that brush scratched at the Jeep's sides as we passed, and bushy branches poked leaves through its open windows. The road—more of a hiking trail—was washboard bumpy, rocky, and crossed over some wide streams we had to drive through slowly, unsure of their depths.

Taillights suddenly appeared through the brown cloud ahead—I jammed on the brakes. We skidded on the loose gravel and dirt, coming to a stop only feet from the back of the guide's pickup.

"Damn, Buck!" Ray hollered from the backseat. "Scared the crap out of me."

The guide materialized from the dust, walking toward us with his eyes squinted. I hung my head out the window.

"End of the line," he said. "We walk from here."

Pierce jumped out. Ray grimaced, then opened his door. Stanley crossed his arms.

"I'm too old for this. I'll wait here." He checked his phone. "I have three bars, should be able to make calls."

Every instinct I had told me that we were getting closer to the treasure now. I glanced back at Stanley. Would I live to be too old to hunt for it?

40

THE TRAIL WINDING UP AND AROUND THE FIRST HILL WAS WORN SMOOTH. As we passed the northernmost end from where we'd left the Jeep, the guide stopped to point through the foliage toward a valley and dark growth beyond it.

"The caves are on that mountain over there."

"Then why're we over here?" Ray was rubbing his heel.

"He wanted to see the caves from a vantage point." The guide stabbed a nod toward me.

"If it doesn't seem promising, we can skip the whole hike," I said. "Time is too important."

The guide put his hands on his hips and looked at each of us.

"If you would be a little more forward with what you're looking for, I could be more helpful."

"Just what I showed you," I said. "That's all we know."

We continued on for another thirty minutes until we reached a rocky outcropping near the top of the hill. We had a clear view of many other green hilltops about the same height—upright green eggs as far as the eye could see.

"This is an area heavy with Taino Indian history," Keith said.

"Are there many petroglyphs here?" I said.

"I can show you some," the guide said.

"Can we see the caves from here?"

We followed the guide to the outside of the rocky clearing. He pointed halfway down the next hill over.

"See the dark spots in the middle of those coconut trees there?"

From my backpack I removed my binoculars. The bush was thick and the distance too great for much detail, but I could see what looked like two, maybe three dark holes. I lowered the binoculars. From this distance, who knew how many caves there were?

"Well?" Keith said.

"Could be."

Ray lowered his canteen from his mouth. "Why'd you bring me up here, Buck? I could have been flying overhead, doing aerial research—"

"Because you're smart, Ray. I'm hoping you'll see or think of something I might miss."

That got me a faint smile and one of Ray's maxims.

"Brains are best exercised with idle feet," he said.

"So do you want to go down?" the guide said.

"Yes, let's get going," I said.

"We can either wind around all the way back down the way we came and cross the valley to that next hill or we follow a wet-weather drainage ditch from here and head straight toward it. That's a little rougher—"

"Let's take the most direct course. Time is—"

"Of the essence, I get it," the guide said.

After passing through some dense brush, we found a dry creek bed that led straight down the mountain. It was slow going, and given Keith's age and Ray's physical condition it took longer than it should have. We had nearly reached the bottom when a sound caught my attention.

"You hear that?" Ray said.

"Radial engines?"

"Not just any radial engines—"

"Everyone get under cover!" I said.

"What's the problem?" the guide said.

"Now, please!"

We all scrambled out of the trough of the creek bed and into the bushes. The origin of the sound appeared a moment later, flying through the valley where we were headed, at maybe one thousand feet above the ground.

"Looky there," Ray said.

I watched the old Grumman Widgeon fly at slow speed between the mountains, the dove gray of her belly well matched against the partially cloudy sky.

"Betty."

"Is it Dodson?" Keith said.

"Something I should know about?" the guide said.

I nodded to Keith, then told the guide it was a competitor looking for the same location.

I had no idea how Jack guessed our destination.

The plane faded into the distance, adjusting course to stay within the valley of the two mountains. I suspected they were cruising through the entire region looking for signs. Had they seen the Jeep? It was out in the open, and Stanley wouldn't know to move it.

Dammit.

We moved on, now at a faster pace. Keith and Ray would have to keep up.

It took another forty-five minutes, but we made it up the mountain to the caves. Surrounded by dense forest, underbrush, and boulders, they were hard to see, much less access. And I still couldn't tell how many there were. Our guide said they'd supposedly been hiding places for the Leeward Maroons back in the days of the first Maroon war.

I glanced toward Keith, who was still breathing hard.

"Yes . . . that's correct." He took a couple breaths. "This whole area was strategic . . . because getting here was so difficult."

Ray had his shoes off again and was sitting on a boulder rubbing his feet. I could see they were blistered and red. "Still is," he said.

While the others rested, I walked around to get a view from different angles—but still couldn't see clearly enough to determine the number of caves or the configuration. No way to tell if they matched the Blue Mountain petroglyph and the mantelpiece.

"Ray, you come with me, we'll check this first cave. Keith and Pierce, why don't you check the next one?"

"What about me?" the guide said.

"Keep watch and listen to see if either group needs help or calls out that they found something."

"What exactly are you looking for?" he said.

"We're not sure," I said, "but we'll know if we find it. If the plane comes back, hide inside one of the caves before it can see you."

He just stared back at me.

We each took a backpack that contained two flashlights, a canteen, a rope with carabiners, and flares. The hike up to the cave entrances took another fifteen minutes.

The opening to the first cave was roughly twenty feet wide and fifteen feet high, but the ceiling dropped down at a sharp angle toward the back of the cave.

"I hate caves, Buck," Ray said. "You know I hate caves."

"They're just holes in the rocks—"

A swarm of bats dropped down from above and swooped toward our lights. The sound of guano slapped like hail against the stone floor.

"Ugh!" Ray said. "I've been hit by bat shit!"

I managed not to laugh and focused ahead on the depth of the cave. I continued forward, scanning my light from side to side, searching for any other openings, offshoots, wall carvings, or paintings. In the back of the cave, maybe sixty feet in, was a small passage that continued deeper into the darkness. We stopped, knelt down, and shined our lights inside.

"Don't even think of asking me to go in there," Ray said.

With only enough room to crawl, I went in—crab walking while still holding the flashlight. Another thirty feet in and it became too narrow for a man to pass through, much less hide treasure. I barely had enough room to turn around and get out.

Back outside we found Keith and Pierce sitting on rocks. They stood up when we stepped into the daylight.

"Anything?" Keith said.

Ray was brushing purple guano from his shirt. "The mother lode—of bat shit, that is. Disgusting." He rubbed his hands in some weeds.

"How about you guys?" I said.

"Wasn't much of a cave, really. More like a ledge."

"Any more past that?"

"One, but it was also shallow and empty," Pierce said.

"Where's the guide?"

Keith glanced around. "I'm not sure—"

"Up here!" The guide was up on top of the rock outcroppings that made up the roof of the cave Ray and I had explored. "Looking for more caves, but nothing so far."

A light rain began to fall.

Lovely.

When the guide returned, we were standing just inside the mouth of the bat-infested cave to avoid getting soaked. The sound of an animal's wail—no, a horn of some kind—made us all look up.

"What was that?" Ray said.

"I don't know—"

"That was an abeng, I'm quite sure," Professor Keith said.

"Which is what?" I said.

"An animal horn, often from a cow or ram, used by our Maroon ancestors to convey information across a wide distance."

"Who would be conveying information—"

The horn sounded again. It blew three distinct blasts.

"Stanley carries an abeng," Keith said. "Warriors alerted others to the presence of British troops with blasts from the abeng. He must be sending us a message—we should return to the car."

"British troops?" Ray said.

"Worse, could be Gunner," I said.

41

THE HIKE BACK TOOK NEARLY NINETY MINUTES, AND AS WE EMERGED FROM the trail on the hill I could see Stanley sitting in the Jeep. Sweat had soaked through my clothing. The wasted morning had me tired and frustrated. The guide was knowledgeable, but this had been a fruitless effort, other than crossing a few caves off the list of a thousand in Jamaica.

Stanley climbed out of the Jeep as we approached.

"Were you using an abeng to warn us about something?" I said.

"Got another call from the kidnappers. They wanted an update and to remind me we only had twenty-eight hours left."

I kicked at a rock—stubbed my toe and nearly fell. I glanced from face to face. Nobody was smiling.

"Anything else?"

Stanley sneered. "They say they mean business, Buck." His voice was flat and his eyes stared blankly past me as he spoke.

I kicked at the rock again and this time it sailed and bounced off the side of the Jeep, leaving a ding in the door. "Dammit!"

Everyone stood staring at me, waiting for some direction or a plan. If only I had one.

"I need to clear my head." I started toward my Jeep, then stopped and turned around. "I'll be back—"

"I need to get to my office near Albert Town," the guide said. Everyone turned to look at him. "There's a jerk stand out front. We could meet there—"

I froze. "That's the same place where Nanny was grabbed," I said. "She said there was an outfitter nearby. Guess that was you."

I pulled out in the Jeep and with the windows open and top down, let the air blow over me to try and cool off. There wasn't time to waste, but I had to clear my head. It felt as if we were chasing our tails, yet my gut still said we were close. Something just had to break for us, and fast.

The potholed road rattled my thoughts as much as the Jeep. My hands were damp on the wheel, and even with the top down the steady breeze couldn't keep sweat from making my body miserable.

The clock was ticking. If we didn't turn up anything by tomorrow, I'd have to leave the island—Stanley had made that clear. He couldn't risk Nanny being hurt because of my being perceived as competition. It wasn't what the kidnappers had asked for, but assuming I couldn't find the Morgan treasure, I'd at least surrender the island to them. I'd argued they could hurt her even if I left and we'd feel just as guilty. It didn't matter. Neither option was good, and we both knew it.

Dammit!

I pulled over, got out my phone and squinted at the photos of circles and ovals from Morgan's mantle at Firefly. The screen was too small to see any details well. I emailed the picture to Stanley and Ray and asked them to study it—maybe they'd see something I hadn't.

Henry fucking Morgan, the greatest privateer in history.

I thought of his victories in Porto Bello, Cartagena, Maracaibo, and finally Panama, each employing hundreds and later up to a thousand men, each campaign utilizing unique strategies. Morgan's creativity as a commander was still studied at war colleges. The use of surprise attacks and unconventional warfare—hell, he even sent hundreds of men in canoes up the Chagres River to reach Panama.

What must that have been like? A fleet of hand-hewn canoes, each with men and weapons, like a swarm of angry crocodiles paddling hard up the river in the deep of night. Their minds would have been focused on the coming battle, their thirst for riches. Morgan had been amongst them, calling the shots.

Did he steal the plunder from his men, or was it all a legend?

Would Nanny die because of it?

The answer's up in the air. The answer's u—

My body jerked and I grabbed the steering wheel tight.

"Son of a bitch! I've got it!"

I stomped on the accelerator—the Jeep responded with a lurch, then sped forward.

THE DRIVE TO THE JERK SHACK WHERE NANNY HAD BEEN JUMPED—WHERE the guide had an office out back—took less than a half hour. I barely braked through the switchbacks that led up the hill.

I flew through the door, causing Ray to jump out of his seat. I spied bottles of clear rum on the table in front of Keith and the guide, who glanced up at me. Pierce was drinking coconut water straight from the husk. Stanley was holding an iPad he and Keith had been studying when I burst in.

"I've got it!" I said. "I had an epiphany."

"And you gave us one," Stanley said. "Come see."

As anxious as I was to share my news, I bent down to see what had them excited. It was the picture I'd sent from my phone. The screen of the iPad was much larger, and the image—

"It looks much brighter than the original," I said.

"We've been enhancing it on the photo app," Keith said.

"The details are sharper," Stanley said. "And look."

He pointed toward the smaller oval shape, second from the right. I leaned closer. The picture had been enlarged to at least four times the original carving. Then he panned from left to right.

"Do you see it?"

I took the iPad and scanned the circles and ovals. The fourth one—second from the right? I saw it.

"This one's filled in with some cross-hatching, or could that be a fat X?"

"Whatever it is, it's something," Keith said.

I handed them back the iPad, my mind busy comparing this realization with my own. If I was right, the two might well be connected.

"What about you?" Ray said. "What did you find out?"

My attention shifted to the guide, now drinking water.

"Do you have your map handy?"

He went out to his truck and returned a moment later. With the restaurant empty aside from us, I dragged over another table and cleared it of salt, pepper, and napkin holder. The guide laid the map out, flattening it with his palm.

"Where are we now?" I said.

He dragged his finger up the road I recognized from earlier, then stopped an inch above where we'd entered the bush this morning. I placed my finger on the map, followed the road toward Albert Town, and stopped in the approximate location of the restaurant where we now were.

"Are there any caves you know of in this area here?" My voice sounded an octave higher.

He started a slow nod. "Yeah, the whole area is full of sinkholes, some caves—"

"Caves that have been connected with Maroons from the 1680s and 90s?"

"The area around Albert Town was a popular hideout. Accompong was the center of the world for the Leeward Maroons, but the area up there was strategic—a gathering place. They stored weapons."

"Where did Njoni live?"

Keith, standing with his arms crossed, answered that one.

"Nobody knows exactly where he lived, but there's a good chance it was in that vicinity."

I turned back to the guide.

"Of the caves you know, are there five that are contiguous?"

The guide studied his map, then looked up, a fresh light in his eyes.

"I have seen some clustered caves there—rarely visited because of sinkholes, a lot of them hidden under thick brush."

Everyone was on their feet now. I checked my watch.

We had a few hours of sunlight left.

"What did you find out, Buck?" Ray said.

"That the twenty-mile radius just got a whole lot smaller."

Lava
Ground

42

"So what's it here that's got you so fired up?" Ray said.

The smile that bent my lips was irrepressible.

"The answer's up in the air," I said.

All three of them looked up, just as the guide and Pierce walked over to see what we were looking at.

"Those old canoes?" Ray said.

"How old would you say they are, Professor?"

Keith stepped closer and stood beneath them. There were two hand-hewn canoes suspended from branches, both hung upside down under a high plastic canopy. One was about two feet shorter than the other. They were faded, cracked, and dried out to a pale gray.

"Very old indeed," he said. "Impossible to say without testing, but they could date back several hundred years—"

"Could they be from the 1670s?" I said.

He glanced up again. "I suppose. Impossible to tell the type of wood they're made from, but they're well preserved—"

"Are there any canoes from when Henry Morgan attacked Panama in any of the museums?"

Keith shook his head. "None that I've seen."

I rubbed my palms together—couldn't help it.

"If my theory's correct, these canoes may have been two of the ones used by Morgan during and after that raid, then used to transport whatever treasure he'd secreted off his ship upon returning to Jamaica—"

"So this is about the legend of Morgan's missing treasure?" the guide said.

I paused, then nodded. No point in hiding it any longer.

"I thought so, but there aren't any navigable rivers near here that connect to the sea," the guide said.

"Exactly," I said. "I think these canoes may well have been carried from as far as the Rio Grande, across water when possible but also over land—to hide the treasure in caves near here. That's how the Spanish used to cross Panama to Porto Bello in those days. They carried everything, including their boats, in portage."

Everyone was staring wide-eyed at me, especially the guide.

"The road that leads toward the caves I mentioned earlier is right behind this restaurant," he said.

I looked from face to face. "This could be it."

BACK IN OUR VEHICLES WE HEADED FOR A TRAIL THE GUIDE SAID WOULD take us closest to the caves. A quick whisper from Stanley—"We may have a rat on-island"—had me grinding my teeth, but given the limited amount of daylight remaining, I had to focus all my energy on the task at hand.

The drive in was on the most rugged of any trail we'd yet traveled. We had to drive around sinkholes and stop several times to clear debris, roll boulders out of the way, hold back tree limbs. We were now deep into Cockpit Country, where the erosion of the limestone plateau had left countless round-topped conical hills and valleys. Diverse tree and plant life made me feel like we were in Jurassic Park.

The trail ended abruptly at the foot of one of the many steep hills.

We'd driven as far as we could, and the sun was descending. The trip had taken an hour.

The group mobilized, donning backpacks, filling the canteens from a fifty-gallon jug the guide had provided. This time I'd brought the bigger duffel bag stocked with a full array of caving and rappelling gear. The guide produced his well-worn map and laid it out on the truck's tailgate.

"We're approximately here." He tapped his finger on an area that seemed pretty close to the restaurant, but then we'd traveled slowly. "The caves I'm thinking of are in this area here." He dragged his finger across multiple topographic circles to what looked like a wide valley.

He took the compass from his belt and adjusted the map so the symbol that pointed north was accurate, then calculated the most straightforward route to minimize climbing, maximize pace, and make the best use of our remaining sunlight.

"I'll stay with the vehicles," Stanley said. He held up his abeng. "I'll let you know if anything comes up."

We set off into the wilderness. A sense of purpose drove us faster than Keith and Ray were comfortable with, but they didn't complain.

The guide led, stopping occasionally to consult the compass and map, which he'd folded small to expose only the area we were in. Birds cried out and flitted from trees as we passed, but human conversation was minimal. We stayed in open areas or followed animal trails where possible. The temperature was mild and there was no humidity—perfect weather for a rigorous hike.

"The valley of the caves is below." Our guide was pointing down from the hill we'd climbed. I managed to get myself atop a large boulder and lifted the binoculars to my eyes.

The valley—maybe two hundred yards wide—was a wasteland of sunken limestone holes, some of which held water. It would be a bitch to cross. I raised the binoculars a bit to scan the hill behind it, starting from the far left and working my way along its length.

A cave filled my vision—then another, and another. Then yet another cave!

The binoculars fell from my hands, the strap yanked at my neck.

"See anything?" Ray yelled up to me.

I turned to hoots and cheers from every one of them. My smile said it all.

43

W E NEARLY LOST KEITH TO A BRUSH-HIDDEN SINKHOLE AS WE CROSSED THE valley, but we made it to the caves in one piece. Everyone now knew we were after Henry Morgan's treasure, and that time was working against us. I hoped we'd have enough light to make it back to Stanley, but that would depend on what we found—or didn't find—ahead.

The broad karst hill ahead stairstepped in plateaus of stone, and carved at the base was a near exact replica of the circles and ovals I'd first found at the Blue Mountain crossroads.

It took several deep breaths to absorb the breadth of the caves—from here it looked like the second and third had eroded into one, so I concentrated my focus on what would have been the second from the right—the one that had been etched in and was different than the others on the mantle's etching at Firefly.

As we closed the distance I went over my mental checklist of notes I'd made from the archives Nanny had shared with me. Though the main texts had been largely undecipherable, there were some key words and phrases I counted on being relevant here—details I had yet to share with anyone. I recalled the symbols:

$$III =III \wedge III \ 0$$

I hoped these were some type of directions, like maybe: third passage or tunnel, third pipe up or chute, third tunnel or pipe or chute. No way to be sure until we checked, but that's what I'd translated the drawing and words to mean.

We walked past each of the other caves—a huge pile of rubble lay in the middle of the second and third cave, confirming my assumption that two had become one. My brain didn't seem to know quite how to react. We had located the mystery caves, but was there anything in them to find?

Outside the fourth cave, we dropped our gear. There were sinkholes on both sides of the cave entrance, and one held water.

"Ray and I will go in—"

"What?" Ray said. "Why me?"

"I can go," Pierce said.

My glare at Ray, at an angle the others couldn't see, caused him to purse his lips.

"No," he said. "I'll go."

"The ground inside isn't stable," the guide said. "All these sinkholes and the collapse of the other two caves. There have been several earthquakes in the past few hundred years—inside may be totally impassible."

"Great," Ray said.

A distant sound echoed through the canyon. Was it wind? It sounded again, three times, in fast succession.

"That's the abeng," Keith said.

"Stanley?" I said.

"Or ghosts of the Maroons who fought and died here," the guide said.

What message was Stanley sending us? Had the kidnappers called again, or worse? While I hoped he wasn't in danger, I knew he'd agree we needed to press on, so I picked up the pace.

The sun was dropping fast.

"If you're following old Maroon directions, " the guide said, "you must know that they often reversed meanings on maps in case of capture or discovery."

I stared at him for a long second, then turned to Keith. The professor nodded.

With that, I pulled the big duffel bag over my right shoulder and with my flashlight in hand and Ray right behind me set off into the cave.

The space inside was tighter than the one we'd checked this morning—God, was that just today? The roof was lower, too, and the cave itself far deeper.

"Do you think what the guide said was true?" I said. "That the Maroons reversed directions on their maps?"

"You're asking me?" Ray said.

Morgan wasn't a Maroon, but what about the notes from the archive? If Njoni made them, would they be reversed? His Port Royal letter had been a total fabrication—another form of reversal.

Damn.

I scratched the symbols from the archive into the dirt:

$$III = III \wedge III\ 0$$

"I'm thinking this could be some type of code for this cave," I said. "I'm hoping the IIIs are Roman numerals for three, and if that's the case, the equals sign could be a tunnel, the carat a turn or chimney, and the zero some kind of chute or other tunnel."

Ray scratched the stubble on his chin. "I read aircraft specs and diagrams, not ancient codes, so okay, if you say so."

I walked deeper into the cave, where the footing consisted of loose gravel and large rocks. The sound of trickling water echoed through the brown stone, and some of the walls dripped with moisture, lichen, and ferns.

"Do you know where you're going, Buck? Should we leave markers?"

"It's okay, Gretel, so far there's just one direction—"

Just then a swarm of bats blew past us. Ray and I ducked.

"Damn bats!" he said.

A whisper of the abeng filtered into the cave, then—

BOOM!

"Was that a gunshot?" Ray said.

BOOM!

Shit!

Could someone be shooting at our team outside the cave? The shots sounded far away, and if it was the kidnappers or Gunner, if not one in the same, the best leverage we'd have would be finding the damn treasure. "Let's move," I said. "We're running out of time."

I picked up the pace and we came to a tunnel leading down. It was narrow and turned to the left, where my light lit the wall.

"What do we do?" Ray said.

I sucked in a deep breath. This could be the first pipe, but did the symbol mean up? And if so was the meaning reversed, in which case we should go down?

There was a chimney just past the turn, leading up. Was that the first of three "^"? Or was it in reverse? I exhaled a deep breath and continued forward—the cave was getting narrower.

We came to another fissure leading down and away. Number two? Or was the chimney number one? We kept going until our lights met a pile of rocks ahead thirty feet away.

There was another shaft above our heads, and the main tunnel was only about seven feet high now.

Ray pointed forward. "Is that the end?"

"Look," I said. There was another chute going down just where the pile of rocks blocked whatever was left of the main tunnel.

"What's so special about that one?"

"It's the third one."

I dropped the duffel.

BOOM.

The shot was muffled, but we were deep inside the cave now.

I shined my light into the hole leading down and saw it was full of water. Good grief.

I thought about the chimney we'd passed. Was the archive written opposite or not?

Damn!

"Okay, we need to dive this hole."

"Are you crazy? Dive with what?"

From the duffel bag I removed a small twenty-PSI pony bottle with an octopus regulator and two masks.

"I'm not going down there," Ray said.

I handed him the mask, turned the knob to release the compressed air into the regulators, and pushed the purge button—a loud rush of air blew Ray's hair back. I handed him the octopus, or second regulator.

"Come on."

I climbed into the water—cold, maybe sixty-five degrees—with the mask on my face and the pony bottle in my right arm, tugging on Ray's shirt with my left hand.

He mumbled, grumbled, and groaned, but he eased in.

"Jesus!" he said. "Is this thing spring fed from the South Pole? I can't believe you're dragging me into this death trap."

We kept moving forward.

Up to my waist now, I let go of him and took the light from my pocket. I eased myself into the water and convulsed from the cold. I shined the light forward.

The passage was narrow but clean of debris. It went down fifteen feet, then seemed to either dead-end or turn to the right. The positive buoyancy caused by breathing compressed air, along with my hands being full and the narrowness of the passage, made progress difficult. I had to pull myself ahead and kick off the rocks. Ray—who had to stay close so the second regulator wouldn't pull out of his mouth—pushed me from behind.

The water got colder.

At the bottom—it was a turn, not a dead end—something caught my eye.

The passage seemed lighter ahead. I pointed, but Ray's mask was fogged and I couldn't read his face. I pulled him forward. The tunnel narrowed and the pony bottle clunked against the rock. I held my breath—if the nozzle sheared off, we'd not only have no air, but the tank would explode inside the tunnel. I hugged it close to my chest.

The temperature had me shaking uncontrollably—or was it fear—but the tunnel had ceased to descend and turned perpendicular. Since we were no longer going down, I could lean forward and crawl. My knee tore against a jagged rock—I screamed out a burst of bubbles.

Ray clutched my right bicep and I felt his hand shaking.

The angle of the tunnel canted upward and the light was now definite. I turned off the flashlight, which made Ray shriek bubbles behind me, but then he must have seen the light too, because he started to press on my back. I turned the flashlight back on and we continued toward the light.

A glance at the air gauge on the pony bottle revealed we'd already used over half the air. I picked up the pace, pulling Ray after me. I didn't want to get stuck with no air, no matter what we found ahead. The guide's warning about Maroons reversing directions, along with the pile of rocks that blocked our progress in the tunnel, made me wonder: had there been another chute upward on the other side of that pile? Or were we in the wrong cave altogether? My worries had me breathing faster than I should.

The light became brighter.

Ray pulled at my shoulder and pointed.

The surface of the water refracted the light into an orange glow. Were we back out to the surface of the valley, coming up from a sinkhole?

We would soon find out if this was the wrong hole or not.

44

CLIMBED UPWARD TOWARD THE LIGHT. THE WEIGHT OF MY WET CLOTHING, icy limbs, and the pony bottle caused me to move awkwardly—I smashed my head into the roof of the chute. Stars shot across the backs of my eyelids and I bit down hard on the regulator.

A shove from behind and I was pushed up out of the water with a splash. Ray pressed past me, his flashlight in my eyes, blinding me.

Heavy breathing followed the sound of him spitting out his regulator.

"God, that was terrifying! I'm claustrophobic, remember?"

"You mind getting the light out of my face?"

We were pressed together in the small opening of the chute, and with the pony bottle wedged between the rocks and me, I couldn't turn to see anything. It was a cavern—so we weren't back outside—and it was filled with dim light. I heard the steady sound of water splattering on rocks.

Ray pulled his arm up from between us. His light just missed my nose, and since I was facing the rock wall, I couldn't see—

"Holy crap," he whispered.

"What? Bats? Are you—"

"Look."

I shoved the pony bottle behind me, then pushed down on the rocks with both my palms and swung around to sit on the edge of what I immediately realized was a huge underground chamber.

"There," Ray said.

I followed the beam from his flashlight and caught a dull glow of bronze—no, not bronze.

Gold.

A heaping pile of gold, mixed with reds, greens, silver . . .

"Holy crap," I said.

We scrambled out of the water. The cavern was twice the height of the cave, and there was a hole in the middle of the domed ceiling where water poured in along with a narrow cone of light that spotlit gold, silver, rubies, and emeralds that shot a rainbow of illumination shimmering across the stone walls.

Ray ran to the pile, his light flashing around the stone room.

I watched him, reliving the many finds I'd made in the past, the joy of discovery, the pride in connecting the miniscule details that led to the find, the rush of unearthing what no other person had been able to find. All the years of failure washed away as I stood in the beam of light and let the trickle of water from above cleanse me of the taint of self-doubt—no more years of wondering whether I could do it again. I pumped my fist silently in the air—redemption!

And with it came negotiating power to get Nanny back.

I ran to join Ray.

With both our lights illuminating the pile, we stood silent, stunned by the gold and silver bars, piles of silver cobb coins, gold plates, jeweled goblets, a wood bin the size of a baby's cradle filled with gold doubloons.

I scanned the chamber with my light. There was no other way out except through the top, which was twenty feet high. Ray was sifting through the edge of the pile, calling out items like a child under the most lucrative Christmas tree in history.

"We need to get out of here, Ray."

"This is a ton of stuff. How are we ever going to—"

"We'll have to come back. Remember those gunshots?"

I flashed my light back toward Ray and saw his eyes wild with treasure-fever, something else I remembered well.

"We have to take something!" He dug his hand into the pile. "Some gold coins—did you see these emeralds?"

"We need to leave—*now*, Ray. If Nanny's captors find us before we can negotiate her release, it may never happen. This is the only leverage we have." I turned and walked back toward the flooded passage to the main cave. Then glanced at the air gauge on the pony bottle.

35 percent remained.

It would have to be enough.

I sat on the edge of the water. It didn't even feel cold anymore. I was numb with discovery yet sick with mounting concern.

What awaited us outside?

Was Stanley okay?

Nanny?

I glanced back. "Ray!"

He jumped up and ran over, his eyes still wide.

"Drop the goblet, Ray."

He glanced at it, then set the gold chalice down carefully.

I picked up the pony bottle.

Before we got in the water I gave him some worst-case instructions, made him repeat them, then discussed the plan for the immediate next steps. He didn't like it but got in the water ahead of me, his light out in front of him like a weapon, his regulator in his mouth, and when I wrapped my arm around his waist, we descended and pressed ahead.

The gloom of the passage darkened the further we got from the treasure chamber. I felt the rocks tear at my skin, and Ray flinched when he cracked his shoulder on one of them. Once we arrived at the turn, which led up into the main cave, I had to pull on his arm to keep him back from ascending.

He glanced back, his eyes wide inside the fogged mask.

I held up three fingers.

His chest lifted with a deep breath, followed by a heavy plume of bubbles.

I held up two fingers.

His arms lifted with the deep breath, then fell when he exhaled hard.

I held up one finger. He sucked in a massive lungful of air, pulled the regulator from his mouth, ripped the mask off his forehead, threw them toward me—then kicked hard off the floor of the stone passage and shot up toward the surface.

My light caught his bubbles—good, he'd remembered to exhale as he went. I couldn't see all the way to the top, but the water settled after a minute, so I repeated the same process he'd just gone through.

When I sucked in my last breath, I secured the pony bottle and regulator to a rock, tucked my mask under another rock with Ray's, and kicked toward the surface. The light and rock walls were blurry ahead.

As my lungs started to burn, I saw the circular opening into the cave—was that Ray standing above it staring down at me?

I broke the surface like a cork. I was breathing heavily—my light flashed up into a face.

Ray's face.

I pulled myself out, put my hands on my knees and caught my breath, then shined my light back down into the hole.

Dammit!

One of the masks had slipped off the ledge and was visible where the chute curved up toward the chamber.

"Crap!"

"What?" Ray said.

I pointed the light down the hole and after a moment, he groaned.

"Is that mine? Sorry—"

"Not your fault, I thought I had them secure." I heard distant voices outside and quickly weighed my options. "Forget it, let's go. The odds are that nobody will spot it, but if they come in here and we're crawling out of the water, game over."

We started back through the cave.

"That was the scariest thing I've ever done," Ray said. "But, man, it was so worth it!"

I squeezed his arm. "Remember, Ray. We found nothing, okay?"

A devilish grin bent his mouth into a half circle.

"Got it."

We made our way back through the cave, but I stopped at the first chimney, which was the widest and appeared to go the highest into the hill above. I shined my light around the perimeter of the opening and saw a handhold.

"I'm going to go take a quick look—"

"Why? I thought we were in a—"

"Trust me, okay? Now, give me a boost."

He bent down and cupped his hands together. I put my foot in his palms, counted to three, and he lifted me as I jumped. The rock ledge was there—I grabbed—my wet hand slipped, but then my forearm caught on the other side. I clawed and pulled myself up into the hole and caught my knee on the small ledge. With my light out of my pocket, I shimmied and climbed onward, up into the chimney, which curved left, then up again.

After a few minutes I found my way into a small chamber. No treasure here—just bones and a familiar smell.

There was a skull. Human.

Another skull.

Some kind of burial chamber?

Bats exploded around me, flopping around, then down through the hole—that explained the smell. And the scream from Ray that followed.

I searched around a moment longer and found some scratches in the stone but couldn't decipher their meaning. I wasn't sure whether the people—men, I assumed by the size of their skulls—had become trapped in here or were buried here.

I kicked the bones around—there wasn't anything else there.

I had no idea whether these were Taino or Maroon remains, or how they came to be here. With one of the skulls tucked between my arm and chest like a football, I began to descend back toward the main tunnel.

The return down the chute was faster—a controlled slide more than a graceful exit. I dropped toward the opening—

"Watch out!"

I fell onto the floor of the cave, my light crashing and breaking against the stone floor, my legs buckling as I hit feet first.

"You okay?" Ray was on me with the light.

My arms and knees were bloodied, I'd been half drowned, but I held fast to the dried-out skull. Ray spotted it and jumped back.

"What the heck?"

"Made a friend up there," I said.

"That's gruesome." He shivered. "And we already found the treasure, why the hell did you do that—and bring that skull out with you?"

"Obfuscation, Ray. Obfuscation."

"Meaning what?"

"You're about to find out."

45

THE SOUND OF VOICES COULD BE HEARD LONG BEFORE WE EXITED THE cave—many voices, but one rose above the rest.

"Buck Reilly, where the fuck are you?"

"Someone's anxious to see you," Ray said.

"Do you recognize the voice?"

"Should I?"

"It's Gunner." Ray deflated instantly.

"It'll be okay, Ray, just follow my lead. We never went into the water. Got it?"

He didn't respond, staring out toward the cave opening.

"Ray? Do you understand?"

"I understand," he said. "But what if he finds the mask?

"Forget the mask. You waited in the cave while I went up into the chute in the ceiling—you boosted me up there, right? We didn't find anything of value, just a couple dead Indians.

"Now let's go, it's almost dark and we have a long hike back to Stanley."

WHEN WE STEPPED BACK INTO THE FADING LIGHT OF DAY, I WAS SURPRISED—there was nobody waiting. Then I glanced to my right and saw several men gathered down by the first cave. To their surprise, we walked toward them.

I spotted uniforms—constables?

There were two other men, Cuffee included, also waiting for us.

Cuffee yelled into the first cave, and a moment later the bulk of Richard "Gunner" Rostenkowski ran from the opening like a crazed guerilla.

"Reilly! Get your ass down here!"

A slight wail came from Ray, who clutched my arm for a moment.

"Sorry, but that guy's scary as they come," he said.

"Follow my lead, Ray—see, there's police here too, so don't worry."

After walking around a sinkhole and climbing over some rocks, we arrived at the first cave. Keith, Pierce, and the guide were standing there, all of them apparently unharmed. And Gunner was unarmed—a real surprise.

"These assholes said you were in this cave, Reilly, what the hell?" Gunner said.

"Aren't you supposed to be out at Port Royal restoring some underwater structures?"

"Very funny—and was that you, fat boy, out there pretending to be your boss? Nice fake out."

"How did you even know where we were, Gunner?"

"Mr. Reilly," the older of the two constables said. "We have a cease and desist order—"

"Relax, fellas. I have desisted." I tossed the skull up in the air toward Gunner. He bobbled and caught it, then his scowl became even more intense.

"What the hell's this?"

"Old Taino burial tomb." I paused and dropped my shoulders. "End of the line for me, Gunner. Those ovals on the petroglyph we found by Blue Mountain—the sketch you stole from me?" I glanced at the constables. "All it led to was some old bones."

"Anything to do with the Morgan treasure is ours!" Gunner slammed the skull against the rocks and shattered it.

"Not that I care at this point, but wasn't your permit exclusively for the designated area at Port Royal—"

"Sorry, asshole. We filed an injunction that covers the Morgan treasure, no matter where it's found."

"No court would provide a blanket permit to cover an entire—"

Gunner took two steps forward, ripped the manila envelope out of the younger constable's hand, and shoved it under my nose.

"Take a look at this!"

I pulled the paperwork from the envelope and scanned it. Yes, it was signed by a court official, but it said that "any treasure pertaining to Henry Morgan's return from Panama would be embargoed subject to a proceeding."

"It just embargoes whatever's found until proper ownership can be established—"

"That's in the works, Reilly. After that bullshit fake letter and the millions we pissed away in that mudhole, the Jamaican government owes us!"

"I really don't care, I'm done with this whole search." I smirked. "*So sorry I lost my bid to dive there.*"

Gunner lunged at me—to the shock and surprise of the constables—but I was coiled and ready. I shoved the butt of my right palm straight into his nose and my left fist into his ribs—blood erupted through my fingers, and the big man's knees buckled. I stepped back, satisfied.

The constables grabbed him—flailing about, screaming, and cursing me. Cuffee and the other man with him stepped closer, their eyes twitching with rage, Cuffee slapping a thick walking stick against his palm. I took a quick glance at the other man but didn't recognize him as one of the three who'd attacked me and taken Nanny.

"You men stand down," the older constable said, hand on his holster.

Gunner settled down and gave everyone an eerie smile.

"I won't forget this, Reilly. Now, what the hell did you and your fat friend *really* find in the caves here?"

I shook my head. "We searched every single one and found nothing but a burial chamber."

"Yeah, right. I saw the sketch from those rock carvings at Blue Mountain too. These caves are the exact—"

"Like I said, it must have just been a map to a Taino burial ground, or cave, I don't really know. I'm done."

"We'll search them ourselves, don't worry. Just remember our injunction, Reilly." His voice was high because he was pinching his nose, which continued to drip blood.

"Good luck, asshole. Nothing here but rocks, bones, and bat shit. You'll be right at home."

I waved to my little group as Cuffee and the other brute circled closer.

"We're out of here," I said.

"And get the hell out of Jamaica, dammit!"

I stopped and pivoted on my heel.

"Where's Nanny?"

"Huh?" Gunner said. "Last I saw her was on the Jamaican five hundred dollar bill. Aside from that, I don't know what you're talking about."

I jerked my head toward Cuffee.

"And you don't know anything about you and him beating up an old man, I suppose." I turned to the constables and again nodded toward Cuffee. "The day before Colonel Grandy of Moore Town was beaten half to death, that man stood outside his house shouting threats so loud you'd have no trouble finding witnesses." One of the constables jotted something in a notebook.

Gunner and I held a lethal stare, one I chose to break.

"As far as I'm concerned, there *is* no treasure. I'm heading back to Key West. You win, asshole. Now fuck off."

Gunner's shrill laugh followed us as we started across the valley. Fortunately, a full moon helped light our way as darkness fell. I turned to Professor Keith.

"Those must have been Gunner's shots we heard earlier. What happened to his gun?"

"The constables confiscated their weapons and left them on the first hill, thank God."

"Nothing in there?" Pierce said.

"Just that skull and ancient human remains. But most of the main tunnel had collapsed, so who the hell knows."

My peripheral vision caught Ray fighting back a smile.

Nothing to smile about, yet.

46

THE HIKE BACK WAS SLOW AND BRUTAL IN THE DARK. IT TOOK TWICE AS long, and by the time we reached the vehicles the men were disappointed over what they believed Ray and I had failed to find in the caves, hungry, and angry at the turn of events with Gunner, Cuffee, and the constables. As for whether or not my gamble to take the high road worked, we wouldn't know until we knew.

It was that simple.

We descended the final hill. The batteries on our lights were nearly spent. The moon was nearly gone, the sky had clouded over, and by the look of the deep black horizon, a storm was coming.

Good. Hopefully it would soak Gunner and his goons.

That thought led me to Gunner reacting with a wisecrack when I threw Nanny's kidnapping at him—if he had her, he wouldn't have wanted to hide it from me, he'd say something non-incriminating that would rub my nose in it. That little insight made me even more worried. Gunner and Jack I could outthink, but I now had no idea who I was dealing with.

Gunner hadn't had any scuba gear I could see, and his finding that submerged cavern was a long shot anyway. He'd have to see the mask or the opening in the roof of the chamber. The circle of knowledge about the caves was getting wider, too: our guide, Keith, Pierce, the constables, Gunner, Cuffee, and their other goon. When competitors and unfriendlies were close to a target, it was like lighting a fuse on a bomb. If the goods couldn't be secured within forty-eight hours, the odds drastically increased that something would go wrong.

Another forty-eight-hour countdown.

Except Nanny's clock was set to expire at three o'clock tomorrow.

The Jeep was now ahead, as was the guide's pickup truck. Beyond them I saw the constable's car and a black Land Cruiser that must be Gunner's. The call of the abeng earlier had me worried, so I pulled open the driver's door on the Jeep. The dome light lit and Stanley Grandy, who had been sound asleep, jerked up and grabbed for a stick he must have scrounged from the forest.

"It's us, Stanley. Sorry to surprise you."

With a hand on his chest, he lay back down in the passenger seat, which was reclined all the way back.

"Damn, boy, thought I was going to have to crush your skull." He rubbed his eyes. "Did Cuffee and his crazy white partner find you? Or the constables?"

"They all did, but we didn't have anything for them other than some harsh words." He held my gaze and I pumped my eyebrows once. "I'm going to check their car, then we'll get out of here."

Everyone else piled gear in the back of the guide's truck, but I continued down the path to Gunner's vehicle. The doors were locked, but using my flashlight I could see pretty clearly what was—and wasn't—in the storage area of the Rover. There was no treasure-hunting gear: no shovels, no scuba or climbing gear. Just some cases. Gun cases.

That was the Gunner I knew. His plan was simple: take the fruits of someone else's labor by force, getting as little dirt on his hands in the process. Blood, however, wasn't a problem. But if he went hunting inside that cave, he'd better be prepared to work. For once.

I was tempted to slash his tires but wanted him away from the caves, not stuck here.

Back at the Jeep, everyone had gathered around Stanley. Keith was explaining how when they heard the shots, they relocated to the opposite end of the cave system to draw the men away from Ray and me. I commended their thinking but still had to disappoint them when Stanley asked if I had found *anything*.

"Nothing in those caves but some old bones."

Everyone's face sagged again except Ray's, whose eyes flickered in the last of the moonlight. Stanley said he'd ride with the guide back to Keith's car down in Accompong.

"But first I need to tell you something, Buck, so take a walk with me," he said.

I glanced up the hill to make sure there were no flashlights coming our way, and we walked to the back of the Jeep.

"So?" he said.

I nodded my head, gave him a thumbs up, then put my finger to my lips.

Stanley's was the lowest-key reaction to a treasure find I'd ever seen. No smile, no jumping up and down, no questions. I figured when a man isn't driven by greed, he keeps the big picture in mind. We had around fifteen hours to find Nanny, and when we did, Morgan's treasure—if still there— could be used for the people of Jamaica.

At least that was the plan.

"Any word from Nanny's captors?"

"Another call—definitely a Jamaican, same one as before." He paused. "Just putting the pressure on."

"What you said after your other call—Stanley, do you have any intel on who has Nanny?"

"I have an idea but will need to confront him face-to-face to know for sure."

We agreed on a plan and returned to the vehicles.

Handshakes, pats on backs, a couple laughs about my breaking Gunner's nose, then we all loaded up and made our way out along the narrow trail toward Albert Town.

Now alone in the Jeep, Ray turned to me.

"Wow! I can't believe we're the only two people who know about that pile of treasure! What are we going to do?"

It was like he'd just had six Cuban coffees.

"If we can't find Nanny well before the three o'clock deadline, we'll have to turn it over to her captors. Of course if we free her first, we get to keep our 10 percent."

"So where we headed?"

"Need to change things up. Gunner's anticipating too many of our moves. We're headed toward Kingston, then up into the mountains. A friend of mine named Clemens Von Merveldt, used to be the general manager at a place on Harbour Island in the Bahamas, and now runs a little beauty called Strawberry Hill. We can hide out there until morning."

A few miles on it occurred to me that I hadn't spoken to Harry Greenbaum since before using his credit card to secure the boats for my charade out at Port Royal. I took a deep breath and dialed his number.

"About time I heard from you, my boy," Harry said. "I trust you're calling with news? I'm just finishing dinner, enjoying a Grand Cru Chablis with my Dover sole."

"I can't say much on the cell, Harry, but we've accomplished our goal—"

The sound of liquid sloshing and Harry swallowing filled my ear.

"Excellent!"

I glanced at Ray. "There are strings. We're capped at 10 percent of the find."

Pause. "Rather paltry, wouldn't you say?"

"Not at all, considering the total worth."

"Splendid, dear boy."

"Right now even that's in jeopardy because our benefactor's been kidnapped. Her captors want the treasure by tomorrow, or they say they'll kill her."

A belch caused me to pull the phone away. It was late, and Harry had said he was just finishing his wine. Knowing him, that meant the entire bottle.

"Why am I not surprised the first mission of our new enterprise is so complicated, Buck?"

"I have a plan, and we have most of tomorrow to sort this out."

"Anything I can do to assist?"

"Not unless you can find a missing woman from over fifteen hundred miles away."

"That would be a smart trick, but alas, not part of my repertoire."

A long silence followed. I was about to ask if Harry was still on the line—

"I don't say this lightly, Buck, but if you're not successful in securing the percentage you negotiated with your colleagues there, my days as your partner will be over. Nothing personal, of course—you're like a son to me—but business is business."

Shit.

"I understand, Harry."

"Goodbye for now, dear boy. And of course you have my best wishes for success."

Although it was nearly midnight when we showed up, Clemens welcomed us in the bar with a vintage bottle of Burgundy decanted and ready to go. He hadn't changed a bit, nor had his lovely wife, Nancy. The two of them and Ray drank the wine, but I was having Blackwell Rum, neat.

"We heard Heather was on-island," Nancy said. "Have you seen her?"

Heather and I had spent a couple New Year's Eve celebrations and several long weekends at Clemens' place in the Bahamas, so it was an innocuous question. But Clemens must have seen my face contort, because he poured me another drink and changed the subject.

"Chris Blackwell mentioned you'd been to GoldenEye, with Nanny Adou no less." His smile was a circumspect as ever. "Impressive."

A deep breath and another gulp of rum pushed me into the back of my chair.

"My luck with women hasn't changed," I said. "Or maybe I should say their luck with me hasn't."

With that, Clemens led Ray and me to a vacant room on top of the property. I was so exhausted I can only assume I fell asleep the moment my head hit the pillow.

47

THE NEXT MORNING I GOT A PREDAWN CALL FROM STANLEY ABOUT THE RAT he suspected was amongst us, which was like a belly punch. I sat suddenly to absorb the news. After that, Ray and I devised a quick plan, made a phone call, then drove out to the very end of Port Royal. Our plan required a quick inventory of both flotillas to start.

The sailors at the coast guard base Cagway, directly adjacent, stared hard at us through the barbed-wire-topped fence. Their barracks were austere, and given the drug trade that passed through Jamaican waters, I understood their vigilance. These men had difficult jobs.

Out at the very end of the park was a hillock and field, and beyond that, the water. To the right was the Coast Guard shooting range, which was bounded by numerous warning signs about the use of live ammunition. Ray stared at one such sign with his eyes wide.

"Cover me," I said.

Ray held his palms up. "With what?"

I continued beyond the perimeter set for tourists. Once up the short hill and through the tall grass, I could see the water clearly. Jack's flotilla was still in place—and so was Betty.

Through the binoculars I could see men moving around on their boats. No sign of divers. Maybe Jack figured he needed to maintain their presence here in order to cinch his preposterous claim on all things related to Henry Morgan, or maybe he was more of an optimist than I had assumed. The moment he pulled anchor on that site, he'd be acknowledging that they'd pissed millions into the water there.

Of all the people I observed, I hadn't spotted Gunner, Jack, or Heather. Gunner's words from yesterday had left a sour taste in my mouth that no amount of Blackwell Rum last night or Blue Mountain coffee this morning could cleanse.

Past Jack's boats I spotted our own smaller group, the tug and barge all prepping to pull anchor. A whistle sounded—a Coast Guardsman at the fence perimeter was waving me back into the approved area. I'd seen what I hoped to and returned to Ray.

"Let's go."

As we walked back through the fort, I made a call.

"Mr. Buck, tell me something good?"

"Are you still out on the water?" I said.

"Wind and waves finally settled. We just clearing out now."

"Damn, Johnny, that cost me an extra ten thousand—"

"Nobody want off this rolling mess more than me, mon."

"I'm almost to Kingston now. Meet me at the harbor."

He paused. "You got news?"

I glanced at Ray. His face soured the minute he knew who I'd called.

"I do, Johnny. But I'm not broadcasting it on a cell phone, so meet me in thirty minutes."

"I'll be there."

Once the phone was back in my pocket, I looked at Ray.

"I still don't like that guy," he said.

"We don't need to like him, but we do need him."

As we drove back past the airport, Ray kept an eye on the harbor.

"Speedboat hauling ass toward Kingston," he said. I assumed that was Johnny.

By the time we were at the harbor he'd already tied up his boat and was talking on his cell phone. He hung up seconds after spotting us, his eyes wary as he watched us approach. It occurred to me that Henry Morgan's men probably wore that expression when they were about to be told their share of the booty was far less than anyone expected. Trust between priva-teers was no doubt as rare a commodity back then as it was today amongst treasure hunters. In any case, that steely taste was back in my mouth.

"What's up, gentlemen?" Johnny's usual smile and effervescent demeanor were gone.

"The boats headed back to port?" I said.

Johnny glanced back over his shoulder. "Should be. That game's over." He crossed his arms, then uncrossed them.

"Come on," I said. "Let's get out of here."

"Why? Where we going?"

I turned back to face him and gave him a smile.

"Moore Town. Colonel Stanley has news for us."

"Grandy? Why we need to go there?"

"You want in on this or not?"

Ray returned to the Jeep and got in the backseat. I followed, then Johnny came a moment later. We began the journey around the coast. The ques-tions I expected from Johnny were slow to come.

"You going to tell me what you found?" he said.

"First, give me an update on Dodson's activities out on the water."

He shrugged. "Nobody diving these past few days. That big bastard left a couple days ago—"

"Gunner?"

"Yeah. Been some screaming and shit we could hear over the water. After the constable told us we had to get out of here, Gunner followed them off. Not been back, neither."

"What about Dodson?"

"Still out there—least I saw him there this morning."

I looked out my side window at the crystal blue ocean.

"And the supermodel?"

"Ain't seen her all week—come on, mon, tell me what's going on?"

Still no "Mr. Buck." Still no smile. He'd been too busy texting—contin-uously—while we were driving.

"Turn that phone off and put it away. We're going into blackout mode."

He held the phone for a moment. When I gave him a side-glance he made a show of holding the power button down until the chime sounded, then put the phone in a pocket.

"I'm all ears, mon."

We still had a long ride ahead of us, so I decided to provide a recap that would set the stage for when we reached Stanley. I gave him details of the meeting with Michael Portland and the colonel , including their demand that the people of Jamaica get 90 percent of whatever we found—

"That's steep, mon. You *agree* to that?"

I nodded and sailed on: finding the petroglyphs at the Blue Mountain crossing, Gunner showing up with Cuffee making threats and taking my sketch of the circles . . . Johnny was on the edge of his seat, soaking up every detail as we turned down the dirt road that led to Moore Town.

"Remember when I told you Nanny and I were headed to meet Henry Kujo at Accompong? That was the same afternoon we got jumped near Albert Town and Nanny was abducted."

"Damn, mon. Lucky they didn't kill you."

"Yeah, I guess. Knocked me silly, though—damn sure have a concussion."

I left out going to Firefly and cut straight to the cave system that resembled the petroglyphs.

"It was a match to the ovals and circles, but like I feared, it was just a Taino reference to a burial ground. But somehow, Gunner and his goons found us out there anyway."

"And here I been stuck out on those damn boats." I glanced in the rearview mirror.

"So that's all you find, mon, a burial ground? The suspense is killing me."

Ray, who'd been quiet in the backseat, caught my eyes in the rearview. His lips were tight and he shook his head. I smiled.

The river disappeared off our right side as we approached the outskirts of the old Maroon village.

"Buck, what the fuck?" Johnny said. "You got something to tell me or not?"

"I don't, but Colonel Grandy called this morning and said *he* did. That's why we're here."

Johnny sat back and crossed his arms.

Just then we pulled into Moore Town and parked in front of Stanley's house.

"Let's go see what the colonel has for us."

When Stanley opened his front door, he greeted us holding a sawed-off shotgun pointed at all of our chests.

48

"**W**ELCOME TO **M**OORE **T**OWN, GENTLEMEN. **N**OW GET YOUR ASSES inside."

"Buck, what the heck—"

"Step inside, Ray. It's okay."

Johnny spun, lowered his shoulder, and bulled past me.

I sprang off the door jamb, caught up to him in maybe three seconds, dove, and hit him square in the back. We went down hard, the air squeezed from Johnny's lungs when I landed on top of him. I got his right arm pinned behind his back and my left arm around his neck.

"Going somewhere, Johnny?"

I yanked him to his feet. When he tried a drop move I jammed my knee into his ass—another groan. I pulled my arm tight around his neck and spun him to the left, back toward Stanley's house. Then marched him inside.

"On the chair," Stanley said.

A final push toward the chair against the wall—Johnny whirled back toward us, only to come face-to-face with Stanley's double-barreled shotgun.

"Don't think I won't use this, punk-ass."

"Sit down," I said.

Johnny looked from face to face, sucked in a deep breath, and lowered himself onto the chair. Slowly.

"What the hell's going on here?" he said. "Why you doing this to me?"

"We need to check out some coincidences," I said.

"Goddamn, mon, you couldn't just ask me whatever the hell you talking about?"

"You're the one who ran," I said. Then to Stanley, "You can lower the gun."

Ray was still back by the front door, and knowing him as I did, he would stay as far away from what was happening here as possible.

"We can have a civil conversation," Stanley said. "But I'm damned mad, as you can see—so we need truthful answers."

Just then a woman who had to be at least a hundred years old carried in a tray of iced drinks. It was Tarrah, the Obeah woman Nanny and I had met downriver on the raft.

"Coconut water?" She placed the tray on the small table, handed glasses to each of us. Parched after the long drive and the action, I guzzled mine. The liquid, thicker than water, was cool and soothing.

Stanley kept his glass tilted up, swallowing until it was empty. Ray sipped at his, savoring the drink. Johnny drank deeply, then wiped his lips on his bare arm.

I did my best to stare at his face the way he'd stared at the side of my head in the car.

"Remember on the ride up here when I was telling you about how Gunner intercepted us at the crossing near Blue Mountain?"

"What about it?" Johnny said.

"And then again when Nanny and I were attacked outside of Albert Town?"

Johnny crossed his arms—tightly, as if he were holding himself together. "Yeah, so?"

"*So*, you were the only person I told about either of those trips."

Johnny slid lower in his seat. He was blinking rapidly.

"How long you been feeding info to Gunner?"

He started smacking and licking his lips.

"Damn, woman, how much you put in his drink?" Stanley had turned to face Tarrah.

Her laugh was a deep cackle that made me shiver.

"I give him enough so he talk to get the antidote, or he die," she said.

Johnny sat back up fast. His eyes bugged out and a rapid shake began in his extremities. Tarrah stepped up to him and bent at the waist to peer in his eyes.

"I say you got ten minutes before you no longer able to breathe. Five or six before you no longer talk."

Johnny tried to jump up but fell out of the chair—his legs no longer functioned. I rolled him onto his back.

"Get him some water!"

When he drained the small water glass, he cleared his throat.

"Four minutes," Tarrah said. "Talk."

The sentences came out jerky and he kept clearing his throat, but Johnny talked.

"When they were selected, he made me an offer—you were gone, so why not?" He cleared his throat. "Then you came back." Again he cleared his throat. "Nanny—she persuade you—but Gunner . . . he . . . had me—"

"Is Nanny safe?" I said.

Everyone leaned closer.

"Yeah, mon. She—"

Johnny's eyes rolled behind his head. Tarrah knelt down and slapped him hard—his entire body convulsed, then his eyes opened.

"She told me about . . . the drawing . . . caves . . ." He tried to clear his throat again. Stanley poured water into his mouth. "Canoes—up in the air."

I signaled Tarrah. "He's telling the truth."

"He don't tell us nothing we don't know, yet," she said.

Dammit!

I grabbed Johnny by both of his biceps and lifted him up to a seated position.

"Where is she, Johnny?"

His eyes rolled around like balls in a pachinko machine.

"Give him the antidote!" I said.

Tarrah shook her head.

"Stanley!" I said. "Tell her!"

"I told Nanny someone would die!" Tarrah dropped her voice to a bone-chilling whisper. "Won't be her alone."

"He said she's alive—she'll die if we don't get to her!"

"Give him the antidote," Stanley said.

Silence. Nobody spoke, nobody moved.

Then Tarrah grimaced, reached into her waistcoat pocket, and took out what looked like coffee beans. She pulled Johnny's head back by his hair, dropped the beans into his mouth, poured a small amount of coconut water in, and massaged his jaw until he swallowed.

But Johnny had drifted out of consciousness—I was terrified she'd waited too long. We sat watching in a circle around him for minutes that seemed like hours. The only sign of life was his breathing—

His body convulsed.

Tarrah slapped him hard on the cheek. His eyes popped open, his eyelids fluttered, and he convulsed again. After a few moments, he balled and then relaxed his fists.

"Where is she, Johnny?" Tarrah said. "Nanny? Who has her?"

He licked his lips and his eyes focused on me.

"No woman, no cry."

I looked at Stanley. "Bob Marley—where was he from?"

"Nine Mile," Stanley said.

Johnny shook his head and closed his eyes.

"Trench Town?" Ray said from behind us.

Johnny's eyes popped open. A slight nod followed.

Tarrah bent over him.

"You take these men to find her?" Tarrah's voice sounded like a challenge from the devil's own lips, at least to me.

Johnny nodded rapidly.

"You best," she said. "If you want to live."

49

THE SKY SWIRLED WITH VAN GOGH SHAPES AND COLORS AS THE SUNSET exploded over Kingston Harbor. We were fully loaded and armed for rescue, but needed recon to confirm the other assholes were occupied and distracted. Johnny had told his cohorts he was on his way, which we would be shortly.

The moon hovered above the water's surface, maroon and rising. We were parked with the motor running at the edge of Port Royal, the Jeep surrounded by Coast Guardsmen holding rifles. Their commander had his fists balled on his hips, his legs spread wide as he faced me from fifty yards away.

I checked the time and rubbed my palms together.

Come on, Ray.

Through the binoculars I could see Jack's crew pulling lines. And then I heard engines starting. Gray-black smoke hovered over the flotilla. They'd finally pulled the plug on the dive and restoration project. Had they given up, or had they found the submerged cavern in the Cockpit Country cave?

Wait.

I adjusted the focus on the binoculars—yes!

Jack was still on the main boat—

A low grumble caught my attention from the north. I turned, and the Coast Guardsman also turned to see—yes!

The Beast flew low. Ray must have gotten clearance this close to the airport—he'd never break the rules. He was maybe a thousand feet above the water, coming hard and fast.

I swallowed, remembering Gunner's men shooting at us the day we'd arrived.

Would Jack?

I forced myself to focus again on the flotilla. Someone pointed toward the sky, weapons were raised—

There! Jack shouted something. More guns were raised. A big man ran out from the salon—

Gunner!

The Beast buzzed them. Everyone ducked except Gunner, who gave Ray the finger.

Now guns were trained on the Beast. I held my breath. But Ray was hauling ass, gaining rapid distance from the fleet.

Gunner shouted something. The men lowered their weapons. My knees stopped shaking and I released the long breath I'd held.

The Beast shrank in size and I retrained the binoculars on Jack—Gunner gave him a high five.

"That's right, assholes, we gave up and are headed back to Key West with our tails between our legs."

Steely stares watched us inside the Jeep.

"Tell Colonel Grandy he owes me," the commander said. "Now get the hell out of here."

"Thanks again for letting us enter the prohibited area." But I really just wanted to make sure that what Johnny had told us was true, that Jack and Gunner were not where Nanny was being held, and then to make sure they saw the Beast depart. Hopefully they bought it and would no longer think they had to race against me.

Pierce sat next to Johnny Blake in the Jeep's backseat. The passenger seat was empty, but hopefully not for long.

"I told you they don't know shit about Nanny," Johnny said. "You always playing misdirection games, Buck. That's what cause all this."

Our eyes caught in the rearview mirror.

"I learned long ago not to trust people in this business," I said. "I let my judgment lapse with you."

"I had her grabbed for her own protection, mon," Johnny said. "Gunner wanted to torture and kill her—after he rape her, he said."

"Very noble, Johnny." I rubbed my palm across my scalp, the lump from the beating I'd taken still tender. "She'd better be okay, for your sake. And your giving Gunner our whereabouts risked our lives."

Pierce slapped the side of Johnny's head, and he flinched.

We set out past the airport, along the waterfront and through Kingston. By the time we arrived in Trench Town, one of the poorest communities in Jamaica, darkness was complete. The sound of dance hall music blared from open doors, men and women roamed the streets looking for action of any kind. I drove fast with my doors locked. The rental Jeep was already a target, but with me behind the wheel it would be an invitation—

"Turn left at the light," Johnny said.

The traffic signal turned red before I could reach the intersection. Three young men rushed the vehicle with a bucket and rags—two began to wash my windshield.

"No thank you! No!"

My voice made them split, then two came toward my door while the third went to the passenger side.

"One thousand dollar, mon!" the one outside my window said. The exchange rate being a hundred to one.

The light changed and I stomped on the gas pedal. A couple more turns as directed by Johnny led us into a neighborhood of squat rundown shacks, several of which had no glass in their window frames.

"Two doors down." Johnny's voice was on edge. "Listen, Buck, you play it like I say and it goes fine, mon. If not, I can't be taking responsibility—"

"Oh, you're responsible, Johnny. Something happens to us, won't be anyplace you can hide." I paused. "That old woman scares the shit out of me, and we're on the same side. She comes at you? Forget about it, *mon*. So *you* play it like we agreed."

We came to a stop in front of the house. The Jeep would be a dead giveaway.

"If Nanny's unharmed, we'll tie you and your friends up, and Pierce will stay here with you until tomorrow when we've finished our business. I can't have you tipping Gunner off. You cooperate, we won't call the police."

Johnny stepped out.

"I've got a bad feeling," Pierce said.

He was a couple inches shorter than me but thirty pounds heavier, and it was all muscle. If *he* was worried . . .

"Come on," I said.

We followed Johnny. Pierce trailed after me, trying to hide the shotgun between us. Johnny stepped to the side of the door to peer inside a window with no glass.

"Yo! It's me," he said.

A voice called back from deep inside. The words were unintelligible to my ear, but the tone sounded friendly.

Soon I heard the sound of someone unbolting the door. I held Johnny's arm—I knew he'd run if he got the chance.

The door cracked open. Pierce kicked hard and it flew wide.

Clunk!

Grunt . . . thud.

Pierce was through the door. I shoved Johnny in ahead of me.

Inside, Pierce was on top of the man who'd answered the door—now out cold, a bloody crease across his forehead.

"Door must've hit him in the face," Pierce said.

I pointed to Johnny.

"Yo! Freddy?" he said.

A muffled voice from another room. The smell of ganja was strong in the air, as if there was a constant fire burning—which I suspected there was. Johnny sauntered ahead, waving us to follow.

As large as Pierce was, he tiptoed silently behind Johnny, his shotgun raised. I walked behind them into a dimly lit corridor—slowly, it being hard to see ahead of us with so little light—the aroma of smoldering weed stronger with every step.

Johnny turned a corner. He shouted something I couldn't follow, jerked his arm free, darted somewhere I couldn't see, and ran—I could hear his damn footsteps. I heard glass breaking, then a rush of air came from our left. I stepped on broken glass and looked out the window: two men were running away from the house. Pierce and I watched them disappear into the night.

"Nanny!"

I waited until all was quiet to make sure nobody else was there, and then with a deep breath I rushed toward the light coming from a partially cracked door. I pushed the door wide and lit into the room—right into a couch. This ended me up on the floor, which was a jumble of fast food cartons and empty water bottles. In the middle of it all was Nanny, blindfolded, shaking like a mountain flower in a stiff breeze. Pierce had skidded to a stop at the other end of the couch.

"Nanny! It's me, Buck."

On my knees, I removed her blindfold.

"Did you figure out my clue?"

I collapsed onto the couch next to her and started laughing while Pierce undid the ropes from her feet and wrists.

"No interest in treasure hunting, huh?" I said.

Wearing the same clothes she'd had on the day she was snatched, she looked rumpled, but her eyes were clear and her smile an incredible relief.

"I just don't want those bastards to get it," she said. "I hope you found the treasure."

My smile answered her question. I threw my arms wide. "Gunner and his goons showed up so we had to leave empty-handed. Haven't been back, so we don't know the status."

The smile left her face. "What are we going to do?"

"I have something in mind. Let's get out of here before your hosts return with help—or beat us out to the cave."

50

STRAWBERRY HILL ONCE AGAIN PROVIDED RESPITE, BUT THIS TIME CLEMENS installed us in the owner's home behind the spa. After a long shower, a fine Châteauneuf-du-Pape, and a frothy reunion in the master suite, Nanny had succumbed to a deep sleep in my arms. Once my heart had settled, my brain labored into the wee hours over the logistics I'd set in motion. And though I wasn't a believer, Tarrah's prediction that somebody would die before this was over didn't help me sleep.

The morning view of the Blue Mountains was enhanced by the aroma of coffee named for the same range where the beans were grown. Nanny had said her captors, who were always masked, had not hurt her in any way but had shotgunned ganja smoke into her face until, high as a kite, she revealed the details of the cave drawing and the canoes suspended in the trees.

She was upset with herself, but I did my best to assuage her concerns with the fact that so far as we knew, Morgan's stash remained intact.

"And who would you bet on?" I said. "Jack and Gunner, or me?"

Her face brightened. "You, Buck Reilly. Anytime."

"Is there anything you can tell me about the men in the masks?" I said.

Definitely Jamaican—she was certain of it thanks to their accents and speech. She never sensed any more than three men in the room where she was tied up, and having met Gunner was sure he hadn't been there.

Nancy Von Merveldt fed us at dawn, and now as the sun cast long shadows over the peaks of the Blue Mountain foothills, the unmistakable loud sound I'd been anticipating cut the air as if tearing it apart. One of the strategic benefits of Strawberry Hill was the helipad built on the edge of the cliff behind the owner's house. Nanny, Pierce, and I watched Michael Portland's green helicopter steer for the pad and set down hard.

I grabbed my backpack. Pierce ran ahead, followed by Nanny, then me. Keith was already aboard, and as we lifted from the helipad I spotted Clemens saluting us from the ground. I took that as a positive omen.

The pilot vectored west and we swung around the mountains as we gained altitude. A vast sea of green was bifurcated by the central north-south highway below us, then gave way to the countryside that led to Cockpit Country. I spotted Albert Town and was searching for the small building I'd convalesced in when I felt a squeeze on my arm. Nanny smiled at me. She was a mind reader, all right. I smiled back.

ONCE IN THE MIDDLE OF THE CONICAL MOUNTAINS IT FELT LIKE I WAS looking at one of those magic eye pictures—if you squinted just right, a word or a face might appear. I squinted and saw the valley Pierce had marked on a GPS when we were there. I scanned the ground and spotted several ATVs with trailers behind them and men watching us begin our descent.

I used my binoculars when one of them waved to us. Colonel Stanley Grandy. Within a few minutes we were on the ground with our gear and the helicopter was rising into the sky.

The plan for how best to handle extracting the treasure was based on the quantity of material Ray and I had assessed when we discovered the stash. It was too massive for the helicopter or the narrow submersed passage. Stanley had brought in the ATVs with trailers early this morning, and a truck awaited us at the trailhead where we'd last left the Jeep. Pierce, Nanny, and two of the ATV drivers—trusted young men from Moore Town—hiked up and got in position while I found the water source that led into the cave system.

Speed was critical at this point. Our entire operation, from the truck at the trailhead to the ATVs and trailers sitting outside the caves, was totally exposed. Almost certainly Johnny had shared the details I told him with Gunner. And even if he hadn't, Gunner's contacts back in Key West would no doubt have told him by now that I wasn't with Ray on the plane. That being the case, he'd most likely come back here.

No way I could see Gunner expend the effort it would take to find the submerged cave, so he had no way to find the treasure. We just had to get it out before he sniffed *us* out.

With the tripod and pulley system set and anchored into the rock, I switched on my headlamp, snapped the rope into the caribiner on my harness, and placed my legs on both sides of the three-foot-wide black hole.

I smiled at the three men and Nanny, who was still climbing into her harness.

"Don't forget about me," I said.

With that, I let my feet slip into the center of the hole and into the stream of cold water, which immediately soaked me. I descended into the blackness, letting rope slide through my gloves as I went. The chute was longer than I expected—I descended maybe six feet before entering the cavern. With over a thousand caves on Jamaica and hundreds of karst hillocks here in Cockpit Country, it was no wonder this treasure had never been found. Had it not been for the carved circles and Jamaican coastline on Henry Morgan's mantelpiece at Firefly, we'd have never discovered the cave system, much less the hidden chamber. Based on the water pouring through the opening and the pile of rocks below, my guess was that this entry hadn't even existed when the Maroons hid the treasure here.

I spun in a slow circle. The light on my headlamp circled around the vast enclosure.

Where's the treasure?

I swallowed—hard.

Had Gunner found the mask? Had someone else—

There! I just hadn't descended quite enough. When the light caught the heaping mound of glowing metal, I exhaled the breath I'd probably held since the start of the descent. I moved around—it looked gargantuan, even bigger from above. And there were a few canoes Ray and I had missed.

A long exhale made my lips flutter.

"Yes!"

The sound of my voice echoed around the cavern and up through the shaft.

Euphoria had every nerve ending in my body tingling. When I touched down, I unclasped the caribiner and pulled twice on the rope, which promptly disappeared back up the hole through the roof. As arranged, I waited until Nanny joined me in the cavern before I touched anything.

51

"OH MY GOD!" HER VOICE ECHOED IN THE CHAMBER AS HER FEET touched down.

"Nothing in the world feels like finding missing treasure—millions of dollars worth of treasure," I said. "Especially your first time."

She spun into my arms and pulled me into a tight hug.

"This would have never happened without you."

"We make a good team," I said.

She stared up into my eyes a moment, when—clunk—the metal basket we would use to send items back up landed hard on the cavern floor.

"I need to document the mass before we start sending any of it up." Nanny began walking around the mound, photographing it from multiple angles. "Make it quick," I said, and a few seconds later she pronounced the job done.

As we loaded basket after basket after basket, I couldn't help but compare this haul to others I'd discovered. It was a massive cache, maybe the largest I'd ever found. Dozens of gold and silver bars, sacks of silver cobb coins and gold doubloons, a set of twelve gold- and jewel-encrusted goblets—the emeralds and rubies on the goblets had to be five carats apiece. There were also silver-plated ornaments, gold bejeweled crosses—I lost track.

When the last basket was lifted, we stood in the musty chamber, the walls dripping with moisture and our backs aching.

"I feel guilty," Nanny said.

"Don't. This isn't helping anyone down here. Your aspirations are a hell of a lot more noble than what anybody else's would be—mine included." I shined my light along the cave wall, above the stack of old canoes. "What's that?"

Nanny leaned in close to see what my light had illuminated.

"It's the crest of Henry Morgan."

"That makes sense."

"Look at the canoe underneath the crest." She glanced back at me. "It has 'Akim' carved into the bow. Njoni's father."

She took a picture of the wall carving and canoe, then I strapped her into the harness and pulled hard on the line.

She pulled me close, kissed me quickly, then rose like an angel, spinning slowly in a circle as she disappeared into the shaft of light and water.

I waited for the rope to be lowered back down.

It didn't come.

"Pierce!" My voice echoed in the hollow chamber. "Nanny!"

I called again and again, but there was no answer. The bones I'd found in the chimney up in the central cave came to mind.

Son of a bitch!

52

'D BEEN IN THE CAVE SO LONG THE LIGHT ON MY HEADLAMP WAS GROWING dim. I searched around for a way to reach the hole in the roof of the cave, but there was nothing—no way to prop the canoes into a ladder, no way to free-climb. I found myself back at the water-filled tunnel Ray and I had first arrived through.

It was too far to swim with one breath, in the dark.

But there was no choice.

They wouldn't leave me here.

But they'd left me here.

I took three deep breaths to expand my lungs and lowered myself into the water. I shivered—from the cold, or the very real possibility that I might not make it through the long, pitch-black tunnel.

I tried to picture the course Ray and I had taken. Couldn't recall how far it had been, but it seemed endless. I closed my eyes and tried to approximate the distance to where the tunnel turned up toward the main cave— maybe twenty feet through the narrow jagged rock chute. I opened my eyes knowing it was time to move.

My light no longer had the strength to penetrate the water and it wasn't waterproof, so I took it off and tossed it aside.

I took one last breath, submerged, and started pulling myself through the cold, dark water, counting as I went. My body shook from the chill and

I scraped my shoulder against rock. I glanced back—the dim light from the chamber was fading . . .

MOVE!

My head struck rock. My lungs burned.

I pulled myself forward using the sharp edges on the rocky bottom of the tunnel into the blackness. Where was the damn turn up?

Twenty, twenty-one, twenty-two, twenty-three—my chest was a cauldron of spent oxygen. Twenty-four, twenty-five—I felt something move and yanked my hand back. I reached forward again, slowly.

The pony bottle!

I grabbed the tank and felt for the line to the regulator—there. I pulled until the mouthpiece was in my hand—sucked hard—nothing!

Dammit!

The tank had been 35 percent full when we left it here, but the air must have leaked out. I hadn't shut off the valve when we left it here.

My eyes fluttered—so dizzy. I rolled against the wall—was I facing up?

Was this how it ended? Left alone to expire in a submerged cave?

Hell no!

My eyes fluttered and I saw a silver glimmer above me—wait! If the air had leaked out of the tank, could that be an air pocket in the rocks above?

With what strength I had left I shoved my face up into the glimmer—yes! It was an air pocket—two deep breaths—then water!

My hands worked furiously now, pulling myself into the darkness, away from the muted light, forward—*crash*—I careened into the end of the perpendicular chute.

Turn now, kick off the bottom.

Rocks scraped at me as I ascended, but I was moving, buoyancy propelling me upward . . . the passage was so long—

Splash!

My head had burst out of the water—I sucked in air like I'd just sprinted five miles. Then crawled across the jagged edge of the chute, out of the water. I stood still and oriented myself, not easy to do since the cave was virtually pitch black.

The liquid chute I'd survived was on the lower side of the wall, which meant the cave exit was to the right.

I hurried, brushing against the walls, then tripped and was on the cave floor. I got up—there was faint light ahead.

In my panic I ran through the darkness, caroming into protruding rocks as I went, until I stepped on the broken glass from my flashlight that had shattered when I fell from the chimney last time I was here. I was close now—there, ahead!

Light!

I increased my speed and burst into the main cavern, oblivious to the screeching bats overhead.

Nobody abandons Buck Reilly!

53

I RAN FROM THE CAVE AND SAW THE FOUR-WHEELERS WERE STILL THERE WITH the people mounted up and engines running.

"Buck?" Stanley was sitting on the lead vehicle. "Why'd you come through the cave?"

I stumbled forward, the light illuminating cuts and abrasions from my hasty exit through the liquid blackness. With my hands on my knees I scanned the area and tried to catch my breath.

"Buck!"

I heard Nanny call my name from what seemed very far away. I stood and looked up toward the top of the hill where we'd descended into the chamber. Nanny and Pierce were bent down staring into the hole, and Nanny was pulling the harness back around her waist.

"Down here!" My voice croaked. I yelled again, and this time Nanny and Pierce stood up—then held their arms up as if to say, how the hell did you get *there*?

Stanley walked up to me. "You okay, Buck?"

"I thought . . . what the hell took so long for them to come back for me?"

Stanley's eyes opened wide. "You thought we *left* you there? Damn, son—no! An airplane flew low through the valley, that other seaplane—we had to hide."

"Jack? Shit!" Johnny had obviously spilled his guts to him and Gunner.

"No doubt they saw the loaded trailers—but damn, Buck Reilly, you really thought we'd left you to die?"

By this time, Nanny and Pierce had scrambled down the side of the hill and were running toward us. Emotions coursed through my body—I felt both like a paranoid fool and relieved that I hadn't been totally gamed, used and abandoned.

Nanny reached me first. "What are you—how did you—lord, you're scratched and bleeding in a thousand places!"

"We need to get the hell out of here," I said.

"Damn, Buck," Pierce said. "That's an amazing amount of shit you found in that cave."

The men had loaded everything into the trailers behind the ATVs. All of the trailers were covered over with tarps and wrapped tight with ropes. My heart raced from the exertion, but also because I knew Jack and Gunner would be hot on our asses.

We needed to move.

"You, sir, have a golden touch," Stanley said. "I can't believe we did it." He glanced back to the ATVs. "This will be tremendous news for both the museum and the Jamaican people. iPads for all schoolchildren!"

"Too soon to celebrate, " I said. "Let's get the hell out of here."

And so we began the long circuitous journey through the hills toward the dead-end road where a lone truck waited—or so we hoped. The trip out was slow and painful, especially for the bigger men, with two of each crammed onto every ATV. Nanny had her arms around my waist, a necessity given the bumpy ride.

A small plane flew along the valley, straight toward us. It wasn't Betty, but the pilot looked interested in us, given his drop in altitude and course directly overhead. Would Jack have additional spotters out to keep track of our progress? I would if I were him.

When there was a clear straightaway I accelerated to twenty miles per hour and passed Stanley, and everyone sped up. Nanny's grip tightened as we bounced hard, dodged a boulder hidden in ferns, and splashed through shallow puddles that sprayed us with muddy water. Goggles would have been nice.

After a twenty-minute span that felt like hours, I heard a honk over the growl of the ATV engine. I braked to a stop and glanced back. Stanley pointed ahead toward two gray hills separated by a narrow valley. I responded with a thumbs-up, then lifted my arm until each of the other drivers had lifted their thumbs. All of them were muddy, none of them were smiling.

We continued forward—the route Stanley pointed to would have been invisible had it not been for the faint tire tracks through the grassy landscape. I followed the tracks straight toward the rocky gap between the hills.

To my surprise, the tracks cut to the right. I let off the accelerator a moment to scan the valley between the hills—it was an impenetrable crevasse of boulders.

A glance back to Stanley found him pointing up the hill.

Nanny nearly slid off the back of the seat when I added power up the incline. We leaned forward, and her fingers dug into my rib cage. What seemed like a goat trail—narrow, rutted, chiseled by erosion—looped around the left side of the hill on a contour approximately halfway up, which afforded a good view of the valley.

I started to feel a ray of hope.

54

WE ROUNDED THE SIDE OF THE GREEN MOUNTAIN AT THE CLOSEST POINT to the hill on our left—it was the final hill from our previous trip here. Sure enough, the dead-end road was below. The huge truck Stanley had driven to tow in the ATVs was there and partially hidden under the forest canopy.

I followed the tire tracks through tall grass, accelerating once out on the dirt road. Nanny held tight until we screeched to a stop behind the truck. The other ATVs pulled up behind us and came to a stop. Everyone climbed off and stretched, muddy messes each of them.

"My butt is killing me," Stanley said.

The truck had a sturdy canvas top supported by rings over its bed, with an enclosed cab in front. I dropped the tailgate and rolled the canvas up, then removed the ramps they'd used to unload two of the ATVs. I glanced around and spotted the trailer in the tall grass, covered over with branches and leaves. That must have carried the other two ATVs.

"Won't be room for ATVs with all this treasure," I said.

"Who cares," Pierce said. "We'll come back for them."

Nanny sat on the lowered tailgate with a pad of paper and pen and took inventory as the men carried over armload after armload of precious metals and jewels. Everyone worked at top speed to hasten our departure. Inside the truck, I secured the booty with ropes so it wouldn't bounce around.

"That's a lot of buying power for Jamaican schoolchildren," Stanley said.

"And a fine collection for the National Maritime Museum," Keith said.

Nanny's face was serious. "We'll set up a nonprofit—"

"Which Nanny will run," Stanley said.

"And use our Maroon heritage of independence and self-determination to revolutionize Jamaica's future," she said.

All the men stared at her with smiles on their faces.

Whether part of her heritage, her own drive, or her DNA, Nanny was a bold visionary—just like the original Mother of us all.

Once we'd unloaded everything, the men stashed their ATVs and trailers in the tall grass, then climbed inside the truck. I closed the tailgate and secured the canvas flaps. Since he promised to drive fast, Stanley took the wheel for the first leg of what would be a long trip, Nanny sat in the middle, and I was on the passenger side keeping watch. Our destination was Moore Town, via Albert Town, Ocho Rios, and then Port Antonio.

The big diesel fired up. In the back, the men laughed and hollered. Stanley hooted and hollered right along with them.

"I'd hold off on the celebration until we're safely back in Moore Town," I said.

Nanny reached down and squeezed my left thigh.

"You two did a hell of a job," Stanley said. "I never thought there was any truth to the legend, much less that you'd be able to find—"

The truck lurched forward, the brakes locked up—Whoa!

The wheels slid on the gravel—toward—uh-oh. . .

A huge crash sounded behind us and the men yelled. I knew the heavy piles I'd tied down neatly were now a massive jumble after Stanley's screeching stop.

Based on what I saw through the windshield, he'd done a heck of job halting the big truck at all.

"Do you have 9-1-1 in Jamaica?" I said. "If not, somebody better call the police."

Five men, multiple dirt bikes, a black Land Rover, and a pickup truck blocked the road. The men held a combination of shotguns and automatic weapons. As soon as we stopped they rushed us, surrounding the truck, shouting for the men to exit the back. Some jammed their guns inside the cab toward us.

"What's going on here?" Stanley's voice quivered.

"Get out—all of you!"

Cuffee stood in front of the truck, a handgun pointed at the windshield.

"Too late," I said.

Nanny shuddered next to me. "What do we do?"

"Exactly as they say," I said. "These men won't think twice about killing us."

I popped the door open and slid out, followed by Nanny. Stanley did the same from the driver's side. There was shouting—a gun butt hit the side of the truck's back bed—until Pierce, Keith, and the other men climbed out of the truck.

"How dare you—" Stanley's admonishment was greeted with Cuffee's handgun pressed into his cheek.

"Don't shoot anybody!" The loud voice came from behind me.

I spun to find Gunner stepping out of the black Land Rover, his square teeth yellow in the bright sunlight, his nose taped from my breaking it. The other men stepped back and made way for him.

He stopped in front of me. The knife on his belt and the pistol in his holster were not lost on me. My fingers wiggled at the end of my arms, which trembled with rage.

"Didn't I warn you, Reilly?"

"You've got no right—"

"*I* got right!" The voice came over my back shoulder. I glanced back at Cuffee, his eyes bulging wide.

"As Njoni's distant relative?" I said.

His mouth fell open, but he recovered quickly.

"Damn straight, mon. He was the one who hid whatever you found—"

"Damn, Cuffee!" A voice came from behind the truck. "Look at all this!"

Cuffee's teeth were white, and he was as big as Gunner, maybe even bigger.

"Njoni's father was Akim!" Nanny shouted. "*He* sailed with Morgan, who entrusted the treasure to—"

"Shut up," Gunner said. "Spare me the semantics."

Nanny stepped toward him. I grabbed her arm and pulled her back—hard—as Gunner exploded in laughter.

"Pointless to argue provenance," I said.

She pulled her arm out of my hand, which made Gunner hoot with more laughter.

"This is Maroon property!" said Stanley, who had hurried to our side of the truck.

Gunner's smile slid to a sneer. "We'll etch that on your tombstone, old man."

"Everybody calm down," I said. "Pierce, you, Keith, and the others step back." I again took Nanny by the arm. "Let's get out of their way." Then, to Gunner: "You can let him go, too."

Stanley had paled and his legs were wobbling. I was afraid he'd collapse at any moment.

Gunner's men collected all our cell phones and the keys to the four-wheelers. We all stepped back, and the sounds of engines roared ahead of us with the ferocity of a Hells Angel's chapter. Vehicles backed out of the way and motocross engines whined loudly as Gunner stepped toward us, pistol drawn.

"We're taking Nanny with us for insurance."

Nanny slapped Gunner's hand away and he grabbed her around the waist and picked her up while keeping his gun aimed at us. She struggled—

"No!" Stanley leapt forward. I grabbed the back of his pants and he collapsed like a jackknife.

Gunner shoved Nanny up into the passenger side of the truck and climbed in after her. Cuffee got behind the wheel and the truck lurched forward as the other vehicles scrambled in front of or behind them.

"My cell phone's in my sock," Stanley said.

I cut a glance back to our men.

"Pierce! Don't let Stanley do anything crazy. Stanley, call the police—Gunner will be heading south."

"What are you going to do?" Stanley said.

"Get our girl back."

"Ride natty ride!" Pierce called out behind me.

I sprinted toward the last of Gunner's men mounting a dirt bike. He saw me coming and tried to gun the accelerator—the rear tire spun fast and slid hard to the left—

I sprinted harder. He cut back to the right—I dove—

We collided in midair. Both of us were knocked to the ground and the bike fell on me.

My arm pressed against the exhaust pipe—hot!

He lunged for me. I shoved the bike at the man and caught him on the side of the head with the gas tank. He tumbled.

I climbed aboard and spun the accelerator down. The bike reared up on its back tire and the unintended wheelie lasted twenty feet until I switched gears.

The front end slammed down as I gunned it, in pursuit of the small convoy.

55

THE TRUCK SWERVED WILDLY TO THE RIGHT, THEN LEFT—

Gunner hung out of the passenger window, waving to his men on motorcycles ahead, then pointing back to where I was following. The biker on the right braked and reached into his jacket, then pulled out a gun and twisted around to his left.

I accelerated toward him and cut to the opposite side. He tried to switch the gun to his other hand and turn to his right—

I sped up, reached out, and grabbed his handlebar. I shoved it left—

BOOM!

He fired a shot as his motorcycle swerved hard into the woods—he over-corrected, his front wheel hit a rock, and he flew over the handlebars.

Gunner waved at the other motorcycle. The driver shifted his attention toward me and swerved. I braked—

BOOM!

The shot from the motorcyclist was at near point blank range but whizzed past my head—had I not braked I'd be—

BOOM!

My tires screeched from locking the brakes, I continued dodging and weaving, then I accelerated up on his blind spot.

He braked. I had to turn sharply—he pulled behind me—I braked hard.

BOOM! BOOM!

The motorcycle had been accelerating and had to swerve past me to avoid a crash, but his gun hand was on the other side. I accelerated up to his rear wheel. There was a curve ahead.

He swung around and aimed his gun. I cut to the left. He craned back to aim again—I cut hard to the right. He flew off the road at the curve and disappeared in thick bushes.

The truck was ahead. I downshifted and accelerated until I was nearly on the back bumper. Gunner hung out the side window, aiming his pistol as I veered to the other side. I saw Cuffee's face reflected in the truck's rearview mirror, accelerated, and glanced through his window at Nanny. She was struggling with Gunner.

Dammit!

Cuffee steered the truck toward me. I drove up onto the shoulder—branches slapped my body and face—then managed to cut back behind the truck. I saw movement in the bed.

One of the men in back had opened the canvas flap. He held a goddamn machine gun. I cut back to the driver's side—

BAMBAMBAMBAM!

They shot at me blindly through the side canvas. I accelerated in front of the truck.

The black Land Rover was in front of us. Now Cuffee accelerated, forcing me forward—

BOOM! BOOM!

Gunner fired at me, the Land Rover braked, the truck accelerated. I cut to the right—

I could see a series of sharp curves descending the steep hill ahead.

BOOM-POP!

Gunner's shot had hit my front tire. Rubber flew apart. The motorcycle flipped through the air, and I sailed toward the bushes.

I careened off thick plants that ripped at my skin before I crashed into a tree.

Pain and the sense of burning surged through me, but a quick inventory revealed nothing broken.

I was up, running down the center of the road—which turned hard to the right, the upper part of a switchback. The truck had just cut the corner back to the left and disappeared from sight below me.

I ran as hard as I could straight into the woods to my left. Daylight sparkled through thick vegetation. I dodged trees—stickers tore at my arms—

I skidded to a stop.

A sheer cliff dropped off from the woods, the road thirty feet below. The truck was coming fast from the right. The Land Rover, well ahead of it, passed by me.

Oh, crap. Thirty feet, aim for the canvas—

I jumped. Landed on the back edge of the canvas top, slid to the right, and clung to the side.

The truck swerved as Gunner opened the door and pointed his pistol at me.

Click.

His clip was empty. A snarl curled his lips. He yelled but I couldn't hear what over the wind whipping past—we had to be going fifty miles per hour—

BAMBAMBAMBAM!

The machine gunner shot through the canvas top, missing me by inches. I pulled myself across the canvas until I was on top of the truck's cab and grabbed hold.

BAMBAMBAMBAM!

Cuffee braked, flinging me forward. My hands caught the front of the truck's cab. He hit the gas—I flopped backward.

"Aaggh!"

Nanny's voice!

Gunner's door swung open. He stood up to face me, the huge knife in his right hand. The wind blew him around and his left hand clutched the canvas.

"Let her go!" I said. "Take the fucking treasure, but let her—"

"I'm tired of your shit, Reilly!"

The wind whipped his blue-mirrored sunglasses off his head and I was momentarily distracted as they disappeared behind the truck. Both his eyes were bruised and the tape across his nose flapped in the fast air.

Gunner jumped off the seat and landed on the canvas roof—his foot tore through the top. He glared at me, the knife still clutched in his hand. I kicked at his face, which he blocked with one arm, and swung the knife at me with the other.

I glanced ahead and saw blue flashing lights down the hill coming toward us.

Gunner's beady black eyes squinted. He pressed his yellow square teeth together, balled his left fist, and lunged toward me. I ducked to the left, away from the knife, but he caught me around the shoulder with his free hand. I tried to spin but he pressed harder. I twisted toward him and bit his hand.

A shriek was lost to the wind as he shook the hand. His eyes were black as a dead man's heart, and this close I could see his pupils dilate.

He raised the knife high. Just as his arm launched forward I spun onto my side, nearly off the roof—and with a heart-stopping rip of material saw the knife buried up to the handle in the thick canvas roof. He pulled hard to withdraw it, and it came out halfway. Blue lights flashed in my periph-eral vision. A final yank and the knife was clear. He raised it back up—I had no more roof left to negotiate.

Just as his arm launched forward I rolled off the driver's side of the truck, my feet landing on the running board. Cuffee shouted, then Gunner cocked his arm back again—

"No!" I said.

Cuffee grabbed me with his left arm around the back of my neck and slammed my head forward into the side of the door. I sensed Gunner getting in position above with the knife—

"Buck!"

The sound of sirens was suddenly loud. Our tires screeched—I was flung forward off the truck—bounced into the truck's hood—Gunner flew forward—crashed into me.

The screech of brakes cut my ear—

He hit the asphalt first. The knife flew from his grip—I crashed onto his chest. We rolled over and over on the asphalt, which ripped at my exposed arms, legs. My shirt shredded as we rolled into the gravel on the side of the road.

We came to a sudden stop, as did the truck just behind us.

There was movement below me, a growl sounded. Gunner stood and I fell off him, face down in the dirt. He jumped to his feet.

I heard tires screeching. My peripheral vision caught blue lights flashing. And then came a shrill whistle.

"Stop right there!" a voice boomed. "Nobody move, and I mean nobody!"

56

STILL FACE DOWN, I LIFTED MY HEAD. THREE POLICE CARS AND A VAN blocked the road. A swarm of blue pants rushed past me.

"Everybody out of the truck!"

Black combat boots stopped by my head. Legs in blue pants. A policeman bent down.

"You alive?" he said.

I coughed.

"Anything broken?"

I rolled onto my back, lifted my head, then dropped it down. Lifted each arm and leg. Every limb was bleeding from a scrape or road rash or both—I felt like a scaled fish.

"No," I said.

"Get up." The officer gave me a gentle nudge with his boot.

"Buck!"

Nanny's voice. And she was running over.

"Hold it, miss!"

Nanny ignored him, bent down, and hovered over me.

"Are you . . . okay? You look . . ."

"A little scratched and dented, but—"

"This is private property!" Gunner, shouting from a distance.

A loud shuffling sound, closer.

"Whoa! Get away from those weapons, all of you—arms in the air!"

The clatter of metal landing hard on tarmac—guns, I assumed.

"Out of the back, everyone. Now!"

A loud crash—the tailgate falling open.

I slowly got to my feet, only to find a dark-skinned police officer pointing a Glock 9mm at me.

I held my hands up. He waved his gun toward the truck.

"Hands on the hood. You too, miss!"

He frisked me—gingerly, but it still hurt like hell. Then he moved to Nanny.

"I'm a professor with the University of the West Indies! These men robbed us—"

"Step to the back of the truck," the officer said.

We joined Cuffee and two other men. All three had their hands up.

"What the hell is all this?" One of the policemen was peering inside the bed of the truck. "You rob a museum, or what?"

"Those are ancient Maroon antiquities these men stole when they attacked us!" Nanny said.

"That's bullshit!" Gunner said.

"My relatives buried all this hundreds of years ago!" Cuffee said, his voice booming with authority.

I just focused on breathing. My skin felt as if I'd been put through a meat grinder.

"Officer, thank God you came when you did," Gunner said. "My name is Richard Rostenkowski, and my company, SCG International, was awarded the contract to restore part of Port Royal. We also have a claim against anything belonging to Captain Morgan."

The officer, who by his demeanor was clearly in charge, put both hands on his hips.

"The rum company?"

Gunner forced a smile. "The former lieutenant governor of Jamaica back in the late 1600s."

"I am Professor Nanny Adou from the University of the West Indies."

Nanny stepped forward with fire in her eyes. "This man is a thief, a liar, and he kidnapped me! He's a thug, not an archaeologist—"

"What about you there?" The officer pointed to me, leaning against the truck behind Nanny. "Who are you, Indiana Jones?" He cracked a smile and all his men snickered.

"I'm just a half-skinned charter pilot trying to help the Mother of us all use Morgan's treasure for the Jamaican people."

The officer looked confused.

"I have a *legal right to this cargo!*" Gunner now spoke through gritted teeth. "I demand you release it to me!"

He stepped toward the officer in charge, who pulled the gun from his holster faster than Josie Wales.

"Step back, right this second. Your so-called cargo includes illegal weapons, and—"

"It's *not* his cargo!" Nanny cried. "The artifacts are ours!"

"Every one of them belonged to Njoni, my great—"

"I have a legal right to this treasure!" Gunner screamed over Cuffee's booming voice.

"He's nothing but a mercenary!" I shouted while jabbing my thumb toward Gunner. "And a thief!"

BOOM!

Everyone froze.

The officer held his gun up in the air, and smoke floated around the end of its barrel.

"Enough!" he said. "All of you are going to jail."

57

"**A**LL RISE," THE BAILIFF SAID.

Everyone in the hearing room at the Hibbert House stood up as the committee entered through a side door. Professors Nanny Adou and Keith Quao had recused themselves. I was at one end of the long table, stomach in my throat. Jack was slumped at the opposite end.

Neither Nanny nor Gunner were in the room, absent for different reasons, and I had Ray Floyd with me now instead of Johnny Blake, with Harry Greenbaum sitting behind us next to Henry Kujo and his trusty sidekick, Clayton. A month had passed since we recovered Morgan's stash, and the jockeying for control had been vicious. The Jamaican government had immediately seized the treasure, and after a barrage of appeals from all sides agreed to allow 50 percent of it, or the value thereof, to be distributed to the appropriate party.

Thanks to word having leaked about what Nanny planned to do with her 50 percent if she were awarded it, public opinion was heavily lopsided in our favor.

But public opinion rarely decided cases like these.

Cuffee's argument was compelling, as was Jack's about the work they'd done to restore the underwater structure at Port Royal while pursuing a claim for the treasure, but neither had any real basis in law. Stanley's team had a similar argument, along with the history of provenance related to Akim's having sailed with Morgan to Panama. The Leeward and Windward

Maroons had agreed to share in the find, since the goal was to use it for all the people.

All in all, it was a complicated imbroglio, as of course it would be given the history and characters that dated all the way back to the 1600s, not to mention the incredible value of the treasure itself.

Harry Greenbaum and our team of Jamaican attorneys, advisors, and Maroon leaders had rigorously lobbied behind the scenes, but so had lawyers and consultants for Jack's side.

Jack stood and argued that SCG International's claim and broader salvage rights agreement made the decision clear. He characterized my efforts and those of "others" from Moore Town (he avoided using Nanny's name) as breaches of the committee's initial instructions to me—breaches committed despite repeated warnings for me to cease and desist from infringing on SCG's claim. There was quiet for a moment after he sat down.

"Colonel Grandy?" the chairman said.

"Buck Reilly will give our closing statement, sir."

He looked at me. Feeling the weight of health, education, and welfare for all Jamaica's children on my back, I stood.

"Members of the committee, you all know me from my previous application, and from my success as an archaeologist—okay, treasure hunter."

There were a few chuckles.

"Bottom line is I'm not here to make a case for myself to receive this treasure. Professor Nanny Adou and Colonel Stanley Grandy, as well as other respected members of the community, asked me to help them connect the disparate pieces of information their community had possessed for hundreds of years." I paused to let that sink in. "I admit I originally argued for a large percentage of the treasure, but their steadfast commitment to dividing the proceeds between the National Maritime Museum and the educational system in Jamaica was extraordinarily compelling."

I glanced at each face on the committee.

"Once I got to know Professor Adou, she shared her vision with me—to use colonial wealth accumulated by Captain Morgan, with the help of Maroon warriors, to establish an educational program that will liberate young Jamaican minds with knowledge for decades to come. Ladies and gentlemen of the committee, of the many treasure hunts I've participated in around the globe, not one has been based on such a noble cause, nor one with an upside for anyone other than myself, or former e-Antiquity shareholders. On behalf of everyone who has risked their lives to recover this astonishingly valuable find, I ask you to consider that in your final deliberation."

With that I sat down.

The room was silent as the committee filed out of the room.

A murmur started to pass through the audience—

"All rise," the bailiff said. The committee was returning, not five minutes after they had left the room.

When the chairman of the committee stood and read their decision "in favor of Professor Nanny Adou," the room exploded in a frenzy of shouts, hoots, applause, questions, and flash photography. I absorbed the decision with wordless satisfaction as Ray slapped his hand on the table.

"Holy crap," he said.

Local reporters and correspondents swarmed the front table, from Jack down to Stanley and me, getting comments from both sides. Stanley had tears streaming down his cheeks, and though I was only five feet away, I couldn't hear what he was saying to the journalists in front of him.

A reporter zeroed in on me.

"Buck Reilly," he said. "So you were able to combine a bunch of microscopic clues and find a treasure few people believed even existed?"

"Something like that," I said.

"But equally as captivating," he said, "is the metamorphosis of King Buck."

"How so?"

"You gave up 90 percent for the good of the Jamaican people. For an educational program? What happened to the shrewd, ruthless negotiator from the e-Antiquity days? What happened to the King Buck we saw on the cover of the *Wall Street Journal*?"

Not one to seek press coverage, I hesitated, but the message was too important to shirk.

"Nanny said it best. With knowledge comes power, and who needs knowledge more than children?"

He jotted that in his notepad. "So you've become King Buck *the Noble?*"

"It's not about me—"

Just then applause burst out behind me. I turned in time for Nanny to wrap her arms around me in a tight squeeze, her cheeks wet from tears pressed against my neck. When she pulled away, she slapped me two high-fives.

Stanley pushed his way through to hug Nanny, Ray, and me.

"Chris Blackwell was right about you," Stanley said. "He said you could be trusted, and that you'd come through for Jamaica."

I'd never met Blackwell until this trip, though we had some mutual friends—hell, he'd been on the plane with Jimmy Buffett when some over-zealous law enforcement officials shot up Buffett's Albatross years ago. But why would—

"He had a sense about you, Buck. Don't try to figure it out. The man picks talent better than anyone."

"Hear, hear," Harry Greenbaum said.

The crowd—media, commissioners, onlookers—began a surge toward the exit. The human funnel was carrying me to the inevitable face-to-face with Jack Dodson.

At least Heather wasn't here.

I felt for the envelope in my back pocket and pulled it free.

Once we emptied out onto the stairs and into the downtown street, I was surprised at the number of people who'd gathered to await the outcome, many of them now cheering. Schoolchildren in adorable uniforms jumped up and down, and one of them started a chant: "iPads! iPads! iPads!"

Jack was making a hasty exit toward the familiar black Land Rover on Duke Street. I had to run, jockeying through the crowd, to reach him.

"Jack!"

He paused and looked over his shoulder just as I broke through the crowd. By the turn of his mouth I knew he'd spotted me. He hesitated, then crossed his arms and waited.

"Your turn to gloat, Buck?"

I stepped close enough to see wrinkles on his face I hadn't noticed before.

"No, I—"

"Congratulations," he said. "You always were the best at finding treasure, just not so good at keeping it."

"That's what I wanted to talk to you about," I said. "But first, answer me a question, honestly. There's no reason to lie—it's all past now."

"What's the question, Buck?"

The passenger window lowered and I saw Gunner behind the wheel.

"Fuck you, Reilly!"

Jack and I stepped away from the Land Rover.

"Did you have anything to do with Nanny getting kidnapped?"

Jack shook his head. "No. Straight up. Believe it or not, that knucklehead didn't either." He jerked a thumb toward the Land Rover. "Johnny had been feeding us info, but when he told us he and some buddies had grabbed her for leverage, I cut him off." He shook his head. "I did five years in the state pen. I'm not doing more time, and certainly not in a place like this."

I believed him. Maybe I'm an idiot, but I believed him.

And being an idiot, I handed him the envelope.

"Take a look at this."

58

Thirty Days Later

THE BEACH AT NEGRIL WAS CALM AND NOT TOO CROWDED YET CHARGED with energy thanks to the special guests assembled at an impromptu celebration. The new *Sports Illustrated* swimsuit edition shot on Jamaica a few months ago had just been released.

Heather Drake was on the cover.

That would have held no attraction for me, except that Thom Shepherd's CD *Saltwater Cowboy* had also just been released, its first track his latest number-one hit "Rum Punch." He'd again persuaded me to fly him down here to partake in the celebration. A video for the song had been filmed using several models from the shoot standing with the Beast, so the song and plane had been co-promoted.

Chronixx and I-Wayne, two Jamaican reggae stars, were also here, and all of the musicians had been jamming with each other, to the small crowd's delight. Ray was having the time of his life, posing with the swimsuit models and basking in his fifteen days of fame for having been a part of the Morgan treasure team. His joy gave me nearly as much pleasure as the beautiful woman at my side.

Nanny was explaining the lyrics of Chronixx's song "Capture Land," which he was playing at the moment, accompanied by Thom Shepherd on guitar.

"He's saying all the places and people mentioned are unclean due to their past exploitation of slaves and the Rasta's descendents—"

Nanny stopped midsentence as another beautiful woman stepped up to us.

Heather.

She wore tight orange shorts and the same skimpy orange bikini top she had on in her cover shot.

"Buck," she said, "I was hoping we could spend some time together while we're both here."

I'd forgotten the subtle freckles on her nose and cheeks you could only see in sunlight. She gave me that smile—once mine, now the world's thanks to magazine covers, advertising campaigns, and talk shows.

"What's it you wanted to talk about?"

Those sky-blue eyes looked directly into mine.

"About how much I miss you." Her eyes fluttered. "Are you free tomorrow?"

I reached around Heather, grabbed Nanny's hand, and pulled her close.

"I don't think so," I said.

Nanny turned and gave me a soft, sweet kiss. I opened my lips and closed my eyes. When I opened them, Heather was gone.

Ray pressed up next to me and handed me a Black and Stormy.

"That was close," he said.

"Not really."

I glanced over at Nanny, who was laughing with Stanley, Harry Greenbaum, Henry Kujo, and Professor Keith.

"Last Resort Charter and Salvage is now capitalized and doubled in size." Ray raised his glass as Thom Shepherd launched into "Rum Punch."

I turned back to Ray. "The future is bright," I said. "Partner."

He scratched his head. "But I still can't believe you did that deal—"

"Don't start, Ray."

"I mean I get it—but, jeez, did you do the math when you gave away 25 percent of your 10 percent? It—"

"Didn't mean a thing to me."

I followed his gaze out to the ocean, turquoise blue with highlights of orange on the wave crests. On the beach was the Beast, resting askew in the sand, a regal old bird indeed.

My face bent in a broad smile when I looked past her—to my other girl. "Betty, however, means everything," I said.

The End

Acknowledgments

WRITING *MAROON RISING* PROVIDED A GREAT OPPORTUNITY TO RESEARCH another wonderful location, this time Jamaica. I studied the island's rich, and varied history, and was able to meet many people who care deeply about their nation's past, future and culture. I'd like to thank several people who contributed significantly to this effort.

First, thank you to Chris Blackwell, who I had the pleasure to meet with at GoldenEye Resort, drink some Blackwell rum, talk music, history, and Buck Reilly. As the founder of Island Records, Chris has touched all of our lives through discovering or helping to make successful many amazing musicians, including Bob Marley, U2, Jethro Tull, Cat Stevens, Tom Waits, Melissa Etheridge, and many others. His family has a long history in Jamaica, and he's involved with and very serious about historic preservation and the future of the country. It was Chris who gave me the idea that school children in Jamaica would benefit by receiving iPads, and he was very generous to allow me to include him in several scenes in *Maroon Rising*.

Also in Jamaica, my friend, Lancelot Thompson, a.k.a. McGyver, was instrumental in introducing me to, and helping me research many of the locations depicted in the story, as well as different foods, stories, trends, music and introductions to key people like Chris Blackwell and I-Wayne. McGyver's knowledge, passion, ability to work around obstacles and his persistence was truly inspirational. And he too allowed me to portray him in the story.

Singer songwriter, Thom Shepherd, who has penned numerous #1 hits, and has over 100 songwriting credits for some of Country Music's top recording artists, and was himself recently awarded the Country Music Association (CMA) of Texas' Songwriter of the Year award, was also very gracious to allow me to portray him in the story. Thom is one of the hardest working and most talented people I know, and he never stops smiling. I also had the pleasure of co-writing a song with him, called "Rum Punch," and accompanied him when he recorded it in Nashville with legendary musician, songwriter and studio owner, Jim "Moose" Brown and Noah Gordon.

Thom tours nonstop and has performed for American Military servicemen and women in 17 different countries. Thom also appeared in *Maroon Rising* and it was a blast to have him ride shotgun with Buck Reilly.

Clemens and Nancy Von Merveldt, the General Managers of Strawberry Hill Resort, located in the heart of the Blue Mountain range, were also very gracious in sharing their perspectives on Jamaica, and to introducing me to other amazing people and facts about the country, as well as appear in the novel. International reggae star, I-Wayne, was kind and generous to allow me to include him in the book, and like all of the other "real people" who agreed to appear, also wanted to first understand what the book was about, and showed concern and care about the moral of the story being positive for the Jamaican people.

Another Jamaican friend, who happens to live in New York, Thremane Henry, helped me to understand history, city details, music, and had some great suggestions on settings and pertinent cultural aspects of the country. As one of a few trusted pre-readers, he also offered insight and encouragement on the plot and storyline for *Maroon Rising*.

Thanks also to my friend and publicist, Ann-Marie Nieves of GetredPR, for her unwavering support, brainstorming, energy, introductions and creativity. You're the best. Also to Tim Harkness illustrator extraordinaire, along with John Wojciech of C-Straight, my webpage designer, and to Cathy Snipper at Island Outpost for her help in Jamaica.

Thank you to the team at The Editorial Department (TED): Renni Browne, Ross Browne, Peter Gelfan, Shannon Roberts, Morgana Gallaway Laurie, Jane Ryder, Liz Felix and Tad Daggerhart. I've worked with TED as my editorial team for 20 years, and they do an amazing job.

One last thing, people often ask me about my writing habits. The reality is that it takes a lot of time and inspiration to write and edit books, and given the amount of time I travel (over 100 commercial flights in 2015, so far), I thought you might enjoy seeing a partial list of cities, countries, airlines, and hotels, aside from my writing barn, where I wrote portions of *Maroon Rising*. Someday I will travel less and write more. Here you go . . .

New York, NY
Key West, FL
Islamorada, FL
Wellington, FL
Blacksburg, VA
Hamilton, VA
Richmond, VA
Ashland, VA
Nashville, TN
Denver, CO
Pasadena, CA
St. Barths
Jamaica
Amtrak Acela
Delta Shuttle
USAir
United Airlines
American Airlines
Frontier Airlines
NoMad Hotel
London NYC Hotel
Pier House Hotel
Strawberry Hill Resort
GoldenEye Resort
Langham Hotel
Ace Hotel
and more...

And finally, to my lovely ladies Holly, Bailey and Cortney, thank you for your love and support. Never give up on your dreams, some day they may actually come true . . .

WWW.JHCUNNINGHAM.COM

The Buck Reilly Series:

 Red Right Return

 Green to Go

 Crystal Blue

 Second Chance Gold

"Rum Punch" by Thom Shepherd, and cowritten by John H. Cunningham, will be released on Amazon and iTunes simultaneously with *Maroon Rising*

THE BALLAD OF BUCK REILLY
(Available for download, along with the album *Workaholic in Recovery* from Amazon and iTunes)

About the Author

JOHN H. CUNNINGHAM IS THE AUTHOR OF THE BEST SELLING, FIVE BOOK, Buck Reilly adventure series, which includes *Red Right Return*, *Green to Go*, *Crystal Blue*, *Second Chance Gold* and *Maroon Rising*. Through the years, John has been a bouncer at a Key West nightclub, a diver, pilot, magazine editor, commercial developer, song writer and global traveler. He has either lived in or visited the many island locations that populate the series, and has experienced or witnessed enough craziness and wild times to keep the Buck Reilly series flowing. John mixes fact with fiction and often includes real people in his novels, like Jimmy Buffett, Matt Hoggatt, Thom Shepherd and Bankie Banx to augment the reader's experience. Adhering to the old maxim, "write what you know," John's books have an authenticity and immediacy that have earned a loyal following and strong reviews.

John lives in Virginia with his wife and two daughters, and spends much of his time traveling. His choices for the places and plots that populate the Buck Reilly series include many subjects that he loves: Key West, Cuba, Jamaica, and multiple Caribbean settings, along with amphibious aircraft, colorful characters, and stories that concern themselves with the same tensions and issues that affect all of our lives.

For John's other books and music, you can go to his website and link from there:

WWW.JHCUNNINGHAM.COM

Rum Punch

By Thom Shepherd and John Cunningham

Lazy afternoon, with Bob Marley on
Got the Beach Bar boogie
And Bacardi in a jar
Mix it on up, and pour it over ice
Smiles all around, yeah

Rum punch on a hot summer day
feeling down island
In a happy kinda way
The sun is-a shining, ain't nobody whining
We're just doing fine

Sand between my toes, and the sun on my nose
Got good friends together, and some nobody knows
It don't matter 'cause everyone agrees
Too many days-a working and not enough of these
Hell-yeah, everybody's fine
Gettin-on a buzz, don't care about the time

Rum punch on a hot summer day
feeling down island
In a crazy kinda way
The sun is-a shining, ain't nobody whining
We're just doing fine
I said, we're just doing fine

What's it really matter
What's it all about
Choosin' to be happy
Drink away the doubt
Laughter is the flavor
With a little pinch of love
Throw it in a pitcher and mix me up some of that

Rum punch on a hot summer day
feeling down island
In a happy kinda way
The sun is-a shining, ain't nobody whining
We're just doing fine, yeah
Living on island time

Mix me up some
Rum punch
Mix you up some
Rum punch
Drink us up some
Rum punch

CPSIA information can be obtained
at www.ICGtesting.com
Printed in the USA
BVHW090238121122
651552BV00001B/115